THE
ROYAL GHOSTS

Books by Samrat Upadhyay

Arresting God in Kathmandu

The Guru of Love

The Royal Ghosts

THE
ROYAL
GHOSTS

Stories

Samrat Upadhyay

A Mariner Original
Houghton Mifflin Company
BOSTON + NEW YORK + 2006

For information about permission to reproduce selections from
this book, write to Permissions, Houghton Mifflin Company,
215 Park Avenue South, New York, New York 10003.

Visit our Web site: www.houghtonmifflinbooks.com.

Library of Congress Cataloging-in-Publication Data
Upadhyay, Samrat, date.
    The royal ghosts : stories / Samrat Upadhyay.
        p. cm.
    "A Mariner original."
    ISBN-13: 978-0-618-51749-7
    ISBN-10: 0-618-51749-9
    1. Nepal—Social life and customs—Fiction. I. Title.

PR9570.N43R69 2006
823'.92 dc22   2005016737

Book design by Melissa Lotfy

Printed in the United States of America

MP 10 9 8 7 6 5 4 3 2 1

To my chhori Shahzadi

Contents

THE
ROYAL GHOSTS

A Refugee

PITAMBER CROSSED THE BRIDGE to Kupondole and found the gift shop where he'd been told Kabita worked. But the man behind the counter said she'd quit after just a few days. "She wasn't right in the head, you know," the man said, "after all that happened to her."

"Where did she go?"

"I don't know. I tried to convince her to stay on, but she just stopped coming."

Pitamber left the shop and stood on the sidewalk, squinting at the sun and noting the intense heat, strange for autumn. This morning he'd woken restless, with a hollowness in his stomach, and thought about the letter he'd received a fortnight ago from his childhood friend Jaikanth. The feeling remained with him throughout the day as he searched for this woman named Kabita, whose story Jaikanth had described to him. "She's in Kathmandu with her daughter, and I know what a kind man you are, Pitamber. Please do what you can to help her. She's suffered immensely."

Now Pitamber made his way to his flat in Dharahara, where his wife, Shailaja, was cooking French toast in the kitchen. She turned to smile at him as he came in. "Any luck?"

He said no and mopped his forehead with a handkerchief. "Why hasn't she contacted us? Jaikanth said he gave her our address. It's been nearly two weeks."

"Maybe other people are already helping her. Didn't Jaikanth mention other people she knew here?"

He nodded, then told her what the man in the gift shop had said. "I hope she's found another job," he told Shailaja, then said that his stomach had been mildly upset all day.

"It must be hunger," she said. "Why don't you go wash your face and I'll give you some French toast. Sumit should be home any minute now."

He went to the bathroom, washed his face, took several deep breaths, then went to find Jaikanth's letter. He read it again, and paused as he did: "They killed him in front of her, Pitamber. Can you imagine what that must have been like?" Jaikanth hadn't explained the details of the killing, but over the past two weeks Pitamber had formed a picture in his mind: three Maobadi rebels, barely past their teens (they were always so young in the news), storming into her house, dragging her husband out to the yard, slitting his throat with a knife. The four-year-old daughter probably inside the house, perhaps sound asleep, perhaps with a nasty cold. And after the men leave, a woman standing there, her palm over her mouth.

The woman's face was never clear, but Pitamber's mind always flashed with these details: the sun's rays glinting on washed pots drying on the porch, one rebel raising his finger to warn the neighbors peeking from the windows of their houses, the men's footprints on the rice paddies through which they escape.

He massaged his temples. Surely she still needed help now. It was clear that Jaikanth was expecting him to house the woman and her daughter for a while, and Pitamber was willing to do this, even though his was only a three-room flat in a small house. He wanted to help her, mostly out of compassion, but partly out of obligation to an old friend of his family, a friend from the village where he grew up.

When Sumit, his twelve-year-old son, returned from school, they drank tea and ate French toast, then Pitamber and the boy settled down to play chess. Pitamber had bought the set two months ago, after the first set, a cheap one with plastic pieces, disappeared from their flat. Pitamber suspected that one of Sumit's friends from the neighborhood, who had a reputation for lifting small objects from the surrounding houses, had swiped it, but he didn't pursue the matter. Sumit had shown remarkable skill in the game, so this time Pitamber bought a marble set with finely carved pieces. It had cost him nine hundred rupees at a tourist shop in Basantapur. His stomach dropped when the shopkeeper first told him the price, but he'd rationalized the purchase, convincing himself that his son would become a master someday. "We should enroll him in the neighborhood chess club," he'd said to Shailaja the other day. "He can play with older kids and learn more quickly." But Shailaja was hesitant. "He might be intimidated. There'll be kids his age better at the game, and you know how he is." She had a point. Sumit was a sensitive kid; he berated himself whenever he lost to his father. Perhaps he should gain more confidence before joining any clubs.

The two played chess that evening for nearly an hour. Sumit made a couple of silly mistakes and slapped his forehead each time. Pitamber deliberately muddled his moves to compensate for Sumit's errors, careful to pretend that the mistakes were genuine. Toward the end of the game, Sumit captured his remaining knight and paralyzed Pitamber's king. "You're getting much better," Pitamber told his son, and suggested the three of them go for a walk.

The air had gotten considerably cooler and more pleasant, but Pitamber soon grew annoyed by the crowds on the pavement and the cars and trucks spewing fumes and blasting their horns beside them. The three walked toward the stadium, and Sumit spotted a large billboard advertising a Hindi action movie. "I want to see that," he said, and he held out his arms as if he were carrying a machine gun. *"Bhut bhut bhut bhut."*

He mock-shot some pedestrians, and Pitamber scolded him. The boy had been watching too many of these movies on video. Shailaja was too lenient with him, and on weekends, when he and Pitamber were not playing chess, Sumit remained glued to the television despite Pitamber's pleas for him to turn it off. He even recognized all the actors and actresses and knew their silly songs by heart.

Chess was better for him. It taught him to think, to strategize, to assess his own strengths and weaknesses. It was a good game for a future statesman or a philosopher. The idea of his son's becoming someone important brought a smile to Pitamber's face, and he ruffled the boy's hair.

After dinner that evening, Pitamber went to his bedroom to read the day's paper. In Rolpa, dozens of policemen had been shot by the Maobadis. In Baglung, two rebels had been beaten to death by villagers, who now feared reprisal. The cold, passive language of the news reports disgusted Pitamber, and he set down the paper. It was hard to believe that this country was becoming a place where people killed each other over differences in ideas about how to govern it. At his office the other day, a colleague openly sympathized with the rebels and said that the Maobadis had no choice. "Think about it," the man had said. "For years we suffered under the kings, then we got so-called democracy, but nothing got better. Most of our country lives in mind-boggling poverty. These Maobadis are only fighting for the poor. It's a simple thing that they're doing."

"Simple?" Pitamber had said. "Your Maobadis are killing the very people they claim they're fighting for—innocent villagers."

"They're casualties of the revolution," the man said. "They are martyrs. But the revolution has to go on."

Pitamber took a deep breath and said, "It's easy for you to blather on about revolutions from your comfortable chair."

The discussion ended with him walking away from his colleague. Later Pitamber barely acknowledged him when they passed in the hallway, even though he knew that what the man said was not entirely untrue: poor people in the country were fed up with how little their conditions had changed, democracy or no democracy.

Pitamber again went to find Jaikanth's letter and reread it, this time stopping at the three names and addresses of the contacts Kabita already had in the city. Through one of these people, Pitamber had learned about the gift shop where she had worked. He had tried reaching another of the contacts but had been told the man was out of town. Pitamber reached for the phone and called the number again. The man answered this time, but said he didn't know the whereabouts of Kabita. "She hasn't been in touch, but I believe she has a distant relative who is a sadhu in the Pashupatinath temple. You might try him."

Early the next morning, after some searching, Pitamber found the communal house for ascetics near the Pashupatinath temple, where Kabita's relative, Ramsharan, lived. When Pitamber announced whom he was looking for, a small old man with soft eyes and full lips said, "That's me." He told Pitamber that Kabita was renting a flat in Baghbazar and gave him directions. "She hasn't come to see me," the man said. "And I'm too old to walk around the city. But I did go to her flat once when she first came to Kathmandu." Ramsharan shook his head sadly. "What can we do? God creates, God destroys. We can only sing his praises."

Pitamber thanked him and left, mildly annoyed by the sadhu's sanctimonious words. It was already nine o'clock, and Pitamber would be late for work. But he felt so close to finding Kabita that he decided he'd risk his new supervisor's irritation. Thus far Pitamber was in Mr. Shrestha's good graces at the municipal branch office in Naxal where he worked—maybe the man would tolerate one day of tardiness.

Kabita's flat was located above a shoe store, and the smell of leather hung in the staircase as Pitamber climbed to the third floor. He knocked on the door. After a few moments, a small woman with sunken eyes opened it. She couldn't have been more than twenty-five or so, and she had on the standard white dhoti that widows wore.

"Kabitaji?"

She nodded. A girl appeared by her side, and Pitamber could hear the sound of a kerosene stove burning inside. He introduced himself, said Jaikanth had written to him about her. "Oh, yes," she said without much expression.

"I don't want to bother you," Pitamber said. "But could we talk?"

She let him in. It was a one-room flat, with a bed in one corner and cooking equipment in another. There were no drapes on the windows, and Pitamber noticed two girls at the window of the neighboring house looking in at them and whispering. "How old is she?" he asked, gesturing toward the girl. He reached into his pocket, took out a lollipop, and extended it to her. She took it shyly.

"She'll be five next month."

"And how are things for you?"

For a moment she looked at him as if he were a complete fool. Then she said, "All right."

"I was saddened to hear what happened," he said, searching for something more comforting to say. "People in this country have simply gone mad."

"It was God's will," she said. "My only worry is for her." She placed her hand on her daughter's head, and the girl reached under the bed and pulled out a doll with yellow hair and blue eyes.

Pitamber said what a nice-looking doll it was and asked the girl her name.

"Priya," she said, staring at her feet.

"What a pretty name. I have a son who's a bit older than you. He's named Sumit."

"Did you do namaste to him?" Kabita suddenly reprimanded her daughter, who halfheartedly joined her palms together for Pitamber.

He again expressed his sorrow, then said that he was willing to offer any help he could. "I heard you had a job, but quit."

"It's hard to work with her around," she said, gesturing toward her daughter. Kabita said she'd taken Priya with her to the gift shop in Kupondole, but after two days the owner said that he couldn't have a child running around a shop frequented by tourists. The owner of the shoe shop below the flat offered to look after her while Kabita worked, but every evening when she returned, she found Priya bawling. "I've thought about returning to my village," she said, "but those men are still there."

It took him a moment to understand that the men she referred to were the Maobadis. "Listen," he said. "There's no reason for you to be all alone in this city. I am here, my family is here. Why don't you come and stay with us while you look for a job? We'll see if we can find a school for your daughter. And once things fall into place, you can move into a flat of your own."

She shook her head. "I couldn't burden you like that."

"It's no burden! What are you talking about? Listen, we don't have much space, but we can certainly manage. How about you talk to your landlord? Or better, I'll talk to him, explain the situation, and maybe he'll return the money you gave him for the rest of the month."

"I wouldn't know how to repay you for this."

"Nonsense."

Kabita's landlord was argumentative when Pitamber went to see him the next evening after work. "With anyone else I'd require at least two months' notice, but with her, because of her situation, I can let her go at the end of the month. But not before."

Pitamber tried to reason with him, said he should consider all that Kabita had endured, that she couldn't possibly afford to let go of almost a month's rent.

But the landlord wouldn't budge. "I also have my own household expenses to think of. Where am I going to find another tenant on such short notice?"

Pitamber looked around the man's room, lowered his voice,

and said, "Listen, muji, you better let her go. Otherwise people will think you're a Maobadi yourself. Why else would you give her such a hard time? A good question, isn't it?" His own words surprised him, how quickly he said them.

The landlord stared at him. "Are you threatening me?"

Pitamber straightened his back, deciding to finish what he'd started. "Take it how you want to take it. I'm just saying your being stubborn makes you suspicious."

"What kind of a world is this? All I'm asking for is a month's rent that's due to me."

"But in a situation like this, you shouldn't be thinking only about the money."

The landlord looked angry but defeated. "All right, how about a week's rent? At least she can give me that much."

"How much?"

"Two hundred rupees."

Pitamber had anticipated something like this and was prepared for it. He didn't want to part with the money, but it was a small price to pay given Kabita's circumstances. He took out his wallet and gave him the money. "She'll move out tomorrow."

"Don't tell her or anyone else about our conversation today. I don't want people to get the wrong idea about me."

"Rest assured," Pitamber said. As he walked back to Kabita's flat, a few houses away, he felt a bit remorseful about how menacing he'd been, but it had to be done, he supposed. People needed to be reminded of what was important when dealing with those who'd suffered.

The next evening, Kabita and Priya moved into Pitamber's flat. She had only one large suitcase, a thin, folding mattress with a blanket, and a couple of bags, so it was easy to fit everything in a taxi. Kabita wanted to repay the money Pitamber had given to the landlord, as well as the taxi fare, but Pitamber wouldn't hear of it.

Initially, Shailaja said he'd been hasty when he told her

that he'd invited Kabita to live with them. "She might not feel comfortable living with strangers like this," she said. "And we don't have much space." But Pitamber said that he'd feel awful if Kabita was forced to return to the village, and that this arrangement was only temporary. Shailaja finally agreed. "You've always been like this," she said, stroking his hair. "You can't bear to see anyone suffering."

Now she offered Priya and Kabita tea and snacks, and they chatted about her village and how expensive it was to live in Kathmandu. Shailaja said that a seamstress who sewed her blouses in New Road was looking for help. "Do you know how to run a sewing machine?" Kabita shook her head. "I'm sure that wouldn't be a problem," Shailaja said. "She actually taught me. I used to work for her until about a year ago, before my fingers began to swell and I could no longer run the machine."

"But what will I do with her when I work?" Kabita asked, gesturing toward Priya.

"I'll look after her until we find a school for her. All right?"

Pitamber was glad Shailaja showed no signs of her earlier doubts about this arrangement, but even then he'd known that once she met Kabita, her heart would take over. He had always admired Shailaja's generous spirit, and in moments like these he considered himself lucky to have her as his wife.

At Shailaja's offer, Kabita lowered her eyes, as if overwhelmed.

Shailaja went to prepare dinner, and Priya began to cling to her mother, who scolded her and said that she needed to help with the cooking.

"Come here, daughter. Why don't you and I play chess with this brilliant fellow here," Pitamber said, pointing to Sumit, who so far had shown little interest in the girl.

"I don't want to play with her," Sumit mumbled.

"And why's that?"

"She's too young."

"What if I help her?"

"Then it'll take me five seconds instead of one to beat her."

"Did you hear that, Shailaja?" Pitamber said loudly. "I think your son is getting arrogant. I think it's time he challenged some real players at the chess club."

The sound of spinach frying in oil filled the flat, and he heard his wife chatting with Kabita.

"Come, daughter, I'll teach you how to play chess," Pitamber said, and Priya came to his side.

He set up the pieces and began teaching her the rules. But she was more interested in admiring the pieces than anything else, and after a while he sighed and gave up. Sumit, who was sitting next to them doing his homework, laughed. "She's too young, buwa. I told you."

"Why don't you two play a game that she'll find more interesting?"

"But I'm doing my homework."

"Do you like to listen to stories?" Pitamber asked Priya.

Shyly chewing the hem of her dress, she nodded.

"Then I'll read to you. Come." He searched in their bookcase for one of Sumit's old children's books and found one about a cat and a rabbit. Priya sat on his lap, and he began reading. Her eyes followed his finger as it moved across the page. Soon Sumit abandoned his homework and sat next to them, and Pitamber felt a strange happiness come over him, as if somehow his family was expanding. He and Shailaja had both wanted a daughter after Sumit, but despite years of trying, Shailaja hadn't gotten pregnant again. In time, they'd become grateful for at least having had a son.

After dinner, they settled down to watch television. Shailaja turned on some comedy show, and soon Pitamber lost interest. Surreptitiously, he watched Kabita, whose eyes were steadily focused on the screen in front of her. What was going through her head right then? he wondered. Did she think about the killers? If she did, what kinds of things did she think? Kabita appeared to sense him watching her, for she quickly glanced at him. He felt something transpire between them, something he couldn't quite define.

He and Shailaja had decided that Kabita and Priya would sleep in Sumit's bed and Sumit would sleep on a mattress on the floor of their room. But when everyone began getting ready for bed, Sumit balked. "I want to sleep in my own bed," he said to his parents. "I don't want to sleep with you two." At twelve years old, he'd already begun acting like a teenager, Pitamber thought and sighed. Kabita said, "Why should Sumit babu relinquish his bed? We can easily spread our mattress right here." She pointed to the living room floor. Pitamber tried to reason with his son, saying he should at least let the guests spread their mattress on his floor, but Sumit stormed off to his room and closed the door. "I don't know what's wrong with your son," Pitamber told Shailaja, who retorted, "Yes, when he doesn't obey he's my son, but when he wins at chess, he's yours."

"This is how it is in our house," Pitamber said to Kabita, trying to smile, and quickly helped her set up her mattress on the living room floor.

Later, in their room, Shailaja said, "Poor thing. With everything that's happened, she's still maintaining a good attitude."

"She seems to be a strong woman," Pitamber said.

"That kind of tragedy—I mean, what did she do to deserve it? And here we are—we still believe in God."

Shailaja regularly worshiped at the city temples, and her words surprised him. "I'm not sure I believe in God anymore," he said.

"You shouldn't say that."

"But you just said it."

"I didn't say I don't believe in God. I meant that we must believe in God no matter what. You know that."

"So adept at twisting your own words," Pitamber muttered.

After a moment she said, "I want to do a puja at the Maitidevi temple."

"Why?"

Her face was very serious. "Why do people do puja? To ask for God's protection."

"Nobody is threatening us," he said. Then, noting his harsh tone, he said, "Okay, go ahead and do it, that's no problem. I was just asking why."

"There doesn't need to be a why when praying to God," she said, and turned off the light.

The seamstress was more than happy to hire Kabita. "These Maobadis! They should all be burned alive for everyone to see," Ratnakumari said to Shailaja and Pitamber when they went to her.

A routine was soon established. Kabita would leave for the seamstress's house early in the morning, around seven. Pitamber would entertain Priya, who inevitably cried and whined after her mother left, while Shailaja cooked the morning meal. Soon it was time for Sumit to go to school, then for Pitamber to head to work. Kabita returned home at around one or two, depending on how busy things were with Ratnakumari. Pitamber left his office at five. In the evening, after dinner, they all sat around the flat, talking or reading or watching television.

Over the days, Pitamber and Shailaja learned more about Kabita. Both her parents had died of illnesses soon after she got married. Her in-laws lived in another village, in Gorkha, which was also subject to attacks by the Maobadis, so she couldn't go there after her husband was killed. She had a sister who worked as a hotel maid in the Indian state of Bihar. Kabita had very little contact with her—they'd never been particularly close—and most likely she wasn't aware of all that had happened to her sister. No one knew for sure why her husband was killed, Kabita said, for he was only a schoolteacher and had no political affiliations. Whenever she mentioned her husband, she grew restless.

"It won't always be this painful to think about," Shailaja frequently consoled her. "You have to focus on your new life here, and your daughter's."

Kabita usually nodded, looking at the floor. Sometimes she pulled her daughter to her side. In these moments Pitamber found it hard to look at Kabita and Priya without something roiling in his stomach, without vividly recalling the photographs of the Maobadi leaders that had recently appeared in the newspapers. The confounding thing was that these men looked so ordinary, like the men he worked with, the men he saw in tea shops across the city.

As it turned out, a school for Priya was hard to come by. She was too young for kindergarten, and preschools were very expensive. "I have no problem looking after her," Shailaja insisted to Kabita. "Look, she's already taken a liking to me." It was true. Priya now clung to Shailaja as much as she did to her own mother. "Auntie," she called Shailaja, and followed her around the house.

Sumit seemed to be the only one having difficulties adjusting to Kabita and Priya in the flat. He hardly said anything to Kabita and never played with Priya. Once Pitamber saw him push the girl away as she was attempting to get something from the floor near him. Pitamber took him to his bedroom and said, "You should treat her like your younger sister. You should be nice to her."

"Don't call her my sister," Sumit said sullenly.

"Why not?"

"They're not part of our family."

"Well, while they're here we have to treat them that way, understand?"

"When are they going to leave?"

"Soon. Now go play with Priya for a while."

But Sumit stayed in his room alone and shut the door. When Pitamber told Shailaja about his talk with Sumit, she said, "This is normal for someone his age. He'll get used to them."

One morning, right after he reached work, Pitamber heard that Mr. Shrestha had called in sick. Because of the man's grouchy demeanor and strict rules, the employees treated this day as if it were a holiday. Some signed in and went home, others sat around and chatted and made personal phone calls. Mr. Shrestha hadn't said anything to Pitamber the morning he arrived late after searching for Kabita, but Pitamber hadn't risked being late since then. Today, though, he and his colleague Neupane decided to go to a restaurant nearby. There, over samosas and jalebis, Pitamber told Neupane about Kabita.

"You're doing the right thing, Pitamberji," Neupane said. "I'd have done the same."

"Can you believe they'd murder a schoolteacher?" Pitamber said.

"Well, the police and the army are just as cruel. Haven't you heard how they raped and killed those two teenage girls, then accused them of being Maobadis?"

Pitamber grew silent, then he said, "Do you suppose Kabita thinks about revenge?"

"Revenge?" Neupane raised his eyebrows. "Do you expect a young widow to go searching in the hills for those men?"

Pitamber gazed out the window. People were walking, laughing, swinging shopping bags, hailing taxis. Across the street, a teenage boy appeared to be teaching another boy some karate moves.

"God will punish them, Pitamberji. God is watching all of this."

He turned to Neupane. "I don't really like thinking about God anymore."

Neupane laughed. "But where would we be without God, eh? Seriously, though, she has a new life, and she should let the past go. And you should stop thinking about it all so much." When Pitamber said nothing, Neupane added, "Thinking about revenge just puts us on their level."

They left the restaurant and started walking back to the office, but, preoccupied and irritated, Pitamber soon decided that he'd rather go home. Neupane slapped him on the back and said, "Pitamberji, you need to relax. Everything is fine. Your job is fine, and everything is going well with your family. So stop all this obsessing."

Pitamber nodded. "You're right, Neupaneji," he said, but he still wanted to go home, so he said goodbye to Neupane and headed off. Clouds were gathering in the sky, and he recalled the morning's weather report forecasting rain. At least the rain would be a distraction.

On the way home, he had to pass by New Road, and he decided to pay a visit to Kabita. Four women worked at the seamstress's shop, all busy running the machines. A steady and fast *click-click-click* filled the room, which overflowed with pieces of cloth and unfinished dresses. Kabita sat in the back, her eyes focused on the needle as her fingers slid the cloth underneath it. He went and stood in front of her, but she seemed unaware of his presence until he said her name. She looked up, gasped, and the stitch on the cloth went askew. "Tch," she said to the machine, then to Pitamber, "Dai?"

"I got the day off," he said. "I thought I'd drop by to see how you were doing."

She managed a smile. The other women in the shop glanced in their direction. "Dai," she said loudly, introducing him to them above the clatter, and they nodded, went back to work.

"Everything going well?"

She nodded.

"Where's Ratnakumariji?"

"She's gone to run some errands."

"Have you had tea?"

She shook her head. "There's no time for tea. I have too much work to do." And she set her hand on the wheel of her machine.

"How about I bring tea to the four of you, then?"

"Dai, you don't have to. There's a boy from the tea shop who comes here sometimes."

"It'd be my pleasure. Besides, maybe the boy won't come today."

The tea shop was just around the corner, and the boy who was rinsing the glasses there offered to take the tea to the women, but Pitamber insisted on doing it himself. Awkwardly carrying a container with five glasses of tea back to the shop, he shouted, "Chai garam," imitating the men who sold tea at Indian railway stations, and Kabita seemed a bit embarrassed. "I'll just have a little tea and be on my way. Not to worry," he said to her. He sat and chatted with them for a while, asking the other women about their lives, how long they'd been working for Ratnakumari. Kabita remained quiet for most of the conversation, offering only a brief yes or no when he directed a question at her. When Ratnakumari came in and saw Pitamber, she teased him that he was bothering her workers. He sensed that she was not entirely joking, so, somewhat self-conscious, he quickly finished his tea and left.

Pitamber made his way through the dense crowd of New Road, where in a side alley he saw a crowd gathered in front of a wall. He went to them, peeked over their shoulders, and saw, pasted on the wall, large photos of the Maobadis who had been listed as "Wanted" by the government. People were talking excitedly, and a man next to Pitamber said, "They should all be tied together and burned in one big pyre."

Some murmured in agreement, but a voice from behind Pitamber said, "What are you saying? Our revolution has arrived! These are our heroes."

"Heroes?" Pitamber swiveled around. "Who said that?"

Someone pointed to a boy of about nineteen, and Pitamber lurched toward him and grabbed his shirt collar. "What did you say?" He could feel the pulse in his own throat as he slapped the boy hard on the right cheek. Encouraged by his slap, other men now crowded around the boy, shoving him, punching him, shaking him. "I wasn't being serious," the boy screamed. "I didn't mean it!" He began pleading for mercy.

His throat still pulsing, Pitamber walked away. He couldn't believe how fast his hand had flown, how thoughtlessly he'd struck the boy. He knew he ought to go back and try to rescue him, but things were already beyond his control now, and the crowd could easily turn its anger on him. He moved rapidly through the market, pushing his way past the shoppers. What did he do that for? For a teenager's stupid joke. And now the boy was probably all bloodied and injured, perhaps left with a broken arm. Pitamber's head was beginning to throb, and he wished he'd gone right home from the restaurant instead of stopping by Kabita's work.

At home Shailaja was feeding Priya, and Pitamber asked them how their day had gone, then said that he felt the need to lie down.

"You came home because you didn't feel well?" Shailaja asked, and he didn't answer her, just continued on to their bedroom and lay down, trying to slow his breathing and forget what had happened in the alley. But he could still hear the boy's panicked pleas.

A little while later, Shailaja came to him and placed her hand on his forehead. "Doesn't feel like you have fever. Are you nauseous?"

"Not really. Just a bit of a headache. I'm sure I'll be fine."

She stayed beside him, and the warmth of her body comforted him. He told her that he'd stopped by Kabita's work. "I think I might have embarrassed her," he said.

"She probably liked that you went to visit her."

Pitamber wanted to tell her what happened next, but he knew it would upset her, and she'd be shocked that he'd hit anyone, let alone a boy. "How is Priya?" he asked instead, his eyes closed.

"If *I* feed her, she'll eat anything. But with her mother, she makes all kinds of excuses."

Pitamber laughed and pressed his hands to his closed eyes. Little stars burst in the darkness there, and for a moment he felt soothed. "She's so happy with you. If we'd had a daughter, I bet she'd have been like her."

"No point in thinking about that now. Come, I'll rub your forehead."

He let her, and her soft fingers felt good on his head.

A while later he woke with a start to sounds of boys arguing outside in the yard. He went to the window, looked out, and saw Sumit tussling with some boys from the neighborhood. "Stop that!" Pitamber shouted. He put on his slippers and hurried downstairs. As soon as they saw him, the other boys ran away, and he grabbed Sumit by the shoulder. "Why were you fighting? What's wrong with you?"

"They were saying things about Kabita auntie," Sumit muttered, looking down.

"What things?" Pitamber's eyes searched for the boys, but he remembered the earlier incident in Indrachowk and immediately controlled himself. "Look at you," he said to Sumit. "Your shirt is torn." Pitamber grabbed his arm and walked him back inside and upstairs.

Shailaja inspected her son's face, and thankfully he didn't have any bruises. She too scolded him, then said, "What did they say to get you so bothered?"

"They were saying bad things about her, about . . ." He looked at Pitamber, then said, "I don't want to live in this house anymore."

Shailaja and Pitamber looked at each other. Finally Shailaja told Sumit, "If they say something bad, just ignore them, okay?"

Sumit glared at her and stormed off to his room. Pitamber shook his head and said, "I have no idea what's going through his mind. Now I have a bigger headache."

"Maybe he's having problems at school," Shailaja said. "I'll go talk to his headmaster."

Shailaja eventually coaxed Sumit out of his room for dinner, and they all sat down to eat. Kabita, who'd gotten home late from work, said, "Dai, my work friends were saying you seem like a fun person."

"Hmm, I don't exactly feel like a fun person right now."

"After dinner, you should go back to sleep," Shailaja said. "Then you'll feel better."

Everyone ate quietly, and about halfway through the meal, Sumit stood and returned to his room. Pitamber was about to follow him, but Shailaja told him to let him be. She then began talking about how the Dashain and Tihar festivals would be more fun this year with Kabita and Priya around. "Now Sumit will have a little sister to do bhai puja with, and Kabita, you can put tika on him." She gestured toward Pitamber.

"I could, but it's only been a few months since my husband died," she said.

"Of course, of course," Shailaja said. "I guess it wouldn't be appropriate."

"What harm would it do? Doing tika doesn't mean you're no longer in mourning," Pitamber said to Kabita.

"That decision is up to her, isn't it?" Shailaja said.

"I don't know," Kabita said. "It might anger God."

Pitamber grew flushed and said, "Why bring God into it? You are starting a new life. Your God should be pleased about it."

"These days the mere mention of God sets you off, doesn't it?" Shailaja said.

Pitamber said to Kabita, "It's your decision. Do what you want to do." Then he stood and went back to bed.

The next morning, a Saturday, Pitamber woke up and went to the living room, where Shailaja was arranging a basket of incense, rice, nuts, and red, orange, and yellow powder. He remembered that today was the day she planned to go to the Maitidevi temple. Despite himself, a groan escaped his lips, and Shailaja, now spooning some curd into a container, said, "You don't have to go if you don't want to."

"I'll go, I'll go," he said.

In the taxi on the way there, Sumit sullenly stared out the window, and Pitamber tried to lighten his mood. "Hey, champion, what happened to your chess game? You don't play these days."

"I don't feel like it anymore," Sumit said.

Pitamber looked sideways at Shailaja, but she was busy rearranging the items in her basket.

"If you stop practicing, how will you become a great player?" Pitamber prodded.

"I don't want to be a great chess player."

"Why not? What do you want to be, a hoodlum, and fight with everyone?" He tried to control his irritation.

"No, I don't want to be a hoodlum," Sumit said. "Anyway, who are you to speak? You're the one who brought a second wife in our house."

Shailaja looked sharply at Sumit, then at Kabita. Pitamber pinched Sumit's left ear, pulling his head toward him. "Say that again?"

Sumit shouted, "Why don't you and Kabita auntie go live somewhere else?"

Pitamber felt his left hand tighten into a fist, make a wide arc, and hit his son on the head. Sumit slumped in his seat, his body limp. The taxi driver braked, then continued. Shailaja gasped something like, "What? What?" and Kabita pressed her hand to her mouth. Pitamber shook his son, said, "Sumit, Sumit?"

Letting the puja basket fall to the floor, Shailaja climbed over Pitamber's lap to her son's side. She too shook Sumit, whose eyes were closed. She pressed her ear against his chest, then said, "I can't hear his heart." Pitamber tried to listen, but he couldn't tell whether the pounding he heard was the rapid beating of his own heart. A wave of panic washed over him, but he managed to tell Shailaja, "He's all right, he's fine." He felt around Sumit's throat with his fingers — there seemed to be a pulse there.

It was the taxi driver who finally said, "Drive to the hospital, hajur?"

Fortunately Bir Hospital was only a stone's throw away, and as they headed inside, a doctor who was on his way to work rushed over to look at Sumit, who was beginning to stir and open his eyes. The doctor fingered the purplish swelling on Sumit's right temple, then guided them into the emergency room. There, he examined Sumit more thoroughly and said, "Nothing serious. Looks like he went unconscious for a few minutes. Did he fall or something?"

Everyone exchanged looks, and the doctor said, "Who hit your son? Did you hit him to discipline him?"

Pitamber knew he ought to step forward and confess, but admitting he'd hit Sumit would further complicate things, so he shook his head and miserably kept quiet.

The doctor said, "Do you know that we've had people die in here from head concussions? Do you parents think before you act?" He looked as if he were about to say something more, but a nurse came to him saying a man had just arrived who'd been injured in a bomb blast. "Take him home and make him rest," the doctor said to Pitamber before he left. "If this type of thing happens again, I'll have to call the police."

The nurse stayed and applied a compress to Sumit's temple, gave him some painkillers, then discharged him.

"We're obviously not going to the temple," Shailaja said as they left the hospital, and during the taxi ride back home, no one spoke. Shailaja didn't look at Pitamber. Sumit lay with his head on her lap, and she murmured to him while stroking his hair. Pitamber glanced at Kabita in the front seat, holding Priya close to her chest, and suddenly he wished he could disappear.

At home Shailaja put Sumit to bed and went to the kitchen to make some soup. Pitamber went to his son's room and sat by his side. He wanted to apologize, to say that he didn't mean to hit him (he'd certainly never hit Sumit before), but as he watched Sumit lying there, his eyes on the ceiling, Pitamber found himself unable to say anything. He had always detested those who hit their children. "Son," Pitamber finally said, and without meeting his eyes Sumit said, "All my friends tease me about her."

Shailaja appeared in the doorway holding a bowl of soup, and without looking at Pitamber, she asked him to leave so she could feed her son. Pitamber went to the living room, where Kabita was trying to mollify her daughter, who was clinging to her, asking her what had happened to Sumit. "Maybe she's hungry," Pitamber said, and Kabita, her eyes cast down, said, "Maybe."

For three days Shailaja didn't sleep with Pitamber in their bedroom; instead, she slept beside Sumit. A heavy silence had permeated the flat, and Pitamber felt constantly ostracized and increasingly guilty. "I didn't mean to hit him," he repeated to Shailaja a few times, but she merely tightened her jaw and refused to look at him. Kabita too seemed wary of him. She averted her eyes whenever he was nearby and instinctively touched her daughter in a gesture of protection. Whenever Pitamber tried to talk to Kabita, she came up with a reason to rush off. It was Sumit who at last broke the silence in the flat one evening, when, after two days of staying home from school, he announced that he was ready for the chess club.

"The chess club?" Shailaja said. "No chess for you, after all that happened."

"But I want to go." They were sitting around the living room. Shailaja was sewing a garland for another attempt at puja the next day.

Pitamber said gently, "Son, don't feel that you have to."

"But I want to. I miss playing."

For a while no one said anything, then Shailaja said, "Son, it's your choice. Don't feel forced to do anything."

"I want to go now," Sumit said. "Buwa, can we go now?"

Pitamber looked at Shailaja, who said, "What's the point of staring at me? It's Sumit who wants to go, not me."

"Okay," Pitamber said to Sumit. "And if you don't like it, you don't have to go anymore." A few months ago, Pitamber had stopped by the club and inquired about its schedule, so he knew it would be open at this time. He had to seize this opportunity — finally here was a break in the gloom and doom of the flat, and Sumit would get a chance to hone his skills with some accomplished players. "All right, let's go," he said to his son.

It turned out that Sumit loved the chess club, and every day after school, he and Pitamber walked to the small brick building, where on the ground floor children and adults of all ages, their eyes intently focused, sat around small tables before chess boards and strategized about how to beat their opponents. After his first time there, Sumit asked Pitamber to wait outside. "I can't concentrate with you in the room," he said, and Pitamber reluctantly obeyed. From outside, he tried to peek through the window and watch his son, but the glass was too dirty and all he could see were blurred figures inside. "He plays well," said Kamal, the man who managed the club, "but he lacks confidence. He needs more encouragement."

That evening as they walked home, Pitamber said to Sumit, "Kamal Sir was saying that you're a marvelous player."

"Really?"

"Of course. You're a natural. You only need a little practice, that's all." He put his hand on his son's shoulder.

Pitamber had sensed it coming—in the past few days Kabita had often mentioned that she and Priya had stayed with them for too long. Still, it surprised him when a week later Kabita announced that she was moving out the next evening, that she and Priya would move in with one of her coworkers, a young woman who lived with her widowed mother and was looking for ways to cut down on their rent. "I can't possibly burden you any longer," she said. In her new flat, her friend's mother would look after Priya while Kabita worked. "I am so grateful for all you gave me," she said to Pitamber and Shailaja.

"I was hoping we'd put tika during Dashain and Tihar," Shailaja said.

"That we'll do, Shailaja didi, I promise. I'll come back for it."

The next evening, Pitamber hurried home after dropping off Sumit at the chess club. Shailaja and Kabita were struggling to get Kabita's belongings down the stairs. "Why didn't you wait for me?" Pitamber said as he grabbed the suitcase and the bedding from them.

"The taxi will be here any minute, dai," Kabita said, smiling. She looked the happiest he'd ever seen her look.

Downstairs, he hauled her things into the trunk of the waiting taxi and said, "Now remember that we're always here for you if things don't work out there." But he knew she wouldn't return—she was too proud to ask for help again. He squatted in front of Priya. "Daughter, you be a good girl to your mother, okay?" She nodded, then opened her palm. He reached into his shirt pocket and handed her a lollipop.

"She has no shame," Kabita said, laughing.

"Don't forget us, you two," Shailaja said as the two stepped into the taxi. Pitamber squeezed Shailaja's shoulder as they watched the car drive away. They trudged back up to the empty flat, and Shailaja immediately headed into the kitchen. He stood inside the door and called, "Shailaja, how long are you going to remain like this?"

She didn't answer, and he heard her start to cry. He went to her and slid his arms around her. "Don't do this to me," he said.

"I thought he was dead," she said between sobs. "I swear, I thought our son had died that day."

He held her tighter.

"You'd never raised your hand against him. Or me."

"I know, I know." He knew that he had no excuse. And maybe he should have seen it coming, given how he'd lost control and slapped that boy in the crowd. "I don't know what came over me," he said.

She squirmed out of his grasp and faced him. "If you do it again, I'll leave you."

He nodded and embraced her again.

The country was soon plunged into mayhem. Maobadis threw bombs at the village homes of several high officials; army men shot at a group of villagers they suspected were aiding the rebels. Rumors spread about rebels stalking the countryside, carrying the severed heads of villagers who refused to give them money. Families abandoned their homes and moved to India. Every day, newspapers announced atrocity after atrocity. Pitamber refused to read the papers or watch the news on television anymore. At the office he began to keep to himself, declining Neupane's occasional offer to go out for a cup of tea or snacks.

Sometimes Pitamber wondered whether Kabita's wounds had begun to heal. Now and then he had the impulse to visit her at her work, and once he actually went, but he couldn't bring himself to walk inside the shop, afraid that his old, dark feelings would resurface.

Every day he went to work, came straight home, and waited for Sumit to return from school so they could play a game of chess before he went to the club. Pitamber found a number of books on the game at a discount store, and he studied them intensely. He taught himself how to anticipate an opponent's moves, how to consider the outcome of his own options and strategize accordingly. And ignoring Sumit's impatient sighs, he often spent long minutes planning his next move.

One evening after work, he ran into Kabita near a busy intersection of New Road. Smiling, she told him that Priya had begun attending a school near where they lived, and that Ratnakumari had asked her to manage a new shop she was opening in Patan. He expressed his pleasure at the good news, then reminded her that he and Shailaja expected her and Priya to visit their home during Dashain, which was only a month away.

"Of course I will, dai," she said.

The Wedding Hero

UMESH, GAURI, AND I JOINED Sagarmatha Bank after it expanded into home and small-business loans. We were part of a staff of about fifteen, newly graduated from commerce college, and our staff had a new building all our own in the bustling tourist district of Thamel. Sagarmatha Bank's head office was in a dilapidated building in Thapathali, a Rana-style monstrosity that leaked during the rainy season, resulting in rooms that were moldy and foul-smelling. The head office's staff had vigorously petitioned to move into the new building, but the board of directors decided that the space in Thamel was too small for the thirty-five or so workers, and that the expansion would be well served by a new staff in a new location.

The three of us had seen one another around the Shanker Dev Campus, but it was at the New Sagarmatha Bank (that's what we called our branch to distinguish it) that our friendship developed. To this day, I can't say exactly why, out of a group of fifteen, the three of us came together. I do remember noticing, the first day at work, how beautiful Gauri was. She had a flawless face, a long, aquiline nose, and soft, delicate eyes. I was not the only one who thought she was beautiful.

The other young men in the office hovered around her, visiting her desk under various pretexts.

I was amused by all the attention Gauri was getting, and when our eyes met across the office, I smiled, and she smiled back. Soon after, she came over to my desk to get my signature for something and addressed me as Jayadev, without the honorific "ji," which I thought was fairly bold but also somewhat refreshing. We exchanged pleasantries, and right at that moment Umesh appeared with a question for us about loan rates. Umesh had a boyish, sad-looking face and bright, shiny hair that frequently fell over his eyes and, as we soon discovered, a melodious voice. He loved to croon the popular Narayan Gopal's songs.

After I signed Gauri's papers and we answered Umesh's query, we began to talk—me sitting in my chair, Gauri leaning against my desk, and Umesh standing with his hands in his trouser pockets, jangling his keys. We talked for what seemed like hours, even though we had work to do. People walked about us, phones rang, we summoned cups of tea and drank them. I remember how pleasant it was, after days of being uneasy in this new office, to find people with whom I could chat effortlessly. What did we talk about? The latest movies, the new dance clubs, the city, buses, our country's relationship with India, government banks, the Maoist rebels, government workers, the Shanker Dev Campus, winter fog, our inept leaders, bits and pieces of personal information. We knew we had to get back to work—our colleagues were giving us sidelong glances—but the branch manager wasn't in, and none of us wanted to break this spell.

This is what I gathered about Umesh: He was twenty-five years old, the only child of well-to-do parents (both drove their own cars). He lived in Lazimpat and had attended St. Xavier's School, so his speech was punctuated with well-pronounced English words. He had a passion for reading novels in Nepali and English. He even admitted that he used to drink heavily in college but had given it up. "I took this job so I wouldn't remain idle at home," he said. Later Gauri told me of a rumor she'd heard about him: a woman had broken his heart, and this had led to his alcoholism.

Gauri herself came from an uneducated family in Janakpur, but had graduated from her high school after performing well on the national School Leaving Certificate exam, which had prompted a Kathmandu benefactor to agree to pay her way through college. The benefactor had wanted to send her to Delhi to study, but Gauri didn't want to live in India, so they'd found a compromise in Shanker Dev Campus in Kathmandu. Gauri rented a flat in Dillibazar. She liked to paint and had taken some art classes, but didn't think she was very good, so she hadn't shown her paintings to anyone.

As for me, it's hard to describe yourself, but I'll try. At that time I was twenty-eight and unmarried, although my parents had been pestering me about this for the past few years. I am of average height, pretty thin, with a mustache that conceals a small cleft on my upper lip. I remained unmarried because I had not come across a woman who was just right for me. My parents thought this was a very modern view, and they clearly disapproved. They had married in their teens, without so much as having looked at each other's photographs beforehand, and they'd had a happy life. I often suggested to them that what worked for them might not work for me. Nevertheless, over the years they'd shown me countless pictures of women. At times I grew fed up and threatened to move out, live in a flat of my own. My threat worked: my parents couldn't bear the thought of what such a move would signal to others about our family's unity. They'd back down for a few weeks, then start hinting about potential women again. Almost all of my classmates from school and college were married and had children, so I understood my parents' anxiety. Still, I felt deep inside that a woman was out there waiting for me, and I knew it had to be only a matter of time before I found her.

At the end of our chat at the bank that day, I wondered whether Umesh and Gauri were as surprised as I was by how quickly we'd taken to each other. Someone complained to the manager about our long conversation, so the next morning he called us into his office. He told us that the old Panchayat practice of drinking tea and chatting all day was unacceptable, that we were setting a bad example for the rest of the workers. We acted contrite, but as soon as we left his office, we smiled at one another and said, "After work? Ramey's tea shop down the road?"

From then on, we concocted excuses to stop by one another's desks during work, and we disbanded as soon as we noticed the manager's disapproving looks. After work and on weekends, we often visited each other at home. Gauri's flat in Dillibazar was small but comfortable, and she made killer tea with cinnamon and cloves. We played cards, listened to songs. We also gathered at my house a few times, but my mother began eyeing Gauri as a potential daughter-in-law, which made us edgy, so we stopped meeting there.

It turned out that Umesh's large house in Lazimpat was the perfect place for us to get together. Busy socialites, his parents were never home. There was a scraggly garden behind his house, with a small gazebo where we could sit when it rained. The garden buzzed with bees and dragonflies, and we could feast our eyes on the bright red and yellow roses, the riotous vines that crawled up the walls of the house. "My parents *pay* the gardener to keep the garden unkempt," Umesh said once, laughing. His parents had two servants, which meant our afternoons there were filled with momos, tea, pakoras, and homemade ice cream. "Treat this as your home," Umesh said, clearly meaning it, so soon Gauri and I didn't feel uncomfortable calling the servants to fetch us something. Once in a while, usually in the evening, we drank rum and Cokes or margaritas. Gauri always took small sips; she drank only to be sociable. Umesh never had more than a glass or two—he explained that he didn't want to go back to his old ways.

Mildly intoxicated, we sometimes talked sentimentally about our friendship.

"I hope we'll never be separated," Umesh said. "I've never had friends like you."

Gauri quoted lines from a ghazal:

> If we break apart,
> At night we won't sleep.
> Remembering each other
> We will always weep.

"Wah, wah," I applauded her, and she stood and bowed.

"Cheers to us," Umesh said, and we clinked our glasses.

Sometimes the three of us went on picnics—to Dhulikhel, Balaju, Swayambhu, anyplace that would give us respite from the smog and crowds in the city. A chauffeur would drive us in one of Umesh's parents' cars. We watched the sunset from Dhulikhel, shivering in the evening cold as the sky became awash with pink and orange. In the Balaju water gardens, to our embarrassed delight, Umesh stripped to his underwear and bathed at one of the twenty-two spouts that gushed fresh water. Under Buddha's eyes in Swayambhunath temple, we chatted with a scantily clad sadhu smeared with ashes and holding a trident. We asked him why he'd renounced the material pleasures of life, and whether he felt any stirrings when he looked at a beautiful woman like Gauri. We went to plays, comedy shows, dance programs. The more time we spent together, the more we enjoyed one another's company. But the moments I remember most from those days were in Umesh's garden gazebo. The rain falling on the leaves and the flowers. Its steady drumbeat on the roof still reminds me of our friendship.

Then Tikaram entered our lives. Our office boy had quit abruptly, and for three days we didn't have anyone to fetch us tea or run errands, so we were glad when Tikaram was hired as the new peon. The day he started, he appeared at my desk, palms together in supplication. "Recognize me, hajur?"

I didn't.

"We used to play together when we were young," he said.

A dim memory came to me of a friend who taught me how to make a slingshot. I remembered searching for sparrows in the woods of Raniban. "Tikaram?"

He smiled, pleased that I'd remembered him without further prompting. It was little wonder that I didn't recognize him immediately: his face had changed drastically. His skin was already beginning to wrinkle, and his lips were now black-blue. Dark circles had formed under his eyes. He looked fifteen years older than me, although he was, from what I recall, only a couple of years older.

He told me he still lived in the old neighborhood of Chhetrapati, where my parents used to live. His wife had died, leaving him with two children to raise, and he was thinking of remarrying.

"You have someone in mind?" I asked.

He appeared embarrassed. "Something like that."

"Who is she?"

"Her name is Kanyakumari."

"Don't both 'kanya' and 'kumari' mean virgin? Is she a double virgin, then?" I couldn't resist asking, then hoped that I hadn't gone too far. But Tikaram merely laughed.

From then on, he frequently stopped by my desk to see if I needed anything. His job was to serve everyone in the office, but I sensed he paid more attention to me. I soon remembered that my parents, themselves not well-to-do at the time, had hired Tikaram's mother during a period of financial difficulty in her life. Her husband had simply vanished, turning her into a single mother overnight. I remembered her sad face, and I suddenly recalled a boy on the street calling her a whore or something like that, and Tikaram next to her, his face bright red.

One day he told me that his mother had passed away a few years ago.

"She was a good woman," I said.

"She devoted her entire life to me, hajur," he said. "She wanted me to study and get a good job, but I was always too stupid for school. You and I were friends when we were young, but look at us now. You are way up high and I have gone nowhere."

His talk made me uncomfortable. "Don't speak like that, Tikaram," I said gently. "Everyone has his own struggle in life."

"I could have done better, hajur," he said.

Once Tikaram saw what close friends Umesh, Gauri, and I were, he gave them the same attention he paid to me. "You'll give us ulcers with so many cups of tea, Tikaram," Gauri told him, and he merely smiled.

A few weeks after he arrived, things changed for Tikaram. One afternoon I heard an argument near the main door. He was talking to a woman whose face I couldn't see, as she was in the hallway. "How can I do that right now?" Tikaram yelled. "I just started here." The woman said something, and Tikaram shouted back, "You bitch, who do you think you are?"

Everyone in the office looked toward the door, and fearing the manager's response, I quickly went to Tikaram. The woman turned her face away when she saw me. I didn't recognize her. "What's going on?" I asked Tikaram. "Why are you making such a ruckus?"

"Sorry, hajur," he said sheepishly. "She's an idiot to come here and argue."

"Let's go out and talk," I said, and led them down the stairs and out to the pavement. I was still unable to see her face, as she kept it hidden. "Who is she?" I asked. "What's the problem here?"

"She is the one I told you about."

"Ah," I said, remembering.

She finally turned toward me, and I saw that she had a strong, bony face and was at least ten years younger than Tikaram.

"Okay, tell me, why are you arguing?" I asked him.

"She's pestering me to marry her, hajur. But I don't have any money for a wedding. I just started working here."

"He'll never marry me," she said. "He's playing with my life, the donkey."

"Well, you can't settle this in the office," I said. "He could get fired. Why don't you discuss this at home?"

"He doesn't want to discuss it. He keeps avoiding it, saying he can't think about it now."

"Shut your mouth!" Tikaram yelled. People on the street glanced our way.

"You shut your mouth, donkey. If you're not going to marry me, I'll find someone else to marry. You think I can't find someone?"

"You see, hajur," Tikaram appealed to me, "how she threatens me?"

I was embarrassed for them, so I said to the woman, "Listen, you go home now. This evening I'll sit down with the two of you and we'll try to work things out." I regretted my offer as soon as I made it. I could not exactly see myself helping much in a relationship where the words "bitch" and "donkey" were common currency. But my offer seemed to have a calming effect on the woman, and she smiled at me. "That'll be good, hajur," she said as she turned to leave. "We should have done this a long time ago. He speaks very highly of you."

Tikaram and I walked back upstairs. "We'll find her after work, okay?" I said, and he nodded hesitantly.

I told Umesh and Gauri about what had happened, and they laughed. "What are you now, a lami? We'll have to see how well you fit the role of go-between."

"Don't laugh."

"I'd like to see your parents' faces when they learn of this," Umesh said. "Their son, whose marriage they haven't been able to fix, is now offering advice on the subject."

Their mocking made me more apprehensive about my offer to help resolve Tikaram's dispute. What was I thinking? I had half a mind to go to Tikaram and back out of the whole thing, but I couldn't renege on my promise so quickly. I looked at Umesh and Gauri—Gauri with her clear, bright eyes—and an idea came to me. "Why don't you two come along? I could use some help."

At first they laughed away my suggestion, saying it had been my decision and I should deal with it. But I made convincing arguments: Gauri would know how to handle any "womanly" issue that might arise (I had no idea what I was talking about), and Tikaram was a stubborn fellow, and I'd need Umesh's fortification. I don't think they were entirely persuaded, but they took pity on me and finally agreed to come.

After work the four of us, Tikaram included (he looked slightly bewildered at the entourage that had assembled to tackle his problem), took a taxi to where Kanyakumari lived. At the door her aunt said she wasn't home, and when I looked at Tikaram, he said, "She works until six o'clock."

"Why didn't you tell us this before?" I asked, annoyed, but he shook his head as if he himself didn't understand why. Gauri and Umesh were trying to suppress their laughter.

Instead of waiting at Kanyakumari's house for her to return from work, we agreed to go to Tikaram's place and meet his children, and we told Kanyakumari's aunt to send her niece over there once she got home. The woman seemed comfortable with Tikaram and her niece's association with him. I have discovered that sometimes "lower-caste" folks (and I put this in quotes because I've never believed in such nonsense) are more open-minded when it comes to social tradition than those of the "upper caste." Take my own mother, a middle-class Brahmin woman, who made a sour face when she first learned that Gauri was a Jaisi Brahmin. Why would such a thing matter to anyone? As if our forefathers hadn't gone far enough with this ridiculous caste business, they had to divide a single caste into lower and higher. The interesting thing was that my mother's disapproval of Jaisi Brahmins didn't stop her from eyeing Gauri as a potential daughter-in-law. But I suspect that was more out of desperation than anything else. She might have been thinking, Better a Jaisi Brahmin than a Newar, or some other caste she considered even lower.

Tikaram's two children, Shanker and Sita, were playing in the courtyard when we reached his house, which was a couple of neighborhoods away. Like most neighborhoods off the main street in inner Kathmandu, this one featured a courtyard surrounded by old houses. The ground was littered with plastic bottles, and a drain ran along the edge of the courtyard, giving off a foul smell. Tikaram's children came running to him, and he gathered them in his arms. He forced them to say "namaste" to us, and we remarked on how well-mannered they were.

We went upstairs to Tikaram's flat, which had three rooms — a bedroom, a kitchen, and a bathroom. The children's clothes were strewn on the floor, and unwashed dishes were piled in the kitchen sink. Tikaram asked his son, only nine years old, to make tea for us, but we declined. Faint noises from the evening crowd beyond the courtyard filtered into the room as we sat on the carpet on the floor, waiting for Kanyakumari.

When she arrived, the children greeted her with as much delight as they'd greeted their father, and we were glad to observe this intimacy, for it made our mission seem more worthwhile. "They already see her as their mother," Gauri whispered to me.

Without a word, Kanyakumari picked up the clothes from the floor, opened the window to let in some air, and made tea for all of us, even though we kept saying we didn't want any. We sat there drinking our tea and waiting for someone to talk. I was about to open my mouth to say something, anything, when Kanyakumari said, "For two years he's been promising to marry me. The children like me, and I've become attached to them. But he only makes excuses. He says he doesn't have money, but I'm not asking for a big wedding."

We turned to Tikaram, who said, "I don't have enough money for a wedding, big or small."

"There's always the court," Kanyakumari said. Court weddings were inexpensive and required minimal planning.

"What's the point in getting married like that?" Tikaram said, shaking his head. "What's a wedding if you don't invite people, don't have a feast, don't have a band? Without these things it'd be more like a funeral procession."

"If it's a funeral, then you must be the corpse, not me."

"You witch!" Tikaram said angrily.

"Will there be a band?" Sita, Tikaram's daughter, asked excitedly. She was sitting on Kanyakumari's lap. Since Tikaram's and Kanyakumari's language didn't faze the children, I assumed they were used to this type of argument.

In a sugary voice, Tikaram asked the children to go outside and play, which they did, reluctantly. It was beginning to get dark, but he didn't turn on the light.

I asked him, "You have no money?"

"None," he said. "I was out of work for a long time."

"Okay," Umesh said, clearing his throat. "Have you calculated how much you'd need for a wedding if you hire a cheap band and serve a simple feast?"

Tikaram and Kanyakumari shook their heads. In the growing darkness of the room, their faces were becoming dimmer. Umesh stood up, turned on the light, and asked for paper and a pen. Tikaram found them on his bedside table, handed them to him, and Umesh began to calculate the cost of the wedding. He seemed suddenly energized, and he pursed his lips as he wrote. "Bhoj with mutton, pulau, and ice cream," he mumbled. "Fifteen thousand rupees. Might be hard, but we can shop around for that price. Band, ten thousand rupees." The final tally came to about sixty thousand rupees. All of us, including Tikaram and Kanyakumari, were relieved he had taken over.

Kanyakumari snatched the piece of paper from Umesh and shoved it in Tikaram's face. "See how easy it is? You needed someone like Umesh dai to make the sun shine on your thick skull."

Umesh sat with a smug smile, hands folded in his lap.

"Shut your mouth," Tikaram told Kanyakumari. "That's all fine and dandy, but I don't have that kind of money."

I began to wonder if they ever had an intimate moment, if they ever whispered sweet nothings to each other.

Umesh said, "Okay, how much do you have, Tikaram? No money, no money, you keep saying. But you must have something."

"I could maybe come up with fifteen thousand, that's all."

We watched Umesh. Something was happening inside him, something ticking, something churning. You could see it on his face. His lips were pressed together, his eyes had narrowed. We stared at the paper with all the calculations, then looked at him.

Finally Umesh opened his mouth, and in the split second before he spoke, I think we all knew what he was going to say. "Tikaram, this is important," Umesh said, enunciating his words carefully. "We have to find a solution to this. You can't keep saying you have no money. You do want to marry her, right?"

Tikaram nodded.

"And you," he asked Kanyakumari, "want to marry him?"

She too gave her yes.

Umesh took a moment to relish the anticipation on our faces. "Then let's fix a date."

"What do you mean?" I asked, afraid of what was coming. "He just said he couldn't afford more than fifteen thousand."

"I'll take care of the rest," Umesh said. "He'll just pay me back when he can."

Tikaram insisted that no, no, he couldn't possibly take a loan from Umesh. How and when would he be able to pay it back? Both Gauri and I tried to gently dissuade Umesh from what he'd just offered. But he didn't listen. "Look," he said. "It's a loan, not a gift. What's the big deal? Can you come up with a better solution?"

We were stumped. I was about to say, "If they don't have the money, they shouldn't get married," but I didn't want to offend anyone. I was annoyed with Umesh, and I saw Gauri was too. What was he trying to be, some kind of hero?

"I want you two to get married," Umesh said with authority. "It would be great for the children."

Tikaram had stopped objecting and was watching Kanya-kumari for her reaction. After a long silence she said, "If we don't get married now, I worry that he'll never marry me."

"That settles it," Umesh said, clapping his hands. Then the three of them—Umesh, Kanyakumari, and Tikaram—started discussing possible dates. Tikaram flipped through a religious calendar for favorable days while Gauri and I looked on in disbelief. They jotted down some dates; a priest would have to choose the one most in accord with godly forces. They discussed money, and Tikaram brought out a stash of cash from somewhere in the kitchen. "Seven thousand," he said, handing it to Umesh, who quickly counted and pocketed it. The remaining eight thousand he'd get from a relative. Umesh held up his palm as if to say, No problem.

As soon as we walked out to the courtyard, Gauri and I gave Umesh a sound tongue-lashing. "What in God's name do you think you are doing?" I exploded. "Have you lost your mind? You just committed yourself to paying for someone's wedding. Sixty thousand rupees! And if it's like any other wedding I know, add another thirty or forty to your original estimate."

As we merged into the crowd on the street, Gauri asked, "What came over you, Umesh? I never knew you wanted to be such a hero." It was as if she had stolen words from my mouth.

Umesh stopped, looking hurt and confused. "What are you saying? I only want to help."

"Helping is fine," I said, "but you're basically wedding them with your money. Why have you suddenly turned into such a philanthropist?"

"Well, I have the money. Why not?"

Gauri and I thought hard for a response. Gauri was quicker in coming up with one. "Then why don't you pay for our wedding too?" She meant, of course, to say our separate weddings, hers and mine, but she pointed her thumb at herself, then me, confusing the matter.

Umesh seized the opportunity. "You two are getting married? Why was I kept in the dark?"

"No, no," we protested. "You know she meant our individual weddings," I said.

But it was too late. Umesh donned the self-important face of a priest, and in crowded Ganabahal, in front of a small shrine of who knows what god or goddess, he chanted some Sanskrit-sounding words and joined Gauri's and my hands. "It's a marriage made for seven incarnations," he declared. I felt a rush of something, embarrassment maybe, and a tingle at the back of my neck. Gauri laughed.

"Let's discuss my handiwork over tea, shall we?" Umesh said.

We slipped into a nearby shop and sat in a corner. On the wall next to us was a movie poster of a starlet with seductive eyes. I stole a glance at Gauri, who was seated next to me, and a young waiter in shorts and a torn vest came to take our order. He sauntered off singing a raunchy song that was popular on the radio. Gauri turned toward me and rolled her eyes.

"You two are mad at me for no reason," Umesh said. "Don't you see that those children need Kanyakumari? And you're going to let a few thousand rupees deprive them of a mother?"

"A few thousand?" Gauri said. "By anyone's standard, sixty thousand is a lot of money."

She sat there in her embroidered blue sari, her large eyes bright, her pink lips full. What was I thinking—she was my friend! I tried to ignore my longing thoughts and addressed Umesh. "Why didn't you at least think about it for a couple of days beforehand?"

"Listen," he said. "Life is too short. God has given me more money than most people have. This is just my way of balancing the wealth. Besides, did you see the faces of those children? How they adored Kanyakumari? Don't you think they need a mother like her?"

We thought about it, and we knew Umesh was right.

+   +   +

Over the next few days, Umesh grew busy with the wedding preparations. He made endless phone calls at work about clothing for the groom, religious paraphernalia for the priest, the printing of the invitations. I don't know how he managed to get his work done, because he always seemed to be badgering someone on the phone, whispering details with Tikaram, or asking me or Gauri a question about some aspect of the wedding we had no clue about. "We've never been married before, remember?" we teased him, and he said, "Oh, yes, you have. I married you two in Ganabahal." Though I laughed him off, I felt my face fill with heat.

Our manager started watching Umesh from his office, but Umesh was unfazed. "Do you think I care about what he thinks?" he said. "I'm getting my job done, so he can't fault me for anything."

Umesh was right. Incredibly, his work had not suffered a bit since this madness over Tikaram's wedding began. On the contrary, Umesh seemed to have more energy than before, and he frequently performed several tasks at once — approving a customer's loan, for example, calling the tailor about the groom's suit, and redrafting the personnel manual for bank employees.

At times we snickered at him. "It's as if he's marrying off his own son," we joked. Other times we scolded him for his bothersome questions. Often he couldn't make it to our after-work tea because he had to rush off and take care of some wedding matter. We missed him, and we resented him a little for neglecting us in favor of Tikaram.

And then something did seem to start happening between Gauri and me. At five o'clock we left the office, never saying much but usually walking close together, and usually with silly smiles on our faces, and whenever our shoulders brushed, our eyes met and our smiles deepened. We sat in the tea shop, and from the silence an intimate conversation would emerge — something that had never happened in Umesh's presence — and we'd get lost in talk about our lives. When Umesh had been with us, the conversation was more energetic, jumping from one topic to another, from laughter to sighs. With just the two of us, though, the conversation was quieter, more reflective, punctuated by long but easy silences. Gauri eventually revealed to me a secret she'd never told anyone: she had been molested by her uncle when she was a young teenager. This had gone on for almost a year, and no one in her immediate family had a clue. Her face turned dark and sad when she spoke, and later she told me that her uncle was one of the reasons she'd left Janakpur, even though she'd have preferred to stay with her family. "I couldn't stand being near him at family gatherings," she said.

The next afternoon, I told her about my lonely childhood. I had often been sickly, and my parents had to take me to the doctor every few weeks. My relatives called me Lurey, the Weakling, and this name had stuck with me throughout my childhood into my early teens. Since playing with other children meant being taunted by them about my thin arms and weak stamina, I often played by myself. Only after entering college had I been able to shed some of these painful memories.

Soon thereafter, Gauri and I kissed in her flat. I had coaxed her into showing me her paintings, and one painting in particular, of an old woman's leathery face with a glinting ring in her nose, caught my attention. "Her features are remarkable," I said, and turned to her. We were sitting on her bed, our bodies touching, so it didn't seem unnatural when I moved my face closer and pressed my lips against hers. She responded softly. After a while I whispered, laughing, "I wonder what Umesh will think of this." I could tell from her face that she, too, felt a pang of guilt, but all she said was "Let's not think about him right now."

As the wedding day approached and Umesh grew even more busy, he enlisted us to help him. In fact, he persuaded us to take a couple of days' leave from the office. At first we were hesitant, because we didn't want to upset our manager, but eventually we realized that Umesh desperately needed our help in handling the numerous last-minute details. "Now all three of you are skipping out of work?" the manager said when we submitted our letters requesting the days off. "What am I going to do with you?"

"Nothing," Umesh said, beaming. "Come and enjoy the feast with us."

In his magnanimity, Umesh had invited not only everyone from our office but everyone from the head office in Thapathali, which meant that the number of guests from Sagarmatha Bank alone approached fifty. By this time it had become obvious that the cost of the wedding had greatly surpassed the budget we had originally discussed. But whenever I asked Umesh about it, he said, "Everything's under control. Don't worry about it. Just enjoy the festivities." Those days he never got a full night's sleep, so his eyes were red. He badly needed a haircut. We *were* worried, but nothing we said or did could slow him down.

In the end, the wedding was, by all accounts, fantastic. A large tent, covering every inch of the sky, had been set up in the courtyard of Tikaram's house. Petromax lamps lit the entire area, and a band, dressed in red, yellow, and black, played Hindi movie tunes. Small colored lights blinked around the periphery of the tent. Attending the wedding were close to three hundred people, not to mention the several passersby who slipped in to take advantage of the feast. At least four varieties of meat dishes and ten vegetable dishes had been laid out on a long serving table, and the desserts included not only ice cream but rasgulla, lalmohan, barfi, and kalakand. We were stunned — only the upper-class people in the city could afford a feast like this. Later I learned that although the food was catered by a small company, Umesh had hired a famous chef from a luxury hotel to supervise everything.

At one point in the evening, amid the hustle and bustle, Gauri and I found ourselves alone upstairs in Tikaram's flat, where Gauri had gone to fetch some coconuts for the priest and I had gone to get a handkerchief for Tikaram.

As we held each other, my heart beat loudly in my chest at the thought that someone could easily walk in on us. The golden bangles on her wrists clinked as she adjusted her arms around my back. Umesh's laughter rose above the conversations of the guests, and I whispered to Gauri, "Shouldn't we tell him about us soon?" After all, it'd already been two weeks since we first kissed.

"Hmmm?" Gauri said dreamily.

"Umesh. Shouldn't he know?"

"He'll find out soon enough."

Someone shouted from downstairs, "Coconuts! The priest needs the coconuts!" I reluctantly let Gauri go, and followed her out a few seconds later. Umesh stood with one of the executives from the bank, and when he spotted me, he called me over. As the three of us chatted, I considered taking Umesh aside and telling him about Gauri and me. I saw myself asking for his priestly blessing, reminding him that he'd already married us the day he'd fixed Tikaram's wedding. But before I could say anything, Umesh was whisked away to the buffet table, where the kalakand was in short supply.

Around seven, the wedding band slowly led the crowd through the narrow lanes of the city center to call upon the bride. Along the route, people watched from the windows of their houses. Tikaram sat in the hired taxi with a couple of his relatives while the children rode in Umesh's car; the rest of us followed on foot. Gauri stayed back at Tikaram's flat so she could help his aunts prepare a customary welcome for the bride. As we walked, the evening crowd parted to let us through. Umesh was beside me, and I put my arm around him. "I salute you today, your highness," I said.

The reception at Kanyakumari's house was modest by comparison, since her family earned a meager income and had rejected Umesh's offer to help. Their tent was patched in places, the buffet table spare, but we were not there to pass judgment, only to fetch the bride, which we did eventually, after hours of wedding rites and rituals. The procession returned with Tikaram and Kanyakumari in the taxi, she in her bright red wedding sari, her face hidden by a veil, and he in his suit and embroidered cap, looking dapper and, for once, young.

For days afterward we talked about the wedding and what a success it had been. Our colleagues congratulated Umesh, and some, even those who were married, jokingly suggested that they wanted to be married, or married again, by him, if only for the obvious financial perks involved. Umesh took it all in with the air of an exhausted father who had just witnessed the birth of his first child. "I did what I could do," he said modestly. "The rest is up to them." Tikaram, who came back to work beaming a couple of days after the wedding, also gracefully absorbed jokes from our colleagues about the wedding night, some of which were quite vulgar.

When the excitement died down, Umesh came back to our fold and we resumed our after-work tea. But now, in his presence, Gauri and I became self-conscious when we looked at each other. We still hadn't told him about us—the right moment just never came. In order to compensate, I suppose, we laughed louder and harder at his jokes, listened to him more attentively.

But it was clear that he sensed something was different. Sometimes, in the middle of talking, he would stop abruptly, stare at us, then say, "I forgot what I was saying." Whenever I spoke, he focused on Gauri's face more than mine, as if to gauge what she was feeling about what I said. I guess a part of me was afraid he'd think that by becoming a couple, Gauri and I had betrayed our larger friendship.

Gauri approached my desk one morning. Umesh hadn't come in yet, and in the past few days we hadn't spoken about him because he'd always been with us. Now, judging from her face, I knew something was wrong.

"What's the matter with Umesh?" she said. "He came to my flat last night at ten o'clock, drunk. I was getting ready to go to bed."

"Really?" I asked. "Has he started drinking again?"

"I don't know," she said. "He kept saying he needed to tell me something, but he never did. Then he held my hand and cried on my shoulder. He kept saying he was so sorry, but he didn't say about what. It was so strange."

Despite myself, I winced at the image of his head on her shoulder. I grew annoyed with him, then annoyed with myself for becoming annoyed in the first place. Was he having some problem he hadn't told us about? Deep inside, I suppose I knew he'd sensed what was going on between Gauri and me, and I resolved to talk to him. But he didn't come to work that day. At around eleven, I called his house but there was no answer. The manager approached my desk a short while later, inquiring after Umesh. "I think he's very sick, sir," I said. "He wasn't feeling well yesterday. Maybe he's too sick to call." The manager shook his head and left.

That evening Gauri and I found ourselves alone as we walked to Ramey's tea shop. She suddenly said, "Let's go somewhere else for a change, someplace we won't be thinking about . . . just someplace different."

We ended up taking a taxi to the Soaltee Hotel, where we walked through several hallways and found a restaurant with plush chairs and tables made of mahogany. Large glass chandeliers hung from the ceiling, and soft sitar tunes drifted from speakers.

The waiter seated us at a table very close to a small stage, where, I discovered, some musicians would soon be playing. Candles in gilded holders burned at our table. We could hear the murmurs of tourists at a table nearby. I had never been inside the Soaltee, let alone such a posh restaurant, and when I asked Gauri how we'd pay for all this, she said, "It's my treat. I just feel like celebrating."

The musicians arrived, and so did our food—chicken chili, lamb kebab, mutton in peanut sauce, naan. It smelled and tasted heavenly, and we chatted as we ate. Neither of us mentioned Umesh. Once the music started, I shifted my chair next to Gauri's and wrapped my arm around her. A harmonium player sang a ghazal in a melodious, almost feminine voice:

> *Yesterday was a night of full moon.*
> *Everywhere there was talk of you.*

The light in the room grew softer, the music even sweeter.

At the office the next day, Umesh avoided us until I confronted him and insisted on a talk downstairs.

"What's happening, Umesh?" I asked when we were outside.

He appeared flushed. "Did Gauri say anything about me?"

"About that night? Of course she did. She's worried about you." His eyes were pink, slightly swollen. "Have you started drinking again?"

At first he vehemently denied it, then admitted that he'd been drinking "a bit" at night, before bed.

"What's eating you?" I asked.

"Nothing, nothing." He looked at me helplessly. "Gauri must think badly of me."

"No," I said. "Listen, why don't you join us for tea today? Everything will be all right."

He stared at me for a moment, then asked, "I won't be interfering?"

"Nonsense," I said, feeling myself blush. "What are you talking about?" I should've confessed to him right then and there.

That evening Umesh walked with us to the tea shop. Initially the conversation was awkward, with long stretches of silence, and Gauri and Umesh kept trying to avoid each other's eyes. By the time we finished our first glass of tea, however, we were all a little more relaxed, and soon we were laughing and joking about work. After a while the topic turned to Tikaram. "I think they're having some problems," Umesh said, taking a bite of a samosa. "He doesn't look happy. The other day he told me that he and Kanyakumari were fighting."

Since the wedding, Tikaram had spent more time with Umesh than with Gauri or me. Now that Umesh mentioned it, I realized that Tikaram had been looking down lately. "So soon?" I asked Umesh. "Over what?"

"Over the children, over money, he wasn't clear."

"A husband and wife arguing—what's unusual about that?" Gauri said.

"I get the impression they argue all the time," Umesh said.

"So much for all your . . . ," Gauri said.

"What do you mean?" Umesh asked.

"Nothing," she said, shaking her head.

After a silence, Umesh said, "Maybe you can talk to Kanyakumari. Maybe that'd help."

"Why should I get involved in their marital problems?" Gauri said. "Anyway, it wouldn't feel right."

"It's obvious they're meant for each other. They're just having difficulties."

"Maybe they weren't meant to be together, Umesh," Gauri said. "Maybe it was only you who thought they were."

I didn't like where the conversation was headed, so I said, "It's been too long since we've had tea together. Let's talk about something else."

But Umesh said, "You don't have to act so high and mighty, Gauri. All I said was that maybe Kanyakumari will listen to you, woman to woman."

Gauri laughed. "High and mighty? Look who's talking. Who is the one going around distributing his parents' wealth?"

"Stop it, you two!" I said.

But the damage was already done. Umesh leaned back against his chair, his jaw clenched. Gauri stared at the table.

"All right," Umesh said. "If that's what you think of me. Anyway, I know what's going on." He looked at me, then at Gauri.

"Umesh, don't talk like this," I said.

"I didn't mean it that way, Umesh," Gauri said. "I'm just a little tired of Tikaram this and Tikaram that."

"You're tired of me, I think," Umesh said, getting up.

"Umesh," I said, but he walked away from us and left the shop.

Gauri and I sipped our tea in silence. Despite myself, I resented her for arguing with Umesh. She could have easily agreed to talk to Kanyakumari, and the conversation might not have been so uncomfortable. My feelings must have shown on my face, for she asked me, "You don't blame *me* for this, do you?"

"Maybe that argument wasn't necessary."

"I might have spoken a bit harshly, but don't you see? He was trying to wheedle me into something I didn't want to do."

"So, he knows about us," I said, defeated. "He probably feels hurt that we didn't tell him earlier."

"Did he give us the chance to tell him?" Gauri said. "Besides, he could have been happy for us instead of acting like a child."

That was true, and some of my resentment toward Gauri dissolved. Umesh, too, could have handled it differently. Still, I felt bad about the whole thing. Only a few weeks ago, all three of us occupied such a different world, sitting around a table in Umesh's garden, humming songs, reading passages from novels. I remembered the three of us laughing—a beautiful thing.

Umesh no longer joined us for tea, and after work Gauri and I began to frequent a restaurant with booths that afforded us some privacy. Sometimes we talked about Umesh—now he smelled of alcohol in the morning, and he kept to himself all day at his desk. He often invented excuses to leave and go to the head office, and a few times I saw him quarreling with the manager.

One morning before Umesh's arrival, the manager called me into his office and said, "You're his good friend. Talk to him. I've already given him a written warning. If this continues, I'll be forced to let him go."

I asked him what exactly was wrong.

"Everything is wrong. He's making serious mistakes. Doesn't come to the office on time. And we all know he's been drinking."

I told him that Umesh was a good worker, that something was troubling him and it'd probably be over soon. Back at my desk, I began blaming myself: maybe if I hadn't gotten involved with Gauri, he wouldn't be acting this way. Soon enough, however, I stopped myself. My logic was absurd. Umesh was responsible for his own actions. How could I be held accountable for his emotions? Or for how much he drank?

When he came in, almost an hour later, I told him that I needed to talk to him, and we went outside. His hair was disheveled, and he was chewing paan paraag, most likely to hide the smell of alcohol.

"That bastard," he barked after I told him what the manager had said. "I have half a mind to go beat him up."

I became annoyed. "Why are you acting like a child? If you don't pull yourself together, he'll fire you."

"I don't care. This isn't the only job in the city."

"A lot of people are talking about your drinking, Umesh." I ought to have grabbed him by his shirt collar and insisted that he stop drinking, that he was ruining his life. But I was no longer sure that I was a close enough friend to take such a liberty.

His face suddenly softened and he said, "Don't worry about me, Jayadev. Worry about yourself. Now you and Gauri have a lot to think about."

For some reason, I couldn't meet his eyes.

Umesh submitted his resignation the next day, and within a few days someone else was hired to replace him. He was gone—just like that.

After he left, Gauri and I grew closer, and we talked about marrying. By this point, Gauri had begun spending much more time at my house, and whatever reservations my mother had about her slightly lower caste status soon disappeared. My mother even offered to go with Gauri to Janakpur when she was to tell her parents our news, but Gauri assured her it would be better if she went alone.

Only hours after she left for Janakpur, I began to miss her, and that day at the office passed very slowly. Every few minutes I half expected to find her at her desk, and that evening I went to Ramey's tea shop by myself, for old times' sake. Being there without Gauri, or Umesh for that matter, made me restless, so I left. I went home and listened to some Narayan Gopal songs on the stereo. During dinner, my mother sensed my mood and smiled at me, even teased me a bit.

That night I lay in bed thinking how lucky I was to have met Gauri—she had such a sharp mind, was so confident about herself, so understanding with me. I slept with a silly smile on my face, but woke in the middle of the night, troubled by a dream in which I saw Umesh and Gauri holding hands. A feeling gradually took hold of me—that I wasn't deserving of Gauri, but Umesh was. It was stupid and self-defeating, but the feeling soon overwhelmed me. Umesh was better-looking and came from a more wealthy family. And that was not all. It seemed as if Umesh *needed* Gauri more than I did. The thought startled me, for I didn't know where it came from. I lay in bed squirming, suddenly feeling that I had snatched her away from him. I couldn't fall back to sleep, and by four o'clock in the morning I was groggy and depressed.

All the next day I was in a lousy mood. When Tikaram came to my desk with tea, I asked him how things were going with Kanyakumari, and he shook his head sadly. "I don't think it's going to work out," he said. I pressed him, but he wouldn't say anything more.

After work, as I was heading home, I decided that I finally needed to talk to Umesh. It'd been more than two weeks since he'd left his job, and I wanted to tell him outright about Gauri and me, and hear him reassure me that he didn't resent us. I walked all the way to Lazimpat, and the cool evening air cleared my head.

I had to bang on Umesh's gate a few times before the servant came to open it. When I asked him where Umesh was, he pointed to the back of the house. I found him sitting inside the gazebo, smoking a cigar and drinking. He didn't seem to be aware of my presence until I called his name, when he looked up with bloodshot eyes, and his face broke into a wild, drunken grin. "Ah, Jayadev. What an honor. What brings you to my humble abode?"

"Hardly humble," I said, laughing. Just hearing his voice, even though he was drunk, made me feel a bit better. "What's with you?"

"First a drink, a toast," he said. He shouted for his servant, who brought a glass. I didn't object when he poured me some whiskey. "How's our good old Gauri?" he asked after we toasted and I took a sip.

"She's fine, but it's you I've been thinking about. The office feels empty now."

"No, no, you two are better off without me," he said. "So, when is the wedding band going to play?"

I told him that Gauri was in Janakpur to talk to her parents.

"Cheers! Cheers!" he said. "What a beautiful day this has turned out to be."

The alcohol eventually relaxed me and turned me sentimental. "What happened, Umesh? What happened to our friendship? What happened to you?"

"I've turned into a drunk again, haven't I?" he said. "Don't worry. This is a phase. It'll pass, just like everything passes."

"I wish things were like they were before."

"You want me to join you two in marriage?" he said, laughing. "Listen, it's obvious Gauri and you were meant to be together." He appeared to be moved by his own words, for he became silent. Then he said, "A nice house, some children—think of how happy you will be. Just don't forget to send me a wedding invitation." He waved his hand, as if dismissing me.

I wanted to stay, to talk more, to mention my ridiculous dream, to try to reignite our old friendship, but he began to stare at his glass and drum his fingers on the table, and before long I knew it was time for me to leave.

When Gauri returned I didn't tell her about my visit to Umesh. Something held me back—I almost felt I'd been disloyal to her. Or maybe I didn't want to sour her mood by talking about the state he was in.

She'd received the approval from her parents, and the wedding plans began in earnest. People joked, "Isn't it too much? You two will work together in the same office, then sleep in the same bed."

Unable to think of a witty response, I simply tried not to blush.

Along with many other people from our office, Tikaram showed up for our wedding, but only with his children. He and Kanyakumari were in the process of getting a divorce. "No more women for me, hajur," he told me. "My children will have to do without a mother." The children looked sad, more grown-up than when I had seen them last.

Despite my hand-delivered invitation, Umesh didn't come. I had a feeling he wouldn't; still, it disappointed me, and I wondered if our friendship had not been as deep as I'd imagined it.

When our wedding party reached Gauri's house, I wanted to tell her that Umesh hadn't come, but she was in a room somewhere inside, getting ready for the ceremony, and it would have been improper for me to seek her out. As I waited in the yard with everyone else for her to appear, I kept glancing at the gate to see if Umesh would show up.

In a few moments people began murmuring that the bride was on her way out. Everyone looked at the front door, and shortly Gauri emerged wearing a bright red sari, her neck and wrists shining with gold jewelry, her face covered by a veil. People remarked on how beautiful she looked. The band played louder. My heart beat insanely, and I wondered what Umesh would say if he saw her now. "Our Gauri," he'd say, his arm on my shoulder, "an ascetic's nightmare." But it was pointless thinking about Umesh. Gauri was on her way to the wedding pyre, where the priests, their hands gesticulating to invoke the gods, had already begun their high-pitched chants.

The Third Stage

ONE MORNING AFTER YOGA, Ranjit was watering the plants in his garden when his old friend Shiva showed up at the gate. Ranjit hadn't seen Shiva in years. When Ranjit was at the height of his acting career, Shiva was gaining acclaim making documentary films, and now had a cult following among educated Nepalis and Western expatriates. Over the years, the two friends had lost touch, especially after Ranjit stopped acting.

"Ah, Shiva!" Ranjit said, and went to greet him. "How long has it been?"

"The last time we saw each other had to be about seven years ago. At some wedding, wasn't it?"

The two friends sat in the garden under an umbrella and chatted about the old days. Ranjit's wife, Kamala, brought tea and snacks. She playfully chastised Shiva for disappearing from their lives altogether, and when she went back inside, Shiva got around to the reason for his visit: he wanted Ranjit to play a lead role in a movie he was going to make — not a documentary this time, but a feature. "Someone else is going to direct it," he said, "but I'm going to produce it. And I very much want you in the movie. It's the perfect role for you."

Ranjit laughed. "I'm an old man. I gave up acting ten years ago, you know that. I'm not going back."

Shiva looked a bit wounded, but he persisted. "Look, Ranjit. I came to you because you're my good friend, always have been, and also because you're the best actor I know of. And look at the state of Nepali cinema. Where have all the good actors gone? Now it's all about how many songs and gaudy group dances you can jam into one movie. That's what the audience wants, these directors and producers keep saying. In your time, at least the songs and the dances were kept to a minimum, or were important parts of the story. Directors didn't compromise their art."

Shiva was becoming more agitated as he spoke, and Ranjit sympathized with him. He recalled a conversation he'd had just a month ago with a Canadian film director who was on a trekking trip in Nepal. He'd been a guest at his daughter Chanda's house. Over dinner the man had asked Ranjit, "Would you call your country's movies musicals? I mean, why else would you have at least five or six song-and-dance routines in every single one of them?"

Ranjit, who'd watched American musicals like *The Sound of Music,* had laughed and said, "It's hard to pinpoint what our movies are about. They're so influenced by Indian movies—you know, Bollywood. Yes, I guess you can call them musicals, but too often these days the song-and-dance is barely connected to the plot."

"I actually enjoy them," the Canadian said. "And you can't help but have fun with all that melodrama—families torn apart, people crying every five minutes, actors bursting into song, the hero overcoming impossible odds. Good stuff."

Embarrassed, Ranjit said, "I can't stand them."

Kamala said, "The last time he and I watched a movie together was four years ago, and that was on video. He doesn't go to the theater anymore."

"Why did you stop acting?" the Canadian asked Ranjit. "Because you no longer liked these formulaic movies?"

"Partly," Ranjit said. "But also I simply got tired of it."

"Papa seems to be on the verge of becoming an ascetic these days," Chanda said. "It's all yoga and meditation and reading the Ramayana and the Bhagavad Gita."

"Ah, the Hindu stages of life," the Canadian said, nodding knowingly. "What are they now? The Bachelor, the House-holder, the Retiree, and the Ascetic? Right now, you must be the Retiree, withdrawing from material life. In the years to come, you'll turn into the Ascetic, am I correct? Renouncing all physical existence and merging into the oneness of God? I find it fascinating!"

"You westerners always seem to know more about our religion than we do," said Bimal, Chanda's husband. "And anyway, I don't know anyone who actually follows these stages from the scriptures."

"But Papa seems to be following them," Chanda said. "He lectures us about our materialism, and one of these days I expect him to don a saffron robe and head into the jungle."

Chanda was referring to how Ranjit had become increasingly critical of what he saw as her flagrant display of wealth. Bimal's business of designing and building Western-style condominiums in Kathmandu was skyrocketing: the three complexes he'd built had filled up instantly, and now he was building five more. Within a short span he'd amassed so much money that he was rumored to be one of the richest men in the city. Their success didn't bother Ranjit so much as Chanda's almost giddy flaunting of their wealth. She never missed an opportunity to mention the enormous checks Bimal wrote to his contractors. She drove her red Mercedes everywhere, even to the shops down the street. For every wedding party she attended, she wore a different diamond necklace, and she made frivolous shopping trips to Singapore and Abu Dhabi, then invited her friends to see what she'd bought — designer clothes, costly toys for her ten-year-old son, Akhil, and perfume and expensive lipstick and watches to give to relatives. She once brought back a cashmere sweater for Ranjit that she admitted cost three hundred American dollars, and he'd refused to accept it. "This old one is fine for me," he'd said, pointing to the sweater he had on, which had been knitted by Kamala a decade ago. Obviously slighted, Chanda had not spoken to him for days, until he'd gone to her house and said that wearing such an expensive item of clothing would not sit well with his conscience. "I don't need it, and frankly neither do you." A small argument had ensued, and finally the two agreed that Chanda wouldn't buy him anything expensive, and he would not chide her for spending money the way she saw fit.

Now, in the garden, Shiva was still going on about the decline of Nepali cinema. Ranjit thought that the commercial greed of the industry—ten times more profitable than it had been during his time—paralleled his daughter's garish show of wealth.

"At least listen to what the role is before you say yes or no," Shiva said. "It's something any actor would kill for. You'll play a father trying to stop his daughter from marrying a boy from a low caste. The father is the central figure, and most of the movie will revolve around the complexities of his emotions— his denial, his anger, ultimately his acceptance. The role will showcase your range of talents. It's a movie made for you, Ranjit, and at just the right time. Imagine, after all these years the public will worship you again."

Kamala came back out and caught the tail end of the conversation. Shiva filled her in on what she'd missed.

"It's up to him," she said, sighing. "People have come here with other offers, you know, but he's always said no. Says he won't be able to stand it. But stand what, I'm never so sure."

"I take it you want him to act again?" Shiva asked Kamala.

"Well," Kamala said, glancing sideways at Ranjit, "when you think about Indian actors like Amitabh Bachchan and Rajesh Khanna, who are acting well into old age and still receiving praise, I think it's not such a bad idea. But I don't want to pressure him to do anything he doesn't want to do."

"Ranjit, what do you think?" Shiva asked. "You're not going to disappoint me, are you?"

"It's not a question of disappointing you," Ranjit said. "It's more a question of whether my heart will be in it. And I don't want to do it halfheartedly. The role sounds intriguing, though, and whoever you get will perform well, I'm sure."

"Is that a no?" Shiva asked.

Ranjit thought for a moment, then said, "I'm sorry, Shiva."

Shiva drummed the arm of his chair with his fingers. "All right, what can I do? I'd heard you had turned away others, that you're becoming some kind of sanyasi, but I thought I'd try. I still think you're the best man for the role, so if you change your mind, give me a call." He jotted down his phone number and left.

"Time to eat?" Ranjit asked Kamala, not wanting to dwell on what had just happened.

"That role sounded really good," she said, getting up from her chair.

"He'll find someone else." He followed Kamala inside and into the dining room, where the two sat and ate their morning meal. Ranjit had switched to a strictly vegetarian diet in the past few years, and although Kamala had initially complained that she couldn't live without meat, she eventually followed suit and now sang the praises of vegetarianism. In silence, the two ate their curried beans and spinach with rice and dal, and Ranjit knew that he'd made the right decision in rejecting Shiva's offer. This was the life he liked — quiet meals with his wife, gardening, his daily routine of yoga and meditation, frequenting the city ashrams to listen to holy men talk about how the whole world was an illusion, watching the sun set behind the Nagarjun hill from his balcony, spending time with his grandson Akhil.

That night in bed, after Kamala had fallen asleep, Ranjit thought about Shiva's proposal again. Even after the two had lost touch, he'd watched all of Shiva's documentaries and admired them. Shiva wasn't afraid to tackle the big social issues, like child marriage, the ostracism of widows, and bonded labor, and his documentaries, instead of being preachy, were infused with an artist's sensibilities. Shiva was certain to bring the same eye to this movie, and the more Ranjit thought about it, the more he wondered whether not being a part of it would be a mistake. The movie had the potential of making a statement about the importance of art and exposing the cheap commercial tactics of contemporary Nepali cinema. Ranjit knew that his appearance in the movie would draw more of an audience, since moviegoers and critics still praised his "presence" on the screen. His name carried a kind of currency; that's undoubtedly why Shiva had come to him.

He woke around four to meditate, but couldn't focus because his thoughts were too scattered. At times he wondered whether he was fooling himself about the movie's significance or his own importance. After five, he went back into the bedroom, woke Kamala, and told her that he was leaning toward accepting Shiva's offer.

"What changed overnight?" she asked him in a sleepy voice.

He was too impatient to explain his thought process. "It's too good a role to pass up, don't you think?"

"That's exactly what I was thinking yesterday. And after this, you'll get other good roles."

"No, no, this is it. I'd only do this film."

"We'll see," she said with a smile.

Later, over morning tea, he told Kamala, "I have no idea what kind of people I'll be working with. Maybe I'm better off not calling Shiva."

"Enough of your indecision. Once the shooting starts you'll feel better." She went to the living room and dragged the phone over to him. "Here, call him."

Ranjit stared at the phone, then picked it up and dialed Shiva's number. Shiva sounded relieved that Ranjit had changed his mind. "To tell you the truth, Ranjit, I didn't know who else I'd have approached for the role. I couldn't really see anyone else doing it."

"Let's hope this will remind people what good movies are all about," Ranjit said.

"Of course it will. Let me tell you something else. I came to you because I had a dream in which you appeared as the character's father. Isn't that amazing? I hadn't seen you in all these years, and then suddenly, the night I read the script, I saw you vividly in the father's role, actually speaking some of his dialogue. I didn't tell you yesterday because I felt a little silly about it."

Ranjit laughed and said, "Well, it must have been fated then." He hung up feeling even better.

Three weeks later, the shooting began on a set made to look like the house of the conservative father that Ranjit was playing. The director was a small mousy man with a nasal voice. He was not Shiva's first choice; the man Shiva had originally approached, a director with two recent hits under his belt, had backed out at the last minute. "I'm sure it was the low budget," Shiva had confided to Ranjit when they met again to discuss the details of the role.

The new director, Diwakar, had only worked as an assistant director, something that didn't inspire much confidence in Ranjit. But strangely, it felt good to be back on the set — good to be fussed over by the makeup artist, good to have young actors and actresses tell him how much they admired his work, how he had been a source of inspiration for them.

On the first day of shooting, early in the morning, Ranjit did a shortened version of his yoga routine, then memorized his lines and arrived on the set at the scheduled time, only to learn that the actor playing the low-caste boy and the actress playing his daughter hadn't arrived. While waiting for them, Ranjit paced the set, talked to the crew, and glanced often at his watch. No one else seemed concerned by the delay, not even Diwakar, who sat on his stool behind the camera and laughed with the assistant director. Trying to appear equally unconcerned, Ranjit went over the script again. He'd read it soon after he'd made that call to Shiva, and was pleased to see that his role was as powerful as Shiva had initially described it. Many critical moments focused on him, but more important, the story was good. There were no unnecessary titillating scenes, the songs didn't involve two dozen scantily clad women shaking their bellies, and there was no violence, not a single punch thrown by anyone. In that respect, it was better than any of Ranjit's earlier movies, most of which climaxed in either a fight scene or a car chase. Rereading the script and going over his lines at least helped pass the time while waiting.

When the actor, Mukesh, and the actress, Priyanka, finally arrived, they inevitably put on airs that made Ranjit uncomfortable. Neither was well known: Mukesh had played a supporting role in an action movie that had flopped miserably, and Priyanka, although a good actress, had garnered only minor roles so far. This movie, with its solid screenplay and Shiva's well-respected name, was their first decent break. Priyanka had a young daughter of four whom she brought to the set, and every time the girl wailed, which she did quite often for a girl that age, Priyanka dropped everything to attend to her, even a few times while the camera was rolling. Mukesh demanded a cold drink every half hour and continually ogled a young woman in the crew.

The shooting of the scenes that took place inside the house was supposed to last two weeks, but it ended up taking a month due to Mukesh's and Priyanka's temperamental behavior. For three days in the middle of shooting, Mukesh refused to appear, citing some vague illness. The young woman from the crew also didn't show up on those days, and Ranjit couldn't believe that no one confronted them about this.

The bigger problem came when Diwakar decided to cut a scene that featured Ranjit growing livid when he discovered his daughter's affair with the lower-caste boy. Ranjit had been looking forward to this scene—he'd throw things around the house, launch into a monologue about how the daughter would be shaming the family for generations. When reading the script for the first time, he had considered this moment pivotal. Now Diwakar wanted to replace the scene with a sleazy one showing Mukesh and Priyanka in a provocative position—on the angry father's own bed.

"That would be out of character for the daughter, don't you think?" Ranjit said to the director. "I mean, she's rebellious and all that, but she still respects her father. I mean, at the beginning she won't let the boy anywhere near the house. This other scene allows people to sympathize with the father's point of view, to connect with his emotions, even as they might be rooting for the couple. It helps amplify the tension."

"No, no, no," Diwakar said. "The father's scene is too melodramatic and predictable. The scene with the two lovers is a symbolic moment. Don't you see, Ranjit Sir, that their making love on his bed eviscerates the father's purity as well as the daughter's? Think about it: the caste barrier is not only a mental or a spiritual one—it's also physical. Their getting together is breaking down this final wall."

Ranjit wished Shiva was there so he could appeal to him. The screenwriter, who Ranjit thought would side with him, agreed with Diwakar: "That's the core of the story—the idea of the physical barrier being erased by physical intimacy."

Ranjit said nothing at that point, thinking that he'd just call Shiva from home and make a plea to him then. For the rest of the day, Ranjit felt irritable, and Priyanka's daughter bawled constantly, giving him a headache.

When he reached home that evening, Chanda was there. She'd just returned from Bombay, and she and Kamala were sifting through shopping bags filled with saris, watches, and jewelry. "Nothing for you, Papa, I'm afraid," she said with a smirk as he sat on the sofa.

"Nothing needed," Ranjit said. "You didn't bring Akhil?"

"He and his father went to buy a table-tennis set."

Trying not to show his disapproval, Ranjit excused himself and went to his study, where he picked up the phone and called Shiva. But he wasn't home, and his wife said that he was in the border town of Birgunj, trying to get some film equipment through customs. He wouldn't be back until the next day.

Chanda ended up staying for dinner, and as the three of them ate in the dining room, Kamala asked him why he had such a long face.

"I'm just tired today," he said. "I'm not used to working long days anymore."

"Akhil wants to challenge you to a game of table tennis," Chanda said. "I told him you were a good player in your younger days."

"Hmmm?"

"What's the matter with you today?" Kamala said. "Something happened on the set?"

Hesitantly, he told them what had happened.

"But that scene is so important for your character," Kamala said. She'd read the script and was visibly upset. "You can't let this happen."

"I'll talk to Shiva tomorrow. He'll take care of it."

"I can't believe a second-rate director has the gall to cut your scene, Papa," Chanda said.

Ranjit stopped eating. "How do you know he's second-rate? He's just doing something he thinks will make the movie better, that's all."

"I can't say anything to you these days," Chanda said. "Maybe I shouldn't have stayed for dinner."

"That's not what I meant, Chanda," Ranjit said. "But you don't know enough about this movie to judge Diwakar."

"Can't I make a comment as your daughter?" Chanda said. "Why do you have to criticize everything I say and do?"

"What's wrong with you two?" Kamala said. "I'm getting tired of it."

For the rest of the meal they talked about other things, but the tension between him and Chanda was palpable. When she finally left to go home, she said goodbye only to her mother.

Ranjit and Kamala went to the living room and turned on the television.

"Don't argue with her so much," Kamala said. "She was complaining to me the other day how you don't love her anymore."

"Of course I love her," Ranjit said. "But I'll never understand her obsession with money. She wasn't like this growing up." In fact, he recalled Chanda as being a modest girl in her teenage years, someone who had many school friends poorer than she. It was after her marriage to Bimal that something had changed.

"There's nothing wrong with enjoying money," Kamala said. "Just because you have changed doesn't mean everyone has to follow in your footsteps."

Not wanting to start another argument, Ranjit kept quiet. That night in bed, when Kamala was asleep, he thought further about what had happened with Diwakar and wondered whether he should bother Shiva about it. Shiva trusted Diwakar, and Ranjit would only be causing trouble and putting his friend in a difficult position. Besides, the more Ranjit thought about it, the more Diwakar's words made sense to him. In a movie that had as its central theme the barriers of caste, wouldn't it be appropriate to be provocative? Could it be that Ranjit was objecting to the replacement of the scene only because he was in it? Was he being too selfish and not thinking about the overall good of the movie? It was true that in his earlier days no director would have done away with a scene featuring him. But those days were gone, and it was foolish of him to hold on to them. Let it go, he told himself. This way it's better for everybody.

The next morning, Kamala asked him whether he still planned to call Shiva, and Ranjit told her that he'd decided not to pursue it.

"Why?"

"It's just one scene. It's not that important."

"So you're going to let him push you around?"

"He's not pushing me around. We all have to think about what's best for the movie."

Kamala seemed about to object, then sighed and said, "Well, it's your movie. I guess I just don't understand what goes on in your mind anymore." For the rest of the morning, it was she who had the long face.

Ranjit wasn't required on the set for the next few days,

and he was glad; it would give him time to collect himself, and he'd be refreshed when he went back. He'd thought more about Chanda and concluded that he needed to be a bit more gentle with her, and this time off was a good chance to spend a few days with the family. With that in mind, he suggested to Kamala that they go over to Chanda's house for lunch that day. "I promise I won't argue with her," he said. Kamala called Chanda, and soon they headed to her house in Lazimpat.

Chanda lived in a new three-story house with carved windows she'd had custom built by one of Bhaktapur's carpenters. A large fountain stood near the entrance, and whenever he visited, Ranjit felt as if he had entered a movie set. The guard at the gate saluted as their Toyota entered the driveway. One of the servants let them in and told them that Chanda was taking a bath, so they went into the living room, where the servant then brought them tea. Elaborate statues and artwork adorned the room. Since their last visit, Chanda had added a tall Buddha in the corner, its head nearly touching the ceiling. Kamala went over to it, touched it, and said that it felt like solid gold.

Akhil came barging in. "Ready for table tennis, Grandpa?"

"After lunch, okay?" Ranjit pulled Akhil toward him and tousled his hair. "Where's your father?"

"Selling condos," Akhil said, giggling. "Condo, condo," he chanted, delighting in the fact that "condo" sounded like the word for ass in Nepali.

Kamala scolded him, saying bad words would rot his tongue. Ranjit merely laughed. He doted on his grandson. "I share a special bond with him," he frequently told Kamala. Akhil too seemed particularly attached to his grandfather, perhaps because he saw Ranjit as a substitute for Bimal, who, constantly busy with his work, rarely had time for his son. Akhil often asked Ranjit questions about his acting days: "Why didn't you act in more movies with lots of fighting?" "Was that villain a bad man in real life too?" Ranjit patiently answered his questions, often providing anecdotes. "Are you thinking about an acting career, grandson?" he'd once asked Akhil. "No!" Akhil had said. "I want to be a rich businessman like my father. I want to make lots of money." Although Ranjit realized that this was just a child talking, he suspected that Chanda was planting warped ideas in her son's head about what life was all about. Ranjit got worried, and the next time his grandson came to visit, he told himself, he'd make sure to talk to him about his career goals. But he soon realized what foolish thinking he'd gotten himself into. The boy was only ten years old, for God's sake.

Chanda soon emerged from the bathroom and they all headed into the dining room, where an enormous lunch of curried lentils and tofu, cauliflower, eggplant, and rice pudding had been laid out on the table. Last year Chanda had hired a cook, and now every meal in her house was a feast. She paid the man fifteen thousand rupees a month, and when she boasted about this to Ranjit and Kamala, Ranjit was aghast. Even at the peak of his career, he never earned enough to hire more than one servant. During his time, actors made a small fraction of what they were paid today. Of course, the cost of living in the city had greatly increased in the past decade or so, but he knew of no household where the cook made more than a top officer in a government job. When he questioned Chanda about it, she said that Bimal entertained many businessmen at home, and it was important to maintain a certain standard.

Now, as they ate, Chanda said, "Don't yell at me for this, Papa, but last night I mentioned to Bimal what your director did, and he came up with a great idea. He wants to produce a movie himself. It would star well-known actors, but he'd give you the central role. He knows a couple of screenwriters he can commission, and you could work with them to develop the kind of story you'd want. Plus, you and Bimal can choose your own director."

Irritated, Ranjit stopped eating. "Starring in my own son-in-law's movie will hardly gain me any respect. Besides, I'm not interested in being in another movie, really."

"Grandpa, please," Akhil pleaded, "can I be your director?

I'd have you beat up ten villains at once." He began jabbing his fist in the air. *"Dhissom! Dhissom!"*

Ranjit patted him on the back. "Why don't you and I make our own movie? You have a video camera, don't you?"

Excited, Akhil nodded and left the lunch table to go get his camera.

"Diwakar is a fine director," Ranjit said to Chanda. "Most good directors are difficult."

"He's known for being particularly difficult, though. Everyone knows this."

"Who is everyone?"

"Well, my college roommate, for example. She's an actress."

Ranjit shook his head. "I don't know why you're poking —getting involved in this."

"I'm worried about you, Papa, that's all. You have such a great reputation, and if your part keeps getting smaller and smaller in this film, what will people think of you?"

Ranjit saw Kamala signal Chanda to drop this line of conversation. Then she asked him, "You'll at least think about Bimal's proposal, won't you?"

"Of course," he said reluctantly. "We'll deal with it when the time comes."

Akhil came back with his video camera, and he and Ranjit walked outside to the fountain, where, under his grandson's direction, Ranjit acted out some scenes. "Act like a villain who's about to die," Akhil shouted from behind the camera, and Ranjit fell to the ground, clutching his heart. "Now, the hero chasing the heroine!" Ranjit scampered around the driveway, one hand behind his ear and the other extended. He crooned a song popular when he was young. "Now be the hero shooting the villain with a machine gun." Ranjit stopped. "No guns in my movies, Director Sab. Think of something else."

They role-played for a while, then went back inside for a few rounds of table tennis in Akhil's game room. "You must be the only boy in town with his own game room," Ranjit said to Akhil, who responded, "Yes, yes, I'm lucky, I know, you've told me that before." Ranjit often played table tennis in his younger days, and now the moves came to him easily. He played with enthusiasm, glad for the distraction. "See, your grandfather's blood is still young," he said to Akhil as they finished the last game.

They joined Chanda and Kamala in the living room for tea, and Chanda turned on the television. An old Hindi movie, *Madhumati*, was showing on Zee TV. It featured the legendary Indian actors Dilip Kumar and Vyjayanthimala. Dilip Kumar, with his large, intoxicating eyes and brooding good looks, walked through a forest, singing, *"Suhana safar aur yeh mausam hansi"*:

> *The journey is pleasant,*
> *The weather gay.*
> *Somewhere, I'm afraid,*
> *I'll lose my way.*

The scene was so simple, so filled with a kind of artistic innocence, that Ranjit grew melancholy.

"Remember, Papa, how people used to call you the Nepali Dilip Kumar?" Chanda asked.

"Yes, those were some strange days," Ranjit said, slightly embarrassed. People had compared him to Dilip Kumar after his performance of a jilted lover in *Memento*. At that time, Ranjit had been pleased at the comparison, but so much time had passed it seemed like ancient history. Besides, it was an exaggeration—Dilip Kumar was in a different league altogether, with so many awards and blockbusters to his credit. Ranjit had won only one award. In his day, Nepali cinema was in its infancy—Indian movies were the rage. Still, many magazines did run interviews and photos of him, and he had been invited to the royal palace for lunch with the king and queen. People often whispered and pointed at him in the streets.

That evening at home, Ranjit rehearsed some of his upcoming scenes after Kamala went to bed. He practiced in front of the mirror in his study so he could observe the movements of his face. He went over the scenes again and again, trying to perfect each expression, each hand gesture. After a while he began to think of Dilip Kumar, of how effortless his acting was, and Ranjit couldn't help but be dissatisfied with his own performance. Had he lost his touch?

This feeling remained with him when he reached the set two days later, and became more acute when he learned that Diwakar had already gone ahead and shot the scene featuring Mukesh and Priyanka in the father's bed. "It went well," Diwakar said. "It's a pretty sexy scene."

Ranjit laughed. "It'll be a sexy movie, eh, Diwakarji? So what's an old man like me doing in a film like this?"

"Don't underestimate your role, Ranjit Sir," Diwakar said. "And anyway, your name will carry this movie." He leaned closer. "Mukesh and Priyanka aren't the big names they think they are. But you, of course, are a legend. That's why, as soon as I learned that you and Shiva were good friends, I asked that you be given the role of the father. You know, Shiva had his eyes on someone else."

"This was not his idea?"

"No, no," Diwakar said, clapping Ranjit on the back. "When I was in college, I went to see your *Darling of My Eyes* five times at the Patan Cinema Hall. I cut classes for it."

Ranjit was so unsettled by this news that he had a hard time concentrating on his acting. "What's wrong, Ranjit Sir?" Diwakar asked at one point. "You not feeling well today?"

In the scene they were shooting, the girl's mother was trying to persuade him not to force their daughter into marriage without her consent. Ranjit knew he wasn't being emphatic enough in the face of her arguments, but he couldn't seem to muster up the energy. Now he shrugged at Diwakar, who threw up his hands in frustration. "I'm not sure it's going to work today, Ranjit Sir. Somehow you're not letting it happen."

"Maybe I've lost my touch," Ranjit muttered.

"If actors like you lose your touch," Diwakar said, "there's no hope for us." He repeatedly ran his hands through his hair, and Ranjit could tell that he was trying not to get annoyed at having to stop early today, and the strain on the budget it would undoubtedly cause.

"I need a drink," Diwakar said. "Care to join me, Ranjit Sir? Maybe a drink or two would relax you."

"I stopped drinking years ago."

"You can still come."

All Ranjit wanted to do was go home and lie down, but he couldn't say no to Diwakar. The assistant director and the cinematographer decided to join them, and Diwakar persuaded Mukesh and Priyanka, who hadn't brought her daughter to the set that day, to come along too.

At a large table in the Shanker Hotel restaurant they ordered drinks and pakoras and sushi. When Ranjit ordered lemon tea for himself, the others objected, saying they wouldn't let him off the hook without at least one drink. Too defeated to put up a fight, he told the waiter, "A small peg of whiskey, please."

Soon the buzz from the whiskey lifted his mood, and he chatted with Priyanka, who was seated next to him. "I personally think your scene was better than the new one," she whispered to him, "but how can you argue with the director?"

"It's not a big thing, really," Ranjit said. The whiskey was making him expansive, and he began to feel warmly toward Priyanka. It was hard for a woman, he knew, to be an actress while raising a young daughter. "The scene will be good for your career, though," he said to her softly. "It's a memorable scene, even if it's a bit risqué. But that's what the public wants these days, isn't it?"

"Sir, sir," the cinematographer was suddenly shouting from the other end of the table. "When you were in *What Happened, How It Happened,* did you have to work out a lot for the role?"

The conversation quickly turned to Ranjit's acting days, and they flooded him with questions. Did that actress really commit suicide while the film was only halfway done? Was it true that the Indian director Raj Kapoor had invited Ranjit to come to Bollywood? More whiskey was poured, glasses were clinked, and Ranjit talked about the old days with relish. The others were transfixed—they gazed at him in admiration and affection. Laughter. Nodding. Groaning and moaning at the recollection of some small but spicy details. He hadn't felt this beloved in a long time. Diwakar was quietly smiling at him from a corner of the table, as if Ranjit were a product of his own creation, as if he were the one who'd turned Ranjit into a star and now could step back and let his great actor bask in this limelight. Ranjit smiled back at Diwakar, not caring whether the director might have been taking too much credit. After all, he had withstood Ranjit's miserable performance today. To-morrow I'll do much better, Ranjit thought, and this thought seemed to be buoyed by the smiling faces around him.

"I have only one complaint, Ranjit Sir," someone said. "You never danced in your movies. What's a movie without some thrilling dance routines?"

Ranjit was about to say that he was not much of a dancer when Diwakar said, raising a finger, "Ranjit Sir danced in *Shakti*. Unfortunately, the movie didn't do too well."

"I bet he hasn't forgotten the moves, though," Priyanka said.

The group erupted, cajoling him into showing them his dancing. Ranjit kept insisting that he barely remembered the moves from *Shakti*, or why he danced in that film in the first place, but they didn't let up, and Priyanka hauled him onto the small dance floor. The restaurant manager was summoned to change the soft music to something more upbeat, and soon the *thump-thump-thump* of a well-known Hindi song reverber-ated in the restaurant.

Ranjit and Priyanka moved around the dance floor, shaking their bodies this way and that. She was a nimble dancer, deftly sliding in and out of his mock grasp. The crowd screamed for Ranjit to reenact the dance from *Shakti*, and suddenly, without thinking, he did a series of struts, the moves coming smoothly as if he were a young actor again. Priyanka matched his steps, and she reminded him of Charu Thapaliya, who had been the heartthrob of young Nepalis. He recalled what a mesmerizing dancer Charu had been, and although she and Ranjit had never acted together, he'd always had a small crush on her. He grabbed Priyanka's hand and twirled her around, causing the others to clap and hoot.

As the evening wore on, Ranjit, though still tipsy, began to feel embarrassed at the way he'd let loose. But as they left the hotel, everyone around him remained upbeat, and he tried not to dwell on it.

At home, Kamala opened the door and immediately leaned back. "Oooph! Did you drink tonight? What came over you?"

"I couldn't say no." He propped himself against the wall. "They kept insisting."

She shook her head and laughed. "I don't think I know you anymore. All these years you don't drink, then you come home reeking. So, I guess our vegetarian days are over too?"

Briefly, Ranjit stopped breathing. Had he eaten meat at the hotel? So many dishes were passed around the table in the course of the evening that he couldn't remember what he ate. A wave of nausea rose in his throat. "No, no, Kamala, of course not," he managed to say after a moment. "Let's go to bed. I'm tired."

That night he frequently woke up as the alcohol gradually wore off. His mind latched on to what Diwakar had said about Shiva initially not wanting him in the movie. So had Shiva concocted that whole business about the dream? Why would he need to lie about such a thing? He rarely visited the set after the first couple of weeks of shooting, and now Ranjit began to wonder if Shiva was as serious about the movie as he'd let on. After all of Shiva's talk about making a quality movie, why hadn't he shown more interest in it? The whole thing troubled Ranjit greatly, and he considered calling Shiva right then, at three o'clock in the morning. Eventually he calmed himself down—he'd just have to wait until a decent hour. His thoughts turned to his lackluster performance that day, and at around four o'clock, he got up and went to his study, where he tried to practice the scene that had given him so much trouble. His hands began to shake as he gesticulated, and when he spoke his lines, his breathing grew erratic. In anger and frustration, he gave up and went to the living room, where he sat on the sofa in the dark. A vigorous session of yoga right now would make him feel better. Since the shooting began, he'd compromised his yoga and meditation. Why had he disrupted his daily spiritual routine for this idiotic venture? Suddenly last night's revelry seemed ridiculous—the attention he'd received, the singing and dancing, the feeling of camaraderie. He'd allowed himself to be seduced, even to do that mindless dance, the very thing he despised in the current movies. He had to regain control of himself.

He went to the bathroom, brushed his teeth and washed his face, then headed to the study for yoga. He took a few deep breaths, then set out to do ten rounds of the Sun Salutation. He moved into other poses, feeling his body gradually relax. While performing the Setu Bandha Sarvangasana, he felt something crack in his right hip, and a piercing pain exploded in his pelvis, making his legs shake. It felt as if the lower part of his body had become unhinged. He shouted for Kamala, and soon heard her thump down the stairs. "What happened?" she shouted, and he said that he'd broken something in his body.

The doctor at Bir Hospital diagnosed a hip fracture and said he'd need surgery. "We'll need to place a large screw in your hip to anchor the bone," the doctor said. "It's a common injury among the elderly."

"I've always worried something like this would happen," Kamala said. "All those crazy contortions."

His mind hazy with painkillers, Ranjit whispered, "Someone needs to tell Diwakar."

Later that morning, Chanda, Bimal, and Akhil visited the

hospital, bearing flowers and fruit, and in the afternoon, Diwakar and Shiva appeared.

"I guess you'll have to shorten my role even more," Ranjit said.

"No, no," Diwakar said. "We'll think of something else. Right now you need to focus on resting and getting better. Don't worry about us."

"Why don't you have the low-caste boy kill the father?" Kamala suggested. "It would make sense. Then the girl and the boy can live happily ever after."

"It's not that kind of movie, bhauju," Shiva said.

Ranjit watched him. The urgency he'd felt last night now dissolved in light of his injury. Still, at some point in the future, he knew he'd ask Shiva what had really happened.

The surgery was performed the next morning, and afterward, Ranjit was dosed up with painkillers and moved to a private ward. The doctor told him he'd have to stay in the hospital for at least a few days. Two days later, Diwakar and Shiva visited early in the morning. The screenwriter had drafted a new screenplay with a revised ending — the father would indeed die, from a heart attack, and the rest of the movie would feature the new couple's struggles to be accepted by the larger society, and end with the birth of their baby boy.

"I'm sorry for all the trouble I've caused," Ranjit said.

The movie was an instant hit when it was released eight months later. Newspapers and magazines raved about it, praising its groundbreaking story and talented actors. "Finally a Nepali film that actually makes a compelling statement about human affairs and how our orthodoxy suffocates us," one critic wrote. Diwakar's name was mentioned with awe, and Mukesh and Priyanka were soon signed up for several big-budget movies. Critics talked about a renewed career for Ranjit, praising his subtlety, his strong presence sorely lacking in contemporary cinema.

Ranjit was back in good health again, though now he had to

walk with a cane. He returned to gardening and began collecting rare stones after he read a book on the subject. He spent hours looking at them through a magnifying glass, observing their detailed surfaces, comparing one to another, reading about their geological origins.

Kamala seemed immensely pleased with the movie's reception and the praise Ranjit had garnered. And when Chanda visited one day and reminded them of her old proposal, Kamala looked at him expectantly. Clearly she wanted him to accept the offer and for the family to work together. Chanda said Bimal was determined to produce a blockbuster that starred Ranjit. He'd already been talking to screenwriters about creating a rich, emotionally complex role for Ranjit. For a brief moment Ranjit was tempted, then he reminded himself of what he'd just gone through. He told Chanda he would think about it, though he knew he wouldn't accept.

"There's a lot of money involved, Papa," Chanda said, and Ranjit couldn't help but laugh inwardly. She was thinking like a businesswoman, a fitting role for not only the wife of a successful businessman, but also someone who had now started her own business. A pashmina factory in her name had just been built outside Ring Road, and she was already talking about expanding it into a major export-import company. These days she was constantly busy, talking on her mobile phone, making deals, zooming away in her chauffeur-driven cars.

"I'll think about it," he lied again. He'd learned to stop butting heads with her, and was trying hard not to begrudge her her ambitions for further prosperity and power. Instead, he devoted a good deal of his time and energy to his grandson. Because his mother was more and more absent, Ranjit visited him often, called him frequently, brought him home and spent whole weekends with him. Akhil had seen Ranjit's movie in the theater several times and had memorized most of the dialogue. "'This wedding will happen over my dead body!'" he'd exclaim, curling his lips and snarling. Or he'd act the part of the daughter and kneel in front of Ranjit, pleading with him to accept her low-caste boyfriend. Videotaping his grandson, Ranjit always encouraged him: "Now lift your arms up as an appeal," he'd say, or "Don't shout, just make your voice sound tough." Later, as they'd sit on the sofa and replay the videotape, Ranjit would praise his performance and say that with more practice he was going to be a teenage heartthrob. Excited, Akhil would study the videotape again by himself.

Ranjit would lean back against the sofa, remembering his own teenage days, years before his first movie role. He used to frequent the cinema halls to study veteran actors like Dilip Kumar and Raj Kapoor, and in the dark of the theater he always imagined himself up there on the big screen, delivering pithy dialogue or expressing complex emotions through one raised eyebrow. He'd leave the theater with a bounce in his walk, dreaming of the moment when he'd be discovered. Ah, the magic of those years! Smiling, Ranjit would again turn his attention to Akhil, whose eyes gleamed as he watched the replay of his own performance.

Supreme Pronouncements

I MET RUMILA AT A FAIR in Bhrikuti Mandap two years ago. One of my friends knew her from college, and as they talked I couldn't stop looking at her. She had a thin, sharp nose, but also these beautiful dark eyes that caught me staring at her and made me blush. It was she who finally asked my friend to introduce us. "This is Suresh," my friend said. "Our master of politics." In the past few years, starting in my college days, I had become something of a political leader. I drafted antigovernment pamphlets, incited others to burn tires on the city streets when I disagreed with the policies of the palace, and organized and led protests.

"I've read about you," Rumila said. "You don't look like your picture." She was probably referring to the fact that I'm quite short—barely five feet tall. My height had earned me the nickname of Pudkay, or Shorty, or the Runt, among my enemies (I was constantly referred to as the Pudkay Leader in tabloid reports), and even my friends called me Pudkay when they were annoyed with me.

"Trust me, this is the same guy," my friend told her with a sidelong glance, as if to warn her to stay away from me, but I asked her to look at my innocent face and judge for herself. She laughed, scrunching her nose.

From then on, I pursued Rumila. I waited for her outside her office at Kitab Mahal, a nongovernmental organization devoted to literacy efforts throughout the country; I telephoned her for silly reasons; I gave her romantic novels; and for a month or so she tried to put me off. "I don't want a relationship right now," she said. Because of my height, I was used to women turning me down, but something about Rumila urged me on, and I told her I just wanted to be a friend, hopeful that something might evolve.

In the weeks that followed, she and I began to spend more time with each other, taking long walks to the Pashupatinath temple, going to foreign films, whiling away whole afternoons cooking momos at her house. Once she even told me that she liked being with me more than her friends, who I knew were rich and convent-educated like her. "Sometimes they're so superficial," she told me. Still, she kept insisting that we were only friends. Occasionally, when we were going for a walk, she'd drift very close, almost touching me, then she'd clearly become aware of it and move away. A strange look would come over her, as if she were struggling with something. Sometimes, in a restaurant or at my house while we were listening to the stereo, I'd notice her staring at me, and she'd avert her eyes when I looked back at her.

One evening I mustered up the nerve to confront her. We had just visited our mutual friend who'd introduced us, and were walking back to her house through an alley near Baghbazar. I stopped and, over the sounds of engines revving at the nearby bus stop, said that she better acknowledge, to me and to herself, that she was rejecting me because of my height. I felt relieved as soon as I'd said it, though she angrily protested that I held her in low esteem if I thought she'd care about such a thing. I responded that it was impossible to arrive at any other conclusion. "That's not it, that's not it," she kept insisting, obviously distraught.

"Then tell me what it is," I said.

But she didn't, and we walked the rest of the way in silence. I said a terse goodbye to her when we reached her house.

That night I felt that I had ruined whatever we had between us, and I worried that she'd never see me again, but early
the next morning, just as I was waking up, my bedroom door
creaked open and there she was. My mother had gone to the
market to buy vegetables, as she usually did in the mornings,
so I was the only one home. Apparently she'd left the door un-
locked, and now Rumila shut my door, locked it, and slipped
into my bed. "This is what I think of you being a pudkay," she
said, and kissed me on the lips.

We lounged around in bed, talking, smiling at each other.
She told me that last night's argument had made her realize
that she'd always felt something for me, starting with that day
at the fair, and that although she still wasn't completely sure
she was ready for a relationship, this morning she became fearful at the thought of losing me. "I've realized that you and I
have gone further than I myself was willing to acknowledge."
I kissed her soft lips then, and she returned the kiss with her
eyes closed.

The sun was streaming into my room, and we went to the
balcony, from where we could see the Swayambhunath temple
in the distance, its spire glinting in the sunlight. "Look, even
Buddha is winking at us," I said.

Rumila and I were a funny sight as a couple: she was three or
four inches taller than I was, and for any other guy that might
have been embarrassing, but I was proud of the fact that she
was tall and beautiful.

In the beginning she showed interest in my political activities. She'd listen attentively as I told her about the shenanigans
of some member of parliament, or talked about how government money allocated for poor districts was being pocketed by
bureaucrats. But after a while I noticed that she looked more
and more preoccupied as I talked. Sometimes she'd reach out
and run a finger across my cheek as I was in the middle of a
sentence. Once I smiled at her and said, "You're not interested
in this anymore, are you?"

She became self-conscious and said, "No, I am. Go on."

But as weeks went by, it became clear that I bored her when I talked of politics. Often she changed the subject. I'd be going on about how it was only a matter of time before the palace would be forced to accept a Western-style democracy, and she'd say, "Have you ever been to Gosainkunda? I've always wanted to make that pilgrimage." I'd feel a twinge of irritation, but I'd try to ignore it as we talked about Gosainkunda and the other pilgrimages she wanted to make. Eventually I started speaking less to her about my work.

The one time that I broached the subject again, she reacted differently. We were in my room with the door shut; my mother was cooking dinner in the kitchen. Somehow I ended up mentioning the first time I went to jail, three years ago.

"What had you done?" she asked.

I told her about the article I'd written about a corrupt home minister. Two policemen came to my house and hauled me off to the home minister's quarters, where the man read my article aloud. He laughed at my assertions, offering his own version of events, and after he finished speaking, he told the policemen, "Show him what happens to writers who lie to the public." The policemen took me to their headquarters, and in a tiny room they smashed the side of my head and my back with a metal pipe. They repeatedly asked me to admit that I was wrong about the home minister, and when I didn't, they hit me more, until I couldn't take it anymore and said that yes, I was wrong about him. They asked me to write a confession, which I did, and then they let me go. The next day, all the government newspapers printed that confession with my signature at the bottom.

"Here, I'll show you my scars," I told Rumila, and began unbuttoning my shirt.

"No, no," she said, grabbing my hands. "I can't look."

"You should," I said. "Then you'll know what these people are capable of."

"Please, Suresh," she said. She looked as if she were about to cry, and strangely I felt almost glad. She embraced me, and through my shirt she caressed my back, her long fingers tracing what she undoubtedly imagined were my scars.

At first I thought that my story had made Rumila appreciate my politics, but it seemed to have had the opposite effect. Now she reacted to my talk almost fearfully, and at times she said, "Could we talk about something else? There are less upsetting things in life too, you know." I felt that she was refusing to acknowledge a big part of me, but I tried hard to put myself in her shoes, and convinced myself that no one, not even a woman who loves you, should have to listen to your rants day in and day out. Still, I thought constantly about the state of our country and continued my work in earnest. There was a strong momentum building against those in power. Riots were breaking out everywhere, antimonarchy slogans had been spray-painted all over the city, and at least once a month an opposition party would declare a nationwide shutdown, called a bandh, which forced the machinery of the entire country — government, businesses, even traffic — to come to a standstill. "I hate it," Rumila said as we lay entangled in my bed. She hadn't been able to get to work because a bandh had been declared that morning, and I joked that at least the closing allowed us to stay in each other's arms.

"Why can't they protest without forcing people to disrupt their everyday business?" she said.

"I know, I know," I said, and tried to change the subject. I asked her if she'd ever had a close relationship with another man. She'd never mentioned anyone, and lately I found myself curious. "Never," she said. But she said it a little too quickly, and I pressed her further, saying that I wouldn't hold it against her.

"Why do you care about the past?" she said. "It's useless. Let's focus on the present and the future."

I joked that she sounded like the so-called Supreme Pronouncements of the kings that were scrawled on billboards across the city: "Use your hands, not your mouth, to build your country." "Our Nation, Culture, King — dearer than our own life."

Rumila said the billboard she liked best was the one in English that exhorted drivers to be Better Late Than Never

—and this in a country where most people barely knew English.

"Come on, you're avoiding my question," I said. "Tell me. Anyone you loved?"

"I just told you no."

"I don't believe you." I turned away from her.

She leaned over and set her chin on my shoulder. "Suresh, this is the most serious I've been with anyone."

Her answer satisfied me, even though I'd have preferred her to say that I was her first love, just as she was mine. I guess it was silly of me to expect an attractive, intelligent girl like her not to have been involved with others before me.

My mother liked Rumila, and frankly I think she was amazed that such a girl had taken a liking to her short, somewhat chunky son. In her desperation to see me married, my mother had become quite liberal, allowing Rumila to come to our house. She even left her alone with me in my room. I think my mother hoped that a girl would make me give up politics. Whenever I led a protest or was hauled off to jail, my mother told me, she grew enormously anxious. Sometimes she refused to speak to me, and I had to sweet-talk her for days before she cracked a smile again. "If only your father were alive," she said. "He'd make you come to your senses." She'd conveniently forgotten that my political awakening had begun while my father was alive—he and I had frequently gotten into arguments about my beliefs.

My father didn't care much about politics. He was a government worker until he died, content with sitting in his office inside that cold, gray building in the city, going over budgets and requests for payments. He was baffled by my rage at those in power. He knew what I had been through at the hands of the police, but he begged me to forget about it. "One day you'll die, and your wrath will vanish with the smoke from your funeral pyre," he often said dramatically. My mother objected to his talk of my death, but I understood what my father meant. All his life he had followed the scriptures, practiced dhyana

and yoga, and he was attempting to make me see the imperma-
nence of my emotions—and consequently the uselessness of
my actions spurred by my emotions. But I had no patience for
his spiritual analysis. No talk of the illusory nature of my existence could blind me to the reality of the scars on my back,
which I would display for him as my answer. "Okay, so you
suffered," he'd say. "There are people who are suffering more.
And your anger will make *you* suffer more." He said the word
"suffer" gently, almost in a whisper.

Despite my disagreements with him, I loved the old man.
He had been a kind father, never raising his voice or a hand
against me or my mother. In our neighborhood and among our
relatives he was regarded as a sort of saint. After his death,
many people came to me and said, "This is a great loss, Suresh,
not only for you but for all of us. We need people like him to
keep us sane." In my mourning I agreed with them, but later
on, I couldn't help thinking that my father's philosophies of
love and peace weren't going to bring about real changes in the
country. I plunged into my political activities with renewed
zeal. I filled up my days organizing meetings, rallies, and sit-
ins, and a few months later, when I met Rumila, she was the
only person who distracted me.

Everything changed for the two of us when I was picked up
late one afternoon for an editorial I had written that questioned
a government contract with an aircraft manufacturer. I had em-
phasized that the middleman for this shady deal was the prime
minister's brother-in-law, a fact other newspapers had already
reported, but somehow my column irked the authorities, and
I was arrested for slander. This time there was no tiny room or
beatings, thankfully, and I was told I'd be in jail for only one
night. Immediately I went to sleep in a corner bunk of a holding cell.

I awoke a few hours later to a flashlight shining in my eyes.
"The electricity went out and the generator broke down. That's
Nepal for you," a guard was saying as he guided another man

into the cell. I couldn't see his face properly; the guard's flash-light jerked around too much. "I'll bring you a candle," the guard said, and left.

"Greetings," the man said. He told me his name, Mohan, that he was from Pokhara, and that he'd been charged with conspiracy against the state. "Who knows what that means anymore," he said, and sat on the opposite bunk.

I felt compelled to offer my name in the dark. He sniffed. "Smells like chicken in here," he said, so I said, "It's my food. You must be hungry. Why don't you eat? I haven't touched it." Somehow I had forgotten to eat the dinner the guard had given me, so I picked up my container and moved it in his direction. Just then the guard returned with the candle, and after he left us, I was able to see Mohan's features: he had a plump face, a broad nose, and a short scruffy beard. He ate the rice and meat with his bare hands. He gave a satisfied burp, leaned forward to light a cigarette using the flame of the candle. "You write for *National Freedom*," he said. "I know you. And I've seen you with Rumila."

"You know her?"

"Well, maybe I shouldn't say anything."

I raised my eyebrows.

"Are you sure you want to hear? You won't write some ar-ticle about me?" He laughed.

I didn't like how relaxed he was with me.

"Sureshji, don't get mad, okay? In other circumstances I wouldn't be telling you this, but look, here we are, guests of the government, in such close quarters and all for who knows how long. Rumila and I were . . . together a few years back." He took long drags from his cigarette.

I knew Rumila had lived in Pokhara and been involved with a children's organization there, though she hadn't talked much about it. I remembered her saying that although she enjoyed the breathtakingly close view of the Annapurna Mountains, she found the community a bit too insular.

"I shouldn't have said anything," Mohan said.

"Rumila already told me about a man from her past," I lied. "We don't hide anything from each other."

"That's good," he said. "But you know, what's written in fate will come to pass. We talked about getting married, having children, but here we are."

He had to be lying. If they had in fact talked about getting married, surely Rumila would have told me about him. "So, what ended your relationship?" I asked. I found myself beginning to feel weak and disoriented. "I mean, she told me her side, but what's yours?"

"What did she tell you?" he asked. The cigarette had burned down to a stub between his thick fingers.

I fumbled for an answer.

"That's all right," he said with a smile. "Some things do have to remain private between couples. She left me because of all my political work. Frankly, I'm surprised she's with you now."

I said nothing. I didn't want to hear his voice anymore. In fact, I didn't want him near me anymore, so I closed my eyes and pretended I was alone.

That night, on the hard bed, I was unable to fall asleep, and all night long I watched the plastic tarp fastened to the ceiling to prevent leaks. Occasionally I heard Mohan cry, "Enough, enough," in his sleep.

The sun was blindingly bright the next morning. Mohan had woken up just as the guard came to our cell to let me out. "I hope I didn't say anything untoward last night," he said, and I shook my head. He asked me to call his wife in Pokhara and let her know that he was fine. "I'll pay you for the call," he said. "No need," I said. "I'll let her know." He handed me a piece of paper with his number on it when the guard wasn't looking.

I was tired, but I didn't want to go home and just fall asleep, so I wandered around the Dharahara area for a while. I assumed my mother had told Rumila of my arrest, and she probably expected me to visit her at work, but this was my first arrest since we'd met, and I didn't know how she'd react. The last few times I'd participated in protests, which sometimes turned violent, she'd grown distressed and irritable. "Every time you go to these things, I hold my breath."

Her concern made me smile, and I'd say, "Not to worry. Nothing will happen to me."

She'd remain upset for a few hours, then things would slowly get back to normal. I realized then that I actually liked the idea of her worrying about my well-being. Perhaps one of these days, I found myself thinking, we'd talk about marrying.

But today I couldn't get my conversation with Mohan out of my mind, and I wasn't quite ready to see her, so I went to New Road, where, under the big pipal tree, I scanned the headlines of the day's newspapers. *National Freedom* carried my arrest on the front page, and I noted that another paper ran a small paragraph about Mohan's arrest. All the papers mentioned the big rally that the opposition parties, including mine, had planned for next week, which was to be followed by a two-day countrywide bandh. I walked around New Road, simply trying to focus on the sights and sounds around me. The area was already crowded, as people rushed to their offices or entered Ranjana Cinema Hall for the morning show or headed to the supermarket. I walked toward Indrachowk, then to Asan and the noisy vegetable market there. By the time I emerged in Ranipokhari, I was so exhausted that I was stumbling.

I slipped into a restaurant and sat there, drinking cup after cup of tea. The more I dwelled on Mohan's words, the more sense they made. I could understand why Rumila avoided talking about her old flame. Maybe she still thought about him. No wonder she insisted that the past was useless.

I made my way back to Jhonche, to the party office that also housed the newspaper, and for the rest of the day I worked, even though I could barely keep my eyes open. Toward evening, Rumila called, asking me why I hadn't phoned her or come by her office. I replied brusquely that I had too much work to do. For a moment she was silent, then she asked, "Did something happen in jail?" When I didn't answer, she said, "You don't want to talk about it?"

"There's not much to talk about. Anyway, I'm too busy."

In a slightly hurt voice she told me that my mother had been worried all day and kept calling her. She said that I should at least phone her at home. "So I guess that's it?" she said. "Should I just hang up?"

When I didn't answer, she said, "Okay, then, I don't know what's—"

"Wait," I said, suddenly afraid of losing the chance to see her.

"I have to go," she said. "I'm getting ready to go to a friend's birthday party."

"I'm not invited?"

"You want to come?"

"If you'll take me."

She said she'd drop by my house in about an hour, so I finished up at the office and caught a taxi home. There, my mother gave me a sound scolding until Rumila appeared. "I'm telling you," she said to Rumila, "I am at my wits' end with this boy. He spends the night in jail, and I'm the one who doesn't sleep."

"I don't know what to tell you," Rumila said, her face strained.

In the taxi on the way to the party, I hoped that she'd pursue the matter of whether anything had happened to me in jail, but she remained quiet. I slipped my hand into hers, and she looked at me. "Don't do this to your mother," she said. "You have to understand how she worries."

"Do you worry?"

She turned her face away.

"Do you worry about me, Rumila?"

She turned to me and said angrily, "What do you want? Do you want me to tell you that I couldn't sleep last night after your mother called me about your arrest? Would that make you feel better?"

I was taken aback by this sudden outburst, which was unusual given her character. Then I couldn't help thinking that her anger had to be false. Did she really worry about me? Or was she thinking about Mohan right now? By the time we reached her friend's house, she had reapplied her makeup, and we were trying to talk normally.

At the party I watched her in her bright yellow sari, making the rounds and chatting with her friends. A couple of times our eyes met across the room, and both of us attempted to smile, although it was obvious that the tense mood still lingered between us. Once a friend standing next to her gave me a distasteful look. I had the feeling that most of her friends didn't like me. They probably couldn't understand why, of all the handsome men from privileged families she knew, she had chosen me, a political columnist who walked around in sandals, a small man with tall ideals. But it didn't bother me much—I didn't really care for her friends, most of whom lived their lives oblivious to how the rest of the country lived. They were only interested in shopping, American pop culture, and the stupid Hindi movies they watched on video. Whenever Rumila was with them, she seemed to become one of them, despite her claim that they often bored her. Now I saw her talking to a good-looking guy named Rakesh, whose father was a high-ranking and corrupt bureaucrat in Nepal Rastra Bank. She put her hand on his arm and leaned forward to whisper in his ear. Then they looked in my direction and smiled. I turned away and watched a couple who were dancing in the middle of the room.

She drank a glass or two of wine at the party, and in the taxi on the way back to my house she seemed more relaxed than before. She placed her head on my shoulder and began to hum. I could smell the wine on her breath, as well as the musky fragrance of her shampoo.

"What were you whispering to Rakesh?" I asked.

"It's a secret," she said, and I saw that she was smiling.

"Got any other secrets?" I asked softly. "Anything you haven't told me yet?"

"You don't need to know every little secret I have."

After a silence I said, "I've been thinking about the guy who shared my jail cell last night. He was talking about this woman he once loved."

"You talked about women in jail?"

"Just to pass the time. He said it didn't work out with her, and he seemed sad, even though he's married now. I guess our past never leaves us, does it?"

She looked at me, almost startled, then said, "At some point you have to move on."

"I wonder if this woman he was thinking about has moved on."

But Rumila was no longer listening to me. She was staring out the window of the taxi, her mind somewhere else. This seemed to confirm my growing suspicion that she had never stopped thinking about Mohan. At that moment something hardened inside me, and I felt it in my chest.

I avoided Rumila for days, pretending that I was busy preparing for the upcoming rally. Then one evening I found her waiting for me outside the party office. A colleague was with me, and on seeing Rumila, he bid me goodbye.

She and I stood facing each other. "You've forgotten me?" she asked with a forced smile.

"How can anyone forget someone like you, Rumi?"

We began walking together. The silence between us grew thick, and finally she stopped. "Is it over, Suresh? Is that what you're trying to tell me?"

"It's only over if you want it to be over."

"When you don't talk to me for days, that's what it feels like."

We were standing in the middle of the pavement, in the way of other people walking by, so I took her arm and we began to walk. "How is your work going?" I asked, trying to move the conversation to safer territory.

"It's fine," she said.

I searched for more things to say, but nothing came. I felt nothing inside.

"You have to decide, Suresh," she said. "You have to make a clear choice."

"About what?"

"You keep pretending nothing is wrong," she said. "But something is definitely wrong, and I can't go on like this."

"Nothing is wrong," I said calmly. "I'm just busy at work, and it is important work."

She stopped again. "So you have made a decision, then," she said.

"That's your conclusion, not mine."

Her lips pursed. She said nothing and resumed walking. I could see that her eyes were beginning to tear. The evening traffic in New Road grew loud and intrusive around us, and we walked in silence again for a few yards. "All right, I'm going home," she said, and crossed the street. I stood there watching her move quickly through the crowd, then disappear.

I walked home slowly, wondering what was going to happen to me now. I felt no urgency, no acute sense that it was really over between us. Somehow I saw this as a kind of interlude in our relationship, and once she confessed to me about Mohan, I would forgive her for keeping him a secret from me. The hardening in my chest would melt, and we'd be able to love each other like before.

That evening I called a party colleague and we chatted about the upcoming rally. We discussed the logistics of bringing together all the different parties, and since this was such a big event, we talked about the possibility of violence. The government had made it clear that the police and the army would be out in full force. After we hung up, I paced my bedroom and envisioned the march winding through the streets and alleys of the city, cries for freedom and democracy echoing in the air, protesters clashing with the police. Then I thought about Rumila, and I sat down, suddenly tired. I lifted the phone and dialed her number. After several rings she picked up and said hello a few times. I had every intention of speaking, but for some reason I could not.

+   +   +

For the next few days, the party office in Jhonche overflowed with constant traffic. The phone rang continuously, people shouted instructions to each other, and cups and cups of tea were consumed as fatigue began to set in. I stayed there late, after most of my colleagues had gone home, and looked over resolutions, copies of news stories, and reports from villages where we were trying to incite people to join our protests. A calmness settled inside me when I was in the office alone, and sometimes I stopped what I was doing and thought about Rumila, who hadn't yet phoned or come to visit me. Each night I asked my mother whether she'd called, and each night she said she hadn't and that I should go and make up with her, even though she had no real idea what was going on between us. But I did nothing. I was convinced Rumila would come to me eventually, and with some prodding own up to what had happened between her and Mohan in Pokhara.

The evening before the rally, I stumbled upon the piece of paper that Mohan had given me. I had forgotten to call his wife. I cursed myself and picked up the phone—I knew that he hadn't been released because just last week in a newspaper column a human rights activist had decried his prolonged imprisonment.

After a couple of rings, a female voice answered, and when I learned that this was Mohan's wife, I told her what he had said and apologized for the delay in contacting her. She said that she had called the jail several times, but was told that Mohan was not there. "And they tell me they don't know where he has been taken," she said. "I've called a number of other places, but no one knows. Or they aren't telling me." I assured her that I'd check into it. She told me she couldn't travel to Kathmandu to search for her husband because her son was sick, and I promised her I'd try to find out where Mohan was being held. Sometimes political prisoners simply disappeared, other times they were held in secret locations; their families went mad trying to figure out where they were; and then the prisoners were suddenly released without warning or explanation. I felt terrible for Mohan's wife and decided that the next day, after the rally,

I'd call some activists I knew, including a woman who worked for Amnesty International.

That night I woke up at around midnight, my throat parched. I took a sip of water from the jug my mother had placed beside my bed and tried to go back to sleep. When I couldn't, I sat up. Rumila had stayed away from me for too long, and I began to feel unsure about everything.

I reached for the phone and dialed her number. When she answered in a sleepy voice, I said, "Long time no see." The silence at the other end was long and awkward.

"Are you sure you dialed the right number, Suresh?"

My chest tightened. I'd missed hearing her voice. What had come over me? All this nonsense about Mohan—what did it matter now? Why had I assumed that she was still hung up on him?

"What's happening in your life?" she asked.

"Let's meet tomorrow and I'll tell you all about it."

"Isn't tomorrow your big rally? You'd have time for me?"

I had momentarily forgotten about the rally, but it didn't start until ten o'clock. I could see her early in the morning before she went to work. I suggested we meet in a coffee shop in Durbar Marg. She agreed, and I wanted to talk more, but she said she wanted to go back to sleep.

I stayed awake for a while, consumed with thoughts of seeing her again.

By eight o'clock, when I reached Durbar Marg, police in riot gear were already in formation on the street. The rally would head this way, to pass in front of the royal palace, and the authorities were girding themselves for an unruly mob.

Rumila was waiting for me in the coffee shop. Something was different about her: she'd cut her hair, I soon realized. "You look nice," I said, standing before her. She smiled. For a few seconds we just looked at each other, then I sat down and said, "You look even more pointy with that short haircut."

"And you're as pudkay as ever," she said.

For a moment I felt that we were back to the way we used to be. This was Rumila, and this was me, and the whole Mohan episode was over and done with. I reached out and clasped her hand over the table. She squeezed mine back and said, "I am going to America in a week."

"America?" My hand went limp in hers.

"Yes, California. Sano Mama has invited me."

Her youngest uncle had settled there, I knew, but she had never expressed any interest in visiting. "For how long?" I asked, withdrawing my hand. The waiter came, and we ordered tea.

"I don't know. I'm going on a tourist visa, but who knows what'll happen. Sano Mama says I should think about applying to some universities there for my master's degree."

"You can't just stay there." I couldn't formulate any more words.

"I can't?" she asked with a tight smile.

Lack of sleep was catching up with me, and my temples were starting to throb. "So I don't count anymore?"

She looked at me for a long time. "You know the answer to that." She sighed.

"Then why are you talking about this?"

"I need to think about myself more than I've been doing."

"You're being selfish," I said before I could stop myself.

She nodded slowly. "I imagine you're right. Maybe I am."

"Listen," I said, trying to control the desperation in my voice, "I know I haven't been able to spend much time with you lately, but that's no reason to give up. What'll happen to us once you go to America?"

"But what's happening now, Suresh?" she said. "Only this." She gestured at the window. I heard a policeman with a megaphone warning people to keep away from the palace.

"Things will change here pretty soon," I said. "This government can't last, then we can start planning our lives together." The waiter brought our tea, but neither of us touched it. Finally I said, "Maybe you're just tired of me."

She touched the teacup with her fingertips, as if gauging its temperature.

"That's it, isn't it?" I pressed. "You've just gotten bored with me and my work and everything I do."

I waited for her to say something, to reassure me, but she didn't. She merely ran her finger along the lip of her cup over and over.

"Rumi, please," I said. "Think hard about what you're doing. You're giving up on us. I always thought you were stronger than this."

She shook her head, then looked up at me. She seemed about to say something, then shook her head again. She picked up her bag, stood up, and came around to me. She kissed me lightly on the cheek and said, "Take care of yourself," and walked out of the restaurant.

I wanted to call her back, but my whole body became too heavy. I sat there for nearly half an hour, soberly finished my cold tea, and headed out.

On the street, a police van drove past me, and threatening messages blared from a loudspeaker on top of it. Many people were hurrying out of Durbar Marg, pushing past one another. Near Tri-Chandra College, a crowd holding banners was already gathering. I was supposed to meet my colleagues in Tundikhel, so I hurried in that direction. In Ratna Park, truckloads of policemen sat waiting. I told myself I wasn't going to let Rumila ruin this important day for me. She had already made her decision, hadn't even given me a chance to change her mind. I told myself that she was no different from those friends of hers who didn't care about anything important.

At the parade ground of Tundikhel, a large number of people were waving placards. I joined them, pushing and shoving my way through them until I reached my colleagues at the front. "Down with fascism!" I shouted, and they echoed my words. Other people joined in, and soon the entire parade ground was chanting my words. My colleagues told me that the army had gathered in full force in Asan, where the rally would pass as it traversed the inner city to reach the palace, a short distance away. "Let them try something," they said, and I replied, "We won't run and hide." The sun beat down, and streams of sweat trickled down my chin.

The procession finally got under way, and the crowd exited the parade ground and headed toward New Road. We were shouting and chanting, and the steady hum of our voices rose into the air. We circled the statue of Juddha Shumshere, and by the time we reached the narrow alleys of Indrachowk and Asan, the crowd was in an absolute frenzy. Some marchers were dancing, as if in the thrall of some religious ecstasy. People in the houses lining the streets had come to their windows, shouting encouragement. One woman threw flowers down at us, and the crowd rushed to grab them. The marchers began to sing, not a protest song but a romantic one, and I joined in.

Suddenly I lost interest in what was happening around me. I was exhausted and, I realized with some disgust, growing weepy. My voice sounded hollow to me. I wanted to leave, but how? The crowd was so dense that we were literally inching along, bodies pressed against one another. I could feel someone's heavy breathing on my back, and I leaned against the shoulders of a colleague in front of me. I could see the pores of his freckled neck, the hair on the back of his arms. The sweat from his shirt, now completely damp, soaked my palms. I took a deep breath. The crowd swirled and the sky rotated. Faces from windows and balconies looked down on me, and I collapsed on the ground.

Later I was told that my colleagues, afraid that I'd be trampled, carried me on their shoulders, two in the front and two in the back, like a corpse. Since they could not squirm out of the crowd, they kept chanting. As everyone pressed on toward Ranipokhari, the roads widened a bit. Evidently that's when people began to notice me, and they jumped to the conclusion that I had been either injured or shot by the police. As my rescuers whisked me through an alley to nearby Bir Hospital, apparently the phrase "they've killed a man" shot through the rally like a jolt of electricity, and the crowd became agitated.

The plan had been for the rally to congregate at the entrance to Durbar Marg, facing the palace, with people spilling out around Tri-Chandra and Ghantaghar. We hoped that those in the palace, including the moronic prime minister, would be forced into agreeing to our seven-point list of demands for stripping away the power of the crown. But as soon as the crowd saw my "corpse," they attacked the bands of police stationed on the side of the street. Rioters hurled bricks and Molotov cocktails at the police. A group of about ten college students broke through an army barricade at the entrance of Durbar Marg and charged the palace. They were immediately gunned down.

A total of fifty people died that day, including two children who'd ventured out of their houses to watch the stampede. I learned of all this later that evening, when I regained consciousness in the hospital. Nothing had happened to me—I had merely collapsed from heat stroke, exhaustion, and an empty stomach—but many people lost their lives partly because they thought I had died. The media had already started referring to the whole thing as the "corpse incident," and my friends and relatives began frantically calling me. My mother soon grew tired of the phone constantly ringing. At first I hoped to hear that Rumila was on the line, wanting to share a laugh with me. "Pudkay corpse," she'd have called me. "Is there a height ban in heaven?" And I'd have retorted, "No, but they do measure people's noses."

Rumila did finally call, a week later, on the morning she was to leave for America. I wasn't home, so she talked to my mother, who told me that she never thought Rumila would betray me like this. "She didn't seem untrustworthy," my mother said. When I dialed Rumila's house later that day, I was told that her plane had already departed.

"Just let her go," my mother said. "You don't need her. I'll find someone else for you, someone prettier, smarter, not someone who'll leave you."

"Yes, please find someone for me," I said. "That's exactly what I need."

Not sensing the sarcasm in my voice, my mother said, "Are you serious, son? You just give me the go-ahead and I'll start looking."

I nodded. Well, why not? Maybe I could send Rumila photos of these women and get her opinion.

Two months have passed since Rumila left, and I haven't heard from her. The government has been dismantled, and a new government has taken its place, one that represents a mixture of political parties. But the new regime is already turning out to be as corrupt and oppressive as the old one, and already those criticizing it are being tossed in jails across the country. I'm sure that one of these days the police will knock on my door and whisk me away for writing one of my increasingly scathing columns. Perhaps I'll disappear like Mohan, whose whereabouts are still unknown.

My mother's attempts to find me a bride are not meeting with much success. Most families she's approached have told her no after learning of my height. A few families reneged after they discovered I was the legendary corpse. I know that Rumila would have laughed at this. "Not only are you a pudkay, Suresh, you are a dead pudkay," she'd have said, and I'd have said, "Better Dead Than Never."

Sometimes I wonder why I allowed her secret to become my secret, why I thought it necessary to hear about Mohan from her own lips. And I wonder how things would've turned out had I told her about Mohan right away, the morning I got out of jail. Much to my dismay, I keep imagining a scene where I tell her what I learned, and she owns up to her past, and we end up laughing about the whole thing. Sometimes this picture makes me restless, especially when I'm at work, and whatever I'm doing at the moment—writing a column, discussing strategy with my colleagues—suddenly I begin to lose interest, and I find myself fighting the urge to simply get up and leave.

The Weight of a Gun

JANAKI WENT TO THE Maru Ganesh temple early in the morning to pray for her son. She stood before the small shrine, her eyes closed, palms together. Bhola often spoke of the voices inside his head. He covered his mouth with his hand as he laughed at the secret jokes he heard throughout the day, and sometimes he spoke into his hand as if it were a walkie-talkie.

She circled the shrine three times and headed back home. Last night, after she'd already gone to sleep, Bhola rapped on her front door, shouting, "Ama, Ama." At first she thought she was dreaming about him, as she often did. But when she opened the door, he barged into her living room and said, "I need to buy a gun. Give me some money, Ama." He'd tied a rope around his waist to hold up his pants and had bunched up his hair on the top of his head with a rubber band. His eyes scanned the room, then he strode into her bedroom.

"What do you need the gun for?" she asked quietly as she followed him. Over the years she had learned to act calmly when he became agitated—her tone baffled him at first, but it sometimes slowed him down.

"I am joining the Maobadis," he said, turning to face her.

"They need me. They'll make me a commander if I can get a gun." He whispered something into his palm.

"A gun costs a lot of money," Janaki said.

"I only need three thousand rupees, Ama."

She talked him into sitting on her bed, then went to get him a plate of dal-bhat from the kitchen. She always had food ready for him, knowing that he often didn't eat enough. Since he'd moved into the single room on the top floor of her house about a year ago, he had started cooking for himself, and Janaki knew that sometimes he went hungry for a day or two. "You can sleep upstairs," she'd told him when he first moved out. "But come downstairs to eat." He'd narrowed his eyes and said, "I know what you're up to. You're going to poison me." Of course that was just his madness talking, and when he came downstairs he did eat her food, with relish, and usually asked for more.

Now when she returned to her bedroom with his food, he was feeling around under her mattress, where she used to stash her money when he was younger.

"First eat," she said. "Then we can talk about money."

"My comrades need me," he said. His desperate look reminded her of when he was about seven or eight and a neighborhood bully had snatched his marbles. "My marbles, Ama," he'd say, "not his." And she'd scour the neighborhood to find the thief, twist his ear, and get her son's marbles back. At that time, Bhola's madness hadn't revealed itself. The only faintly suspect thing he did was stare at the picture of Lord Shiva in the kitchen for minutes on end.

In those days, both Janaki and Bhola's father, Ananda, who now lived with his new wife in another part of the city, didn't make much of it. "He's a thinker," Ananda used to say. "He's just contemplating." But over the years, Bhola developed a religiosity that surprised his parents. By the time he turned fifteen, he was constantly praying. He'd memorized Hanuman Chalisa, the Gayatri mantra, and a host of other sacred invocations. His lips seemed to move silently all the time. "He's going to be a priest," Ananda said, only half jokingly. By that time Janaki sensed something was wrong with her son. "What do you need to pray for?" she asked him once. "We've given you everything. What can God give you that we can't?"

"You think you're better than God?" Bhola said testily. "You want to go to hell?"

When he began to say that there were people inside his head who threatened to kill him if he didn't pray hard enough, and when he accused strangers on the street of plotting to imprison him, Janaki took him to a local clairvoyant one afternoon, suspecting that her son was haunted by an evil spirit. She persuaded him to go by telling him that the clairvoyant specialized in prayer and could help him. A relative had suggested she consult a psychiatrist, but Janaki was afraid that doing such a thing would brand Bhola as crazy, stigmatizing him for life.

The clairvoyant was a college girl who was said to be possessed by a goddess, and she answered the door dressed in a saffron Padma Kanya College sari, a tube of lipstick in her hand. "I have to go to class now," the girl said. "I only see people in the early morning." But when Janaki insisted, the girl set down her lipstick, went to wash her hands, and sat on a straw mat on a dais in the corner of the room. Small statues and pictures of gods and goddesses surrounded her. Janaki and Bhola followed her and sat on the floor in front of her. Instantly, the girl's eyes fluttered and a voice came out of her mouth that was different—hoarser, faster. "You like to play marbles, huh? Do you go to school? Do you get good grades?" she asked Bhola.

"He's become very religious," Janaki said.

The girl spoke in a rapid burst of Newari that Janaki didn't understand.

"Is everything . . . all right with him?" Janaki asked.

The girl let out a sigh and said, "He'll have problems." She pointed to her own head. "Bad spirits have pushed themselves into his mind."

Bhola was staring at the girl, his mouth slightly open as if transfixed by her face.

"What should I do? Can you do anything?" Janaki asked.

"Wait," the girl said. Then her lips began to move. With her fingers she drew circles in the air around Bhola's head, then said, "His father. His father will leave you. Go to the Dakshinkali temple and make an offering of a goat, then feed him fish soup with some ginger."

"Feed my husband?"

"No, no, your son. Feed him fish soup every day for a month."

"He'll be fine then?"

The girl's eyes fluttered and her earlier voice emerged. "I'll be late for class. I have an exam today—I have to go."

When sacrificing a goat at Dakshinkali and feeding Bhola fish soup did nothing, Janaki did take him to a psychiatrist, who met with them and prescribed some pills. But the pills only made Bhola more restless, more fearful and paranoid. A second psychiatrist said that Bhola suffered from a debilitating mental disease, schizophrenia, that had no known cure. He prescribed a medication that he hoped would help control it. These pills seemed to calm Bhola down, but after a few days he abruptly refused to keep taking them, saying they were shrinking his stomach and would starve him to death. Desperate, Janaki once again turned to shamans and soothsayers. But no matter how many chickens she sacrificed to goddesses, no matter what strange concoctions she made to drive the evil spirits away, the voices inside his head continued their harangue.

Now he refused to touch the dal-bhat she'd brought him. "My comrades have forbidden me to accept food or drink from you," he said.

"Who are your comrades?"

"That's top secret," Bhola said with a sly smile. "You might tell the government, and then they'd get caught. So, no, that question I cannot oblige."

It didn't completely surprise Janaki that he was obsessed

with the Maobadis. After all, everyone talked about them—in the shops, on the radio and television. The newspapers continually printed their photos: the top leader with his solemn eyes; the second-in-command, the tall doctor. Janaki didn't understand how these ordinary-looking men could be responsible for spilling so much blood. Finally she said to Bhola, "I can't give you money for a gun."

"You're a worthless mother. That's why Baba left you."

Janaki flinched. "Don't speak to me that way, Bhola."

"Are you giving me the money or not?" Something flickered in his eyes. He'd never been violent, but if he thought those rebels were his friends, who knew what he might do?

"I can't give you money," she said quietly.

Bhola hurled the plate of food across the room, and rice and dal scattered all over the floor. "The comrades will hear about this," he said and stood. "I've an appointment to meet them in the hills tomorrow." And then he left.

Janaki stared at the food, her head reeling, then she took a deep breath, stood, and tidied the floor. When Ananda was with her, she at least had someone to talk to about Bhola, but a year ago Ananda left her, after twenty years of marriage, for a woman who worked in his office. He'd announced it bluntly in the kitchen, right after they'd finished dinner. Bhola was at the window, watching passersby on the street below and speaking into a pen.

"How long?" she'd asked. She meant to ask him how long he'd been seeing this woman, but the rest of the words remained inside her.

Ananda shook his head. "I've known her about a year. Please forgive me, Janaki. I didn't know it would come to this, but Sukumaya and I have decided to live together now."

Janaki stood there. "What about Bhola?"

"He will be fine. He'll come and visit me." Ananda told her that she could continue to live in the house—he'd pay the mortgage—and that she could keep the rent from the shop on the bottom floor for her monthly expenses. She didn't ask him what he'd live on, but he explained, "I'm going to sell that land in the village." She was too numb to argue with him that they'd talked about transferring his family's land to Bhola's name, in case something happened to the two of them.

Later that night, as she lay down in bed and turned off the light, she felt Ananda slide next to her. She quietly got up, went to the living room sofa, and lay down there, shivering a bit because she hadn't taken the blanket with her. A few minutes later, he came to her and gently placed the blanket on her body. She lay still, and he said, "It has nothing to do with you, Janaki."

She didn't speak.

"It's just that . . . with her I've begun to feel a lot of things." In the dark he seemed to be searching for words to explain more, but when he spoke, he only said, "I'll move out the day after tomorrow. Our house will be ready by then."

Bhola was seventeen then and didn't fully understand what was happening. "What did you say to Baba?" he asked the morning Ananda packed his things and took a taxi to his new house. "Why is he leaving us?"

"He has something important to take care of for a while," Janaki said. "You can go visit him."

"You're a bad person," Bhola said, and with his index finger drew a circle around her head. After his father moved out, Bhola got worse. He refused to bathe, brush his teeth, or comb his hair. One day he disappeared for two nights, and when he returned home, his clothes were in tatters. After that, Janaki took him to the hospital and checked him into the psychiatric ward for three weeks. There he developed a fantasy about running away to Bombay to become a movie star. "Amitabh Bachchan has promised me a role in his next movie," he said to the doctors and nurses. Janaki visited him daily and stayed by his bed, reading him stories or playing cards with him, and one afternoon Ananda dropped by with a small cassette player, which he presented to his son. The two listened to songs on the new player, and Janaki went down to the yard, where she sat under a tree and watched some ducks bathe in a large puddle of water. When she went back up an hour later, Bhola was asleep and Ananda had left. He didn't visit his son in the hospital again.

After Bhola returned home from the hospital, he told Janaki that he didn't want to live with her anymore, and when he started shoving his clothes into a large plastic bag, Janaki panicked and offered him the room on the third floor that she'd been using for storage. After some persuasion, Bhola agreed, on the condition that she'd never come up and that he'd cook his own food on a portable stove, as if he worried she'd poison him. She feared he would leave the stove on and burn down the house, but she had no choice. From then on, she listened closely to his loud footsteps on the stairs, and when she was sure he'd left, she slinked upstairs, opened his door with an extra key, tidied up the room, and made sure everything was okay.

A few months later, at the crowded market in Asan, Janaki saw Ananda with Sukumaya, a thin woman with smooth skin and large, attractive eyes. She wore a bright orange sari, her wrists crowded with bracelets and bangles. She was bargaining with a vegetable vendor, and Janaki watched them with a feeling of detachment. She stood there, a packet of cumin seeds in her hands, and when Ananda turned and spotted her, he quickly ushered his new wife away.

Back home from the Maru Ganesh temple, Janaki went up to Bhola's room. After he left the house in a huff last night, he hadn't returned. On the floor was his filthy bedding, and two giant cockroaches, feelers twitching, scurried across the room. Janaki swept and mopped the floor, then tidied up his clothes. As she was making his bed, her fingers touched something hard. She lifted the mattress, then froze at what she saw. She gingerly lifted the thing with two fingers; it was heavier than she thought—she'd never seen one before except in movies. It had a brown handle and was rusted in spots. There was a bulge in the middle where she imagined the bullets went. Did it even work? Where did he get the money to buy it? Who sold it to him? And why had he asked her for a gun? Holding it carefully, she peeked out the window. People were going about their business. Two women carrying babies on their backs laughed as they talked. A young man, his hands in his pockets, sang loudly as he passed by. Voices drifted up. Fear tightened her stomach: Bhola might use the gun on himself.

She found a plastic bag under the bed and wrapped it around the gun with great caution, terrified that it would suddenly fire. She left the house and found herself thrust into the cacophony of the Makhan Tole marketplace. I should have gone another way, she thought, brushing against the pedestrians, fearful that the package would slip from her hands. She headed toward Ratna Park, where she boarded a minibus to go to Ananda, who lived in Balaju. On the minibus, Janaki clutched the gun under her shawl, feeling the cold metal against her belly.

When she knocked on Ananda's door, Sukumaya answered. Janaki had never spoken to her, although she had run into her and Ananda a couple of times in the city after that first day at the market. Janaki and Ananda had done all the talking, mostly about Bhola, while Sukumaya had stood timidly behind him. "Is he home?" Janaki asked now. Her eyes fell on Sukumaya's large belly, and Janaki swallowed. Soon Ananda would have even less time for Bhola.

Playing nervously with her hair, Sukumaya said he was visiting a friend.

"I'll come back, then," Janaki said.

Sukumaya said something so softly Janaki could barely hear her. "Please have some tea first," Sukumaya repeated, louder this time.

What a strange woman, thought Janaki, who had expected Sukumaya to act at least a little sullen. Well, why not? Janaki thought. Let's see what this woman is all about. And maybe Ananda would come home soon, and she could show him the gun.

She followed her into the living room and took a seat on a plush velvet sofa while Sukumaya went to the kitchen. The walls were covered with photos of Ananda and Sukumaya together: at their wedding, with mountains in the background, outside a temple. Janaki's eyes fell on the one picture of Bhola, when he was five. She remembered that one—he'd refused to smile, and when they'd forced him to, he'd bared his teeth. She peered at the photo to see if she could detect something different in his eyes that might indicate how he'd turn out later. But she found nothing.

Sukumaya came back with two glasses of tea and a plate of biscuits. An awkward silence hung in the air as they sipped their tea, then Janaki said, "And you are well? Your health is well?" She almost asked whether she was pregnant, but she barely knew the woman, and she certainly didn't want to be mistaken.

Sukumaya nodded.

She can't be more than a few years younger than me, Janaki thought. Ananda had never mentioned her age.

Sukumaya blurted out, "I am expecting!"

"That's what I thought. How far along are you?"

"Already five months. When you were carrying your son," Sukumaya said, setting her cup of tea down and leaning forward, "did you feel like something horrible was growing inside you?"

"No," Janaki said, nearly choking on her tea at the odd question.

"Did you ever feel that the baby would come out all wrong, perhaps missing an eye or a leg?"

Janaki said no. She wondered whether Sukumaya, too, was touched in the head.

"I feel like that all the time." Her face became slightly contorted.

"If you feel like that, why don't you ask your mother to come stay with you for a while? Let her take care of you."

"My parents don't come here," Sukumaya said. "They were against this marriage."

"Don't you have anyone else you could talk to, lean on? Friends?"

"Even my friends don't talk to me much anymore. I do have a good friend who moved to Chitwan after she married, but we only talk on the phone."

The gun poked at Janaki's stomach as she moved closer to Sukumaya. "Look, strange things happen to pregnant women, especially women who have children at a slightly later age. You should also remember that there's a new person growing inside you, so it's natural that your body would feel awkward."

"Did you feel anything different with . . . Bhola babu?"

Janaki understood what she was insinuating, and she didn't like it. "You mean, did I know that he would be different? No."

Sukumaya failed to catch the irritation in her tone. "To be honest, I'm a little terrified."

"You can't worry about such things," Janaki said. "Though I guess that's what a pregnancy does, it makes you worry, but you should talk about it with someone close to you. Do you talk to Ananda about it at all?"

She shook her head. "I don't know why. I guess I'm afraid that if I tell him how I'm feeling, he'll either get annoyed with me or brush me off."

Ananda has married a child, Janaki thought. He's isolated her from her family, her friends, and left her to deal with her pregnancy on her own. "Listen," Janaki said. "Whenever you feel lonely, call me on the phone. Do you know my number?"

She nodded. "But I won't call you when he is around, as he might not like it."

Suddenly Ananda came in and stood in the doorway, apparently shocked to see Janaki. "Oh," he said. "Everything all right? What brings you here?"

Janaki showed him the gun. Sukumaya gave a start, moved away from Janaki, and went to stand by her husband. "I don't know where Bhola got the money to buy it," Janaki said. "Did you give it to him?"

Ananda and Sukumaya exchanged glances. "I don't know what happened," Ananda said.

"He came to me," Sukumaya said, looking at the floor. "He said he needed money for new clothes. I didn't know he was going to buy a gun with it."

Janaki grew annoyed. "How much did you give him?"

"Two thousand rupees."

Ananda took the gun from Janaki and inspected it. He rolled the bulge in the middle. "There are bullets in here. What does he want a gun for?"

Janaki told him about Bhola's coming to her the night before, about his throwing the plate of food and telling her all his ideas of joining the insurgents.

Ananda laughed. "Then they'll really be a bunch of crazies."

Janaki was irritated by his casual attitude. "What if he does something to himself?"

"Leave this here with me," he said. "I'll talk to him."

"When? He'll be outraged when he discovers that I stole it from his room."

"Then tell him I stole it, and when he comes here, I'll deal with him."

"Why don't you go and talk to him instead of waiting for him to come to you?"

"I guess I could do that," Ananda said, and he and Sukumaya went to sit on the sofa. He reached his arm around her. Before Sukumaya, as far as Janaki knew, Ananda hadn't cheated on her. He'd never expressed any major dissatisfaction with their marriage, though he was by nature a bit distant and aloof. Even on their wedding night, he fell asleep as soon as they were alone together. During Bhola's childhood, Ananda had been a devoted father, but once their son's mental illness became apparent, he grew more remote. Now he said, "I'm getting hungry."

"Shall we eat?" Sukumaya asked. She turned to Janaki. "Janaki didi, you will join us for dinner?"

Didi. Now I'm her sister, Janaki thought. "I should probably go."

"Please," Sukumaya said. "You came all the way here, you might as well stay. I'll go get everything ready." Despite Janaki's protests, she went off to the kitchen.

For a moment, Janaki and Ananda just glanced at each other. Then she said softly, "You should spend more time with her."

Ananda looked at Janaki. "What do you mean? I do spend time with her."

"When a woman is pregnant, she needs people to talk to."

"What did she say to you?"

"She's worried about the baby."

"All pregnant women are like that. You were worried, remember?"

"Yes, but I had people around to take care of me. Remember, my mother was alive then, and she came to see me almost every day."

Ananda stretched his legs and placed them on a small stool in front of the sofa. "We're hoping it's a son."

"What would be wrong with a daughter?"

He shrugged. "I just want another son. Another try, maybe."

"She told me she's worried the child will turn out to be like Bhola."

Ananda shook his head, then recalled how Bhola was as a child, before his illness took over. The way he threw a fit when Ananda had to leave for the office, saying, "Baba, no work, no work." How, as Bhola got older, Ananda used to wrestle playfully with him. He smiled as he spoke, and despite herself Janaki was a little moved.

Sukumaya called them in for dinner, and reluctantly Janaki followed Ananda into the kitchen.

All that night Janaki stayed awake, expecting Bhola to bang loudly on her front door. At the slightest noise, she jerked upright. At four o'clock she finally fell asleep, only to awaken an hour later in the middle of a terrible nightmare, about Bhola hanging from a tree by the side of a hill, a noose around his neck. She scanned her dark room, breathless, and it took her a while to calm down and fall back to sleep.

He didn't come home that night, or the night after, and the following day she scoured the city. Sometimes he hung out with the teenagers in Jhonche, so she walked through that neighborhood, peeking into restaurants and alleys. When she was younger, this area bustled with hippies, and the smell of ganja perpetually filled the air. Once she and Ananda had spotted two hippies sloppily groping in the middle of the street, and Janaki averted her eyes in embarrassment. That night, Ananda jokingly tried to kiss her the same way, squeezing her buttocks with his palms, but she pushed him away. She remembered this now, and at first felt a pang over her failed marriage, then realized what she was truly mourning was her life before Bhola began to slip away. Back then, Bhola's dimpled smile, the way he clung to her and called her "Jana," made tolerable the emotional distance she felt between herself and Ananda. She played peekaboo with Bhola in their garden, and the rapt attention on his face when she told him bedtime stories filled her with a pleasure she had never experienced with Ananda.

After about two hours of fruitless searching, she headed toward Ananda's house again. Had Bhola indeed left the city in search of the Maobadis? How would he know where to find them? Still on the lookout for him, she walked all the way to Balaju, which took her nearly half an hour, and, exhausted, she stood in front of Ananda's house and knocked on the door. No one answered, so she knocked again. A faint sound drifted out from inside: the television was on. She went to the back of the house and peeked in through the kitchen window, but couldn't see anyone at first. She craned to look beyond the kitchen, into the living room, and she spotted a body on the floor. Sukumaya. Janaki ran to the front door, pounded on it, and shouted Sukumaya's name. Eventually the woman came to the door, wearing only a petticoat and a bra, her hair disheveled. The kohl on her eyes had run down her face.

"What's wrong? Why do you look like this?" Janaki asked, pushing herself inside.

Sukumaya walked back to the living room, where she sat on the sofa, her eyes lowered. On the small table next to her was a bottle, and next to it pills, laid out neatly, five in a row. Janaki grabbed the bottle and read the label—they were sleeping pills. "What is this?" she asked.

"I need them to sleep," Sukumaya said in a soft voice.

"This many?"

After a silence, Sukumaya said, "I worry that I won't love this child, didi."

"The child hasn't even been born yet. How can you say this?"

"I don't know," she said. "I just hate my body right now."

Janaki sat down next to Sukumaya and wrapped an arm around her shoulders. Sukumaya leaned against her, her eyes closed. "He doesn't understand the way I feel," she said. "I tried to tell him, but he never really listens to me. I don't know what to do."

"Try to calm yourself down. Everything will be all right."

"I keep thinking of my parents," Sukumaya said, "my friends."

"Everything will be fine," Janaki said, patting her head. She scooped up the pills and slipped them back inside the bottle. "Go wash your face, put on your dhoti, and I'll make us some tea." Sukumaya slowly stood and shuffled off.

In the kitchen, Janaki filled the kettle, and by the time Sukumaya emerged, wearing a fresh dhoti, her face washed and her hair combed, the tea was ready. They sat at the table, and Janaki tried to make small talk—complimenting Sukumaya's earrings, saying the sky was supposed to clear later today. The tea and Janaki's soft voice appeared to have rejuvenated Sukumaya, and when Janaki suggested they go outside to get some fresh air, Sukumaya sprang to her feet. "There are woods in Balaju Park. Why don't we go for a walk there? It's quite nice."

Janaki wanted to ask her when Ananda was going to come home so she could tell him about Bhola, but she knew the mention of either man might change Sukumaya's mood, so she remained quiet as they walked the street. Sukumaya began telling her about a picnic she'd had with her friends in Dhulikhel before the wedding, how the mountain view there was so stunning. And just as she spoke of the mountains, the clouds to the north of the city began to clear and they caught a glimpse of the Langtang range. Sukumaya squeezed Janaki's arm. "Look, didi. How gorgeous it looks!" But Janaki found herself watching Sukumaya's excited face rather than the mountains. Indeed, Ananda had married a child.

Then Janaki's thoughts turned back to Bhola. She desperately wanted to talk to someone about him, even Sukumaya, but as soon as they reached the woods, Sukumaya became consumed in reciting the names of the trees and plants they were passing. A group of young boys went by, singing lewd songs at the two women. "Idiots," Sukumaya said. "Young boys these days. Aren't they so ridiculous?"

"Some are," Janaki replied. How she wished Bhola had turned out to be like one of these boys—ridiculous but sane.

On their way back, she again tried to convince Sukumaya that she shouldn't entertain negative thoughts about her baby. "You have joyful days ahead of you, especially after the baby is born," Janaki said. "Don't give in to such pointless thinking. Come talk to me if you are feeling low."

Sukumaya nodded and thanked her. "Spending time with you today has made me feel so much better, didi," she said.

Janaki finally told her the reason she'd come, and Sukumaya said, "I'm so selfish. Here you are, all worried about Bhola babu, and you have to deal with my nonsense."

"It's not nonsense. You know, I am thinking that once you have the baby, your parents will probably come around. Who can resist a grandchild?"

Back at the house, they saw that Ananda had returned, and when he learned that they'd gone out together, he didn't look pleased. When Sukumaya went to the kitchen to make tea for him, he told Janaki, as he sat on the sofa, "I don't know what you're thinking, but please don't put ideas into her head."

She shook her head. "You should talk to your wife more, I'm telling you." But she hadn't come here to lecture him about her. She drew a deep breath. "Bhola hasn't been home for two days."

"He's done this in the past, and he always comes back before too long."

"I know, I know, but I feel like something really bad is going to happen to him this time."

"Well, I'll go out and look for him tomorrow," Ananda said, then stood. She sensed that he wanted her to leave.

The next day, Janaki went to the police station in her neighborhood to file a report. She didn't mention Bhola's talk about joining the insurgents to the police inspector. "We'll do what we can," he said, "although, to be frank, so many people are disappearing these days, we don't have enough policemen to search for them."

"But my son has some mental problems and can't take care of himself very well," Janaki said. She handed him Bhola's photo, which the inspector said he'd circulate to the police departments in and around the Kathmandu Valley.

Back at home, Janaki went up to Bhola's room, pulled a chair to the window, and sat there, looking out. Across the street, two children were playing football in their yard. A young girl in a frilly dress with embroidered flowers walked below, holding her mother's hand. Janaki closed her eyes and rocked in the chair, forcing herself to remember Bhola in his younger days—how he used to splash in the mud on the street after rain, how easily he recited the multiplication tables, how he used a tall bamboo stick to pole-vault around the neighborhood, swinging high into the air and landing nimbly on his feet.

The days turned into weeks. Janaki fell into a depression that made her unable to leave the house. Ananda called days later to say that he had searched all over the city but hadn't found Bhola. "I'll keep trying," he said. "He'll turn up sooner or later." Every week Janaki called the police inspector, but all he said was that his men were on alert. She no longer turned on the radio, and she avoided newspapers, which these days were filled with pictures of widows holding their children.

Late one morning, Ananda called Janaki, saying that they were in the hospital, that Sukumaya had given birth to a baby boy and had been asking for her. "For me?" Janaki said. "Why me?"

"I don't know," Ananda said, his voice thick. "She's been whispering your name all morning."

"I can't come. What happens if Bhola shows up while I'm gone?"

For a moment Ananda was silent. "I don't know what to do about him," he said gravely. "Where could he be?" When she didn't answer, he said gently, "Don't worry too much. And listen, I'll give some excuse to Sukumaya for your not being able to come."

"No, no," Janaki said, "I'll come. She must be missing her family."

With some effort, she washed her face, changed her clothes, and left the house. The sun seemed too bright, and the people walking about too cheerful. She hailed a three-wheeler, and on the way she tried to muster happy thoughts for Sukumaya.

In the hospital, Sukumaya lay on a narrow bed, looking pale and exhausted. The room smelled of milk and soiled clothes, and briefly Janaki was transported back to her time in the hospital when Bhola was born. He had been a big baby, with thick arms, and she'd marveled that he'd managed to squeeze himself out of her womb. Sukumaya didn't say anything when she first saw Janaki. She just pointed to the baby, who was sleeping in the crook of her arm. Ananda stood and left the room, and Janaki asked Sukumaya how she was feeling.

"I guess I'm all right, didi. Do you want to hold him?" she asked, gazing at the baby. Gingerly, Janaki reached over and took the baby from Sukumaya's arms. He was tiny, with a small face and red lips. "He looks just like you," Janaki managed to say.

"No, he looks like his father, doesn't he? The same broad forehead, the same small mouth. But I don't care. He's my son." Sukumaya suddenly looked as if she were about to weep.

"Calm down now," Janaki said. "Fathers pass along their faces to their sons." She set the baby back beside Sukumaya, who didn't glance down at him. Janaki asked her what they'd decided to name the boy, but Sukumaya didn't answer. She just stared out the window, her forehead creased.

Janaki sat down beside her. "Everything will be all right," she told Sukumaya. "Listen, Ananda is a good father. He always was to Bhola. You have nothing to worry about." Then she couldn't help herself: she told Sukumaya that Bhola still hadn't come home, and she feared that he would never come back. As soon as she said it, she knew she shouldn't have, for Sukumaya lowered her eyes. "But these are just a worried mother's fears," Janaki said, wanting to salvage the mood. "I'm sure he'll be back."

For the next fifteen minutes, Janaki continued to try to cheer her up by saying how great Sukumaya would feel once the baby began crawling and when he took his first steps. But when the baby started crying, Sukumaya didn't attend to him, and Janaki had to pick up the boy again and rock him. Ananda finally came back into the room, and Janaki handed him his son. "You'll be a fine young man," he said, gently rubbing his nose against the baby's face. Janaki told Sukumaya that she'd visit her at home, and then she stood and left the hospital. On the bus ride back, she remembered when she and Ananda brought Bhola home from the hospital. Ananda spent hours with him, pinching his nose, making faces at him, picking him up and singing to him, watching as she gave him an oil bath, outside under the hot sun.

"I have no idea where your son is," the police inspector said testily to Janaki. "I'm sorry, but you can't imagine how busy we are. Do you know how many of my brothers on the force are getting killed these days?" He held his head in his hands. "I'm sorry, I really am, but please just leave, and I'll call you if I hear anything."

Janaki left the police station and passed by a newsstand. On the cover of a magazine were photos of the insurgents in uniforms that looked like the ones worn by the army. They were holding guns, marching. They all looked so young with their smooth cheeks — like schoolchildren.

At home she closed the curtains and bolted the door. Bhola wasn't going to come home, and she wasn't going to open it for anyone else. She lay down on the kitchen floor, resting her forehead on the cool tiles. Her mind was heavy, her body ached, and soon she slept.

It didn't wholly surprise her when she found out, two days later, that Sukumaya had left Ananda and the baby. Janaki took the news calmly, even tried to console Ananda, who was weeping on the phone as he told her. Early that morning they had returned home from the hospital, and since Sukumaya refused to nurse the baby, he carried his son with him to the market to fetch formula. When he returned, she was gone. "How could she do this to me?" Ananda said. "To her own child?"

Janaki had to restrain herself from reminding him of what he'd done to her and Bhola, and when he asked her to come to him, she reluctantly agreed.

When she got near the front door of his house, she could hear the baby crying. She rushed in and saw Ananda on the phone, talking frantically. She picked up the baby from the sofa, and instantly he stopped crying and searched her face. The bottle of formula was on a table nearby, so she picked it up and slipped it into the baby's mouth. Ananda hung up. "She's left the city."

"How did you find out?"

"Someone saw her at the bus station, boarding a bus to Chitwan."

"Who lives there?" Janaki asked, vaguely recalling Suku-maya saying something about Chitwan.

"I don't know," Ananda said. "Wait, I think she has a friend there. Listen, I've got to go find her. I've got to bring her back."

The baby's eyes were closed now, and he was breathing heavily. Janaki met Ananda's gaze and knew instantly what he was thinking.

"No, no," she said, handing the baby to him. "Take him with you. He'll need his mother when you find her."

He pleaded with her, saying traveling with an infant would be a nightmare. "And what if I don't find her?"

Janaki began walking to the door, but Ananda grabbed her arm. The baby, shaken by his move, awoke and began to cry again. "Janaki, I swear to you, it'll only be a few days. If after three days I can't locate her, I'll return. I wouldn't ask this of you, of all people, if I had anyone else to go to."

"Inform her parents," Janaki said. "They are the immediate kin, after all. Tell them they have to accept the baby, whether they like it or not."

"You don't know what kind of people they are, Janaki. They'll slam the door in my face."

The baby wailed, and she couldn't help but take him from Ananda. She sighed. Ananda's parents lived halfway across the country, in Biratnagar; he couldn't possibly take the baby there.

"I'll be forever grateful to you, Janaki, please," Ananda said. "I have to leave now. Maybe I'll find her in Chitwan by tonight."

Back at home, Janaki held the baby until he fell asleep, then set him down on her bed. She looked at him. He was ador-able, with his nose the size of a little button, and after all, he knew nothing. She watched his curled fists as he slept, and she touched his arm. Briefly he opened his eyes, gurgled happily, then closed them again.

After a week, Ananda hadn't returned or called. The baby got used to Janaki, and he seemed to smile whenever she hovered over him. Sometimes he played with her nose, just as Bhola did when he was that small. Before long, she remembered exactly how to clean and change a baby, and all the work that was involved in tending to a newborn. The thought lingered at the back of her mind that the boy's mother should be doing this, but she didn't feel so resentful when she was playing peekaboo with him and laughing.

One evening after dinner, as she watched the baby sleep on her bed, she gave in and cried. So much sadness had seeped into her bones. The baby opened his eyes and watched her, and weeping, she stroked his hairy scalp. She reached for him, took him to the open window, and showed him the outside world. Darkness was approaching. Shops had turned on their lights, and people hurried home. The evening breeze felt good on her face, and she talked to the baby, saying, "A nice evening, isn't it? When I was a young girl, you could see the stars, but now it's impossible to glimpse the sky through this smog."

Someone was climbing the stairs in her building. The heavy thumps made her hold her breath. It was certainly not Ananda, who had a lighter step. Had Bhola returned to her after all these days? With a thudding heart she went to open the door, but found she couldn't move. Who knew where he'd been? Who knew what crazy thoughts now cluttered his mind? Who knew how he'd react to the baby?

Quickly she bolted the door and, clasping the baby tighter to her chest, told him not to be afraid.

Chintamani's Women

As he approached his office building in Lazimpat, Chintamani grew apprehensive. He glanced up at the third floor, where Buddha Publishing was located. Normally his boss, Mr. Somnath, could be seen from here, sitting in his chair, but today the chair was empty. Beginning to sweat a little, Chintamani walked inside and climbed the stairs. Sushmita met him at the top. "Where were you?" she whispered. "Mr. Somnath is in a state."

"I had to take Buwaba to the hospital," Chintamani said, wiping his forehead with his handkerchief. "He had heart palpitations earlier this morning."

"Is he okay now?"

"Yes, but it took up my entire morning."

Mr. Somnath was leaning against Chintamani's desk, his arms crossed, and it looked as if he'd been in this position for hours. As Chintamani approached, his boss said, "Listen . . . ," then he clearly made the decision not to accost him in front of his colleagues, who were all watching. He motioned for Chintamani to follow him into his office. Once inside, Mr. Somnath said, "This is too much. You're late again."

"What's too much, sir?" he asked, exasperated. "You know

I have a very ill father. You know his situation is unpredictable." He told Mr. Somnath what had happened that morning. "Thankfully it was nothing big and he's resting at home now. I hurried to work as soon as I could, sir."

"I'm sorry about your father," Mr. Somnath said. "But just this month you've missed eight days of work. Coming in late has become normal for you. You're not getting your work done, and I can't sit back and allow this to go on. Maybe you can find another job more suited to your situation."

"Sir, where would I find a job like that?"

"I don't know. That's something you'll have to figure out for yourself. I'm sorry to be doing this, but I'm your manager, and you have to understand."

Chintamani pressed his lips together. "I'm a very hard worker. But people have families, and sometimes family members get sick. You are a human being, you should understand that."

"A human being! A human being!" Mr. Somnath seemed at a loss for words.

"Yes, a human being," Chintamani said, strangely fortified. "A human being should understand other human beings."

"What do you want me to do, Chintamani?" Mr. Somnath said. "What will the others think if I don't do something? What will happen to this office if everyone starts behaving like you do, missing days of work, arriving late, leaving early?"

"I'll stay late today to make up for this morning."

Mr. Somnath shook his head.

Chintamani grew desperate. There were hardly any jobs in the city these days, let alone one that would accommodate his life. And this job was good: it paid as much as any work at this level would, his duties as a junior accountant were easy, and his colleagues were mostly pleasant. After he finished his intermediate degree five years ago, Chintamani had been without a job and miserable for several months, and the thought of returning to that state, with Buwaba's medical expenses now increasing, was unbearable. "Sir, I swear I'll be on time from now on," he said, "and I won't miss any more work." An idea came to him. "Listen, I'll put myself on probation. For the next six months, if I don't come in at nine and leave at five, you can fire me."

The man looked at him.

"I just want to prove to you what a committed worker I am."

"Probation, eh?" Mr. Somnath said, lingering on the word. "That's not such a bad idea. Actually, everyone in this office should be on probation. Maybe we can adopt it as an official policy."

"Sir, don't punish others when they haven't done anything wrong. It's my problem and should be my solution."

"All right, all right," Mr. Somnath said. "But I want to put something in writing that you'll need to sign. That way there'll be no misunderstanding later." He turned to his computer and typed up a contract, reiterating what Chintamani had suggested. Chintamani signed it, and Mr. Somnath slipped it into a folder.

"May I also request that none of this gets revealed to the others in the office?"

"Why? I think it would set a good precedent for people here."

"Please, it's a little humiliating for me."

Mr. Somnath looked at him hard, then said, "All right, but if you violate this probation, I'll have to announce it."

Chintamani agreed, went straight to his desk, and began working. He suddenly started to worry what would happen if Buwaba needed to go to the hospital again, but he told himself not to think that way—after all, he had no choice. Sushmita, who sat a few desks away, kept trying to make eye contact with him, but he ignored her. She had always shown an interest in his life, and sometimes, when he was feeling anxious or down, he welcomed her attention. But at other times she made him feel claustrophobic. Some of his colleagues confirmed that she had a soft spot for him, but he wasn't attracted to her. She wore black-framed glasses too large for her face, she was a touch pudgy, and she breathed a bit too heavily. She also had the habit of staring at him when he spoke, which he found unnerving. She certainly didn't come close to the kind of beauty he envisioned spending his life with. He knew enough to realize that a pretty woman didn't necessarily make a good wife, yet he had to be physically attracted to the woman with whom he shared his bed, ate meals, raised children. Chintamani was willing to wait until he found someone who'd make his heart warm, his pulse quicken, every time he looked at her.

The problem was that he'd had little luck in finding such a girl. He used to be friendly with one pretty girl in college, and he was on the verge of confessing his romantic feelings for her when one day she began talking about a new boyfriend she had, someone who soon asked her to marry him. Since then, he'd asked out a couple of other girls, but both told him they were already seeing other people. He worried that his shyness put them off, or that they couldn't see themselves with a lowly accountant who had to take care of his ill father, or that—and this was the hardest thing to acknowledge—they didn't find him attractive. He wasn't bad-looking, he knew, but there was nothing striking about his appearance or personality. He was a fairly small man, with thin hair and a downturned mouth. He'd tried to change this by practicing wide smiles in front of the mirror, but after weeks of practice, nothing happened: when he caught his reflection in shop windows, he found that he looked as glum as before.

After repeated failed attempts at attracting a girlfriend, he'd resigned himself to daydreaming about good-looking women he happened to see on his way to and from work, and lately, to his dismay, even actresses and models he saw in magazines or on television. Too often he found himself fantasizing about the Indian actress Manisha Koirala—he saw himself in a hotel room with her, languishing on the bed, running his fingers through her dark, wavy hair. These were foolish thoughts for a twenty-five-year-old man, he knew, but he couldn't help it, and these fantasies tended to intensify when he got bogged down with worries about Buwaba.

His father's heart palpitations were the latest in a series of illnesses. Soon after his mother's death two years ago, Buwaba was diagnosed with diabetes. It took months to get that under control, and then he began to suffer from acute diarrhea, causing him to lose weight rapidly. Lately he'd been struck with so many ailments that Chintamani could hardly keep track of them. The chair by Buwaba's bed was covered with bottles of syrups, pills, tablets, and syringes, and in the past few weeks he'd remained mostly bedridden. Sometimes he needed Chintamani's help to go to the bathroom.

Now Chintamani thought about calling Sarla, the neighbor he had hired to check in on his father, to find out how he was doing, but Chintamani was acutely aware of Mr. Somnath's gaze from inside his glassed-in office, and didn't want his boss to overhear him making any personal calls.

At two o'clock that afternoon, Sushmita came to his desk. "Isn't it time for tea?" she asked, her eyes large behind her glasses. "Shall we go downstairs?"

"No tea for me today."

She leaned against his desk, breathing audibly. "What happened?" she whispered.

"Nothing," he said. "I'll tell you later."

He sensed her watching him, but he kept his head down, and soon enough she went with other coworkers to the tea shop downstairs.

He was still working after everyone had left the office that evening. Mr. Somnath, who was always the last to leave, stopped by his desk. "Aren't you going home?"

"I'm making up for this morning, sir."

"Right, right," he said, and then he too left. After about an hour, the office attendant who was responsible for locking up became impatient with Chintamani, so he decided to leave.

When he stepped out onto the street below, he was surprised to see Sushmita leaning against the lamppost there. "I thought you went home," he said, and began walking, and she caught up to him. They'd left the office together before, and they usually parted ways in Ranipokhari, Sushmita heading toward Putalisadak and he toward Tripureswor. Now he walked quickly, and she too quickened her pace, and asked, "So, what happened with Mr. Somnath?"

"What do you think happened? He's fed up with me, and he lectured me."

"Something else had to happen," she said. "You look so worried. Why don't you talk to me about it?"

"What's there to talk about? You know my father's situation. You know how Mr. Somnath is."

"He's not that bad," she said. "He is our manager, so he has to say something." It was known in the office that Sushmita was Mr. Somnath's favorite employee. He sang her praises to the other workers, and had once taken her home for dinner with his wife and kids. For a few minutes Chintamani and Sushmita walked quietly, then she said, "When will I ever get to meet Buwaba? You always say you'll bring me home with you soon, but you never do. I'll probably never get to meet him."

She had at times mentioned her own father's death, when she was a teenager, and how it had left a big hole in her life, but Chintamani feared her meeting Buwaba would give him the wrong idea. "He's too ill right now for anyone to visit," he said.

"That's what you always say," she said.

"Be patient," he said. "One of these days I'll arrange it."

"How about I come this Saturday?"

"I don't know. I'd have to ask him first."

"I'll plan on coming unless your father says no."

"Let's just see how he's feeling then."

After they parted ways in Ranipokhari, he changed his mind—it might not be such a bad idea for Sushmita to meet Buwaba. Lately his father had been complaining about the lack of a "feminine presence" in the house, and Sushmita's visit might rejuvenate him. But Chintamani would have to make clear that her visit didn't signal anything significant, that she was merely a coworker who'd become a friend. Not even a close friend, he'd tell Buwaba. And it was true—after all, he and Sushmita rarely talked about personal matters. He did know that she had an elderly mother who sewed clothes for women in her neighborhood, and he knew about her father, but that was about it.

Though Chintamani wasn't attracted to her, he didn't always mind spending time with her. Sushmita was quite intelligent, that much he had gathered quickly. He liked to listen to her argue with their colleagues about politics, discuss books, or explain the latest technological developments in America or Japan. Once, after work, the two stopped by an electronics store because she was thinking about buying a camera. She didn't know what type to buy or which brand would be best for her, but within minutes after the store clerk had explained the basics of two or three cameras, she began discussing such complicated details that the clerk gazed at her in admiration. "Your wife could run an electronics shop all by herself," he told Chintamani. This embarrassed him, and after they left, Sushmita said, "People just jump to conclusions." At any rate, Chintamani wondered why she held this modest job as a junior accountant—she seemed capable of so much more. He guessed that, like everyone else, she clung to her job because decent jobs were so scarce.

Chintamani lived in Tripureswor, in a flat on the second floor of an old house. He stopped by Sarla's tea shop across the street from his house to ask how his father's day went. Chintamani paid Sarla three hundred rupees a month to check on Buwaba while he was at the office—to give him his daily medicine, make his afternoon tea, and see that he was comfortable.

"He's fine," Sarla said as she poured steaming tea from a large black kettle into glasses set out on her counter, filling them to the brim. Sarla's shop was poorly lit and stuffy, but she attracted regular customers because of her warm personality and her fragrant, milky tea. "But he was asking me why you were late. I was upstairs just fifteen minutes ago."

Chintamani mumbled that his workload had been heavy at the office today, and went up to his flat. Buwaba attempted to sit up in bed as he entered. The flat had only one large room, which served as a bedroom for both of them. There was a small, separate kitchen off in one corner and a bathroom in the other. "Son, why so late?" Buwaba asked.

"Too much work at the office," he said. "Sarla gave you your medicine?" He rearranged his father's pillows.

"She talks too much," Buwaba said, his eyes on the floor. It was clear that his father still missed his mother, and at times Chintamani suspected that many of the man's ailments were more mental than physical. One of Buwaba's doctors had told Chintamani, "Be prepared to hear these complaints about his aches and pains until he passes away. It's common for old folks who lose their spouses." In fact, it seemed to him that his father's problems ran deeper than simple grief—some days Buwaba appeared to be gradually giving up on life. He had begun talking about his own death, and snapped at Chintamani whenever he tried to change the subject. Buwaba resisted being shaved anymore, a task Chintamani had to do for him because his hands shook too much, and he no longer played solitaire, a game he'd loved all his life, even when his wife was alive.

Chintamani's eyes fell on the picture of Lord Ganesh on the kitchen wall, and he uttered a prayer that his mother's soul was at peace in heaven. Then he prayed that Buwaba's heart never suffer palpitations again. As he turned on the stove to warm up some catfish soup for his father, Chintamani again thought about Buwaba's getting to know Sushmita. The more he thought about it, the better the idea seemed. She was outgoing and would ask him plenty of questions, maybe help him become engaged in his life again.

When the soup was ready, he carried a tray with two bowls to his father, who was sleeping now, his mouth slightly open, spittle on his lips. Chintamani wiped his mouth, which woke him up. They ate together, Buwaba sitting up in his bed and

Chintamani on the floor, but after a few spoonfuls, Buwaba stopped eating, and a faraway look came over his face.

"Someone's coming to visit this Saturday," Chintamani said.

"Hmmm," Buwaba said absently.

"She works in my office."

Buwaba looked at Chintamani. "It's a woman?"

"Yes, her name is Sushmita."

Buwaba watched him closely. "That's good," he said. "It's nice to have friends at work."

"Yes, and she's been wanting to meet you for a long time." Chintamani worried he'd said too much.

"I wish your mother were here."

"It's not a big thing. Sushmita is just a friend."

Buwaba said nothing more, and Chintamani was relieved.

Later, as they were watching television, Buwaba suddenly said, "What are you going to feed her?"

Chintamani had to think a moment about whom he was referring to. "I don't know, I'll cook something," he said. He kept his eyes on the television. They were watching a program that showed clips from the latest Hindi movies, often the songs and the dances in them, and when Manisha appeared, dancing her way through a garden, he felt himself smile a little.

"Cook something special, okay?" Buwaba said. "It's not every day that a guest comes to our house."

Chintamani nodded. On the screen now, Amir Khan was singing a song about how his heart soared at the thought of his girl. Chintamani missed going to the movies—in the past two years he'd gone only twice.

"Is she from a good family?"

Chintamani nodded, absorbed in the program.

Buwaba reached for the remote, which was lying on the edge of the bed, and turned off the television.

"Why did you do that?" Chintamani asked.

"When I'm asking you something, answer me. I'm still your father. I haven't died yet."

"Don't talk nonsense, Buwaba." Chintamani reached for the

remote, which Buwaba passed from one trembling hand to the other.

"I asked you a question. Is she from a good family?"

Chintamani stood up. "What difference does it make?"

"Answer my question!"

"I don't know!"

"Then why are you inviting her here?"

"Because she wants to meet you."

"Why does she want to meet me? What am I to her?"

"Forget it. This was a bad idea. I'll tell her not to come." He walked over to the television, pushed the power button. The song had ended, and a commercial for an expensive clothing shop was on. Young models paraded down a runway in tailored suits and colorful saris and salwar kameezes. Chintamani turned off the set and went to the window—it had begun to rain, and he saw people scurrying into Sarla's tea shop. The Red Bag Girl appeared and ran into the shop. She always came at this time of the evening, carrying a bright red bag, possibly on her way home from work. From what he could see, she was quite pretty; she was slim and had a broad smile. A few times he'd tried to catch her eye as she went into the shop, but she never looked up. Now he wondered whether he should go down to talk to Sarla, linger at the counter, see if anything would happen. Perhaps he could bring an umbrella and offer to walk the girl home. He sighed—he knew he'd never have the courage to speak to her.

When he turned, he saw that tears were running down Buwaba's face. He still held the remote in his hand.

"What's wrong now?" Chintamani asked.

Buwaba didn't answer, so Chintamani went to him and sat on the bed beside him. He put his arm around his father. "Don't do this."

"No one cares about me anymore," Buwaba said, wiping his tears.

"I do." He had half a mind to tell his father about his probation, about all the trouble he'd gotten into at work because of him, but he held back.

"No you don't."

Chintamani knew that trying to convince his father otherwise was useless, so he merely stroked his back and kept saying, "Everything is fine." In moments like these, his heart went out to his father. One day, before his mother died, Chintamani overheard his parents talking about who was going to pass away first. "I don't know why, but I know it's going to be me," his mother said, and Buwaba reprimanded her and grew quiet. She teased him about his sullenness, and then he said, "I wouldn't be able to live without you." "You will — you know why?" his mother said. "Before I die, I'll make sure Chintamani has brought a daughter-in-law into our house, and you won't feel my absence so much."

At that time Chintamani was struck, as he often was, by how openly affectionate his parents were toward each other — it was, as far as he knew, quite unusual for old people of their generation. This was the kind of married life Chintamani envisioned for himself, and he knew that his own ideals of beauty or physical attraction were shallow in the face of the deep fondness his parents had shared. But a part of him clung to the conviction that he could have both: a beautiful woman with whom he'd be sharing his deepest fears and joys in his old age.

True to her word, his mother had earnestly started looking for a bride for him, but the photos of girls that she showed him disappointed him. The girls were all homely, some of them chubby, some with bland expressions — and none, judging from his mother's descriptions, had particularly interesting jobs or hobbies. He kept shaking his head at these photos, and one night his mother suddenly died in her sleep. During the mourning period, Chintamani became racked with guilt about not fulfilling his mother's wishes, and it took weeks to get over it. In his grief, Buwaba seemed to have forgotten about the search for Chintamani's bride, but lately he was talking about it more and more. He'd put the word out among his relatives who visited, but nothing ended up happening.

After Buwaba fell asleep, Chintamani went to his own bed,

lay down, and flipped through a film magazine. He read about the love lives of some actors and actresses, then began to worry about his probation once more, hoping nothing drastic would happen to Buwaba again.

Chintamani got to work early the next morning, and again, in the afternoon, he turned down Sushmita's invitation to go for tea. Throughout the day, he kept catching Mr. Somnath glancing at him through the glass windows of his office. Chintamani hoped the man appreciated the effort he was making.

At five o'clock Sushmita approached his desk hesitantly. "Do you still want me to come to your house tomorrow?"

"Yes," he mumbled.

"I'm thinking it might not be such a good idea. Your father might think I'm . . ."

"He'll be glad for the company." He attempted a smile.

She stood watching him, then said, "All right, if you want me to."

"I want you to."

The next afternoon he went to the market and bought a kilo of goat meat, two squashes, and a bag of black lentils. As he watched the grocer scoop up the lentils and pour them into a plastic bag, he wondered what the three of them would talk about. He began to worry that Buwaba might say something to her that would put ideas into *her* head. As he walked back to his flat, he grew annoyed with both of them. Then, with a sinking feeling, he remembered his probation and reminded himself that he had to handle this carefully, that he couldn't show his irritation lest it upset his father.

A mirror in one hand, Buwaba was combing his hair in bed. Earlier he'd asked Chintamani to shave him, and hadn't been satisfied with the job he did, so Buwaba asked him to run the razor over his chin again. His father's wrinkles made this a difficult task, and Chintamani's arms were aching by the time he was done.

Now he went to the kitchen and set his bags on the counter. He pulled the paper from around the meat, and using his mother's favorite knife, he cut the meat into smaller pieces and set them in a pan. He poured some oil and red chili powder into the pan and stirred the meat.

"Are you cooking goat meat?" Buwaba called from the bedroom as the sharp smell filled the flat.

Chintamani responded that he was.

"Make sure you don't overcook it. The last time you made it, the bones dissolved in my mouth."

Chintamani clearly recalled Buwaba sucking eagerly on the bones and licking his fingers afterward, but he said in a cheery voice, "I'm being extra careful this time," and filled a pot with water for the lentils.

At six o'clock there was a knock on the door. Chintamani went to open it, and Sushmita stood there wearing a pink sari, lipstick, kohl on her eyes, and light rouge on her cheeks. He'd never seen her wear makeup, or in that sari, and he thought she looked much better than she usually did—she even looked a little pretty. "Come in, come in," he said.

Buwaba attempted to climb out of his bed. "Who is this?" he asked, feigning ignorance. Before he could get to the door, Sushmita was beside him, joining her palms in namaste. "I work with your son at the office," she said.

Buwaba stared at her, smiling. "Come here, my daughter." Chintamani cringed at his obvious attempt to establish intimacy. "It's not every day that such a fine-looking woman comes to visit us."

Sushmita seemed momentarily flustered by Buwaba's sugary words, but she maintained her composure. "Such a delicious smell in here," she said. She looked around for a place to sit. Chintamani had forgotten to remove the medicine bottles from the chair near Buwaba's bed, and now he hastily did so and offered her the seat and helped Buwaba back into bed.

"How are you feeling?" Sushmita asked him. "Your son always talks about you."

"Who knows when God will take me."

"Don't talk like that when our guest is here," Chintamani said.

"I'm sure you still have many years left," Sushmita said. Her eyes moved around the room and fell upon a magazine on Chintamani's bed, open to a photo of Manisha. The actress's head was tilted back and her perfect teeth were revealed in a smile. Sushmita looked down at her palms. Chintamani wished he'd gotten rid of the magazine; it made him look like a schoolboy. He'd certainly never talked about Manisha to Sushmita, who didn't seem as interested in films as he was.

Blushing, he went to the kitchen and added some crushed garlic to the meat, stirred it, and sprinkled salt over the squash. He opened a jar of pickled radishes—Sushmita had once said it was her favorite achar. Buwaba asked her about her family, and judging from his voice, he was thrilled to learn that she too was a Brahmin. Chintamani stayed in the kitchen, tasted the squash and lentils, then glanced back into the bedroom. Buwaba wasn't taking his eyes off her face, and in a moment he said to her what Chintamani had been fearing he might: "I've been begging him to get married, but he doesn't listen." Buwaba asked her if she was married. She shook her head.

"And why aren't you married yet?" he said.

"I don't know why." Her voice was coy.

Clapping his hands loudly once, Chintamani stepped into the bedroom. "Dinner is ready!"

Buwaba kept gazing at Sushmita. "He's not married, you're not married," he said, and Chintamani interrupted him, saying that the food would get cold.

"Well, bring it out to the table," Buwaba said. "You don't expect us to go to the kitchen, do you?"

"I should be helping," Sushmita said, and stood. "What can I do?" she asked Chintamani as he followed her into the kitchen. She inspected what was in the pots and said, "Looks like you spent a lot of time on this."

He stood next to her in front of the stove and whispered, "He's in the habit of talking nonsense. Just ignore him."

"I don't mind," she whispered back. "He kind of reminds me of my own father."

As he reached for a ladle, their shoulders touched, and he flinched a little. She looked at him and smiled, and he said, "I hope the meat tastes okay."

Over dinner, Buwaba plied Sushmita with questions about work, what she liked to do in her free time, her mother. Chintamani edged in a word or two, but Buwaba often interjected, addressing only her. After they were done eating, Chintamani and Sushmita carried the dishes to the kitchen, where, despite her repeated offers to help wash them, he wouldn't let her. "You're our guest, I'll do them later," he told her, then whispered, "It's getting late. Perhaps I should take you home."

Hesitantly, she nodded, then said, "You never told me you were such a good cook. I'm lousy in the kitchen, so my mother does all the cooking."

"I want to meet your mother," Buwaba said loudly from the bedroom.

Chintamani rolled his eyes, but Sushmita called back, "Maybe one day I can bring her here."

Chintamani wetted a towel and went to the bedroom. He wiped Buwaba's face and hands, then said, "Why would her mother want to come here? People have their own things to do, you know."

"I want to talk to her," Buwaba said.

Chintamani looked at Sushmita. "Ready to go now?"

Sushmita went to Buwaba and clasped his hand. "Buwaba, I'm very happy that I got to meet you today. You remind me so much of my own father."

"And you remind me of what's missing in this house, my daughter."

Sushmita blushed, then bid him goodbye, and she and Chintamani walked down the stairs. Once on the street, he let out a big sigh, and she laughed. "Sounds like a huge load off your shoulders," she said.

"I don't know what to do when he starts talking like that."

She opened her mouth, but said nothing. He scanned the

street for a three-wheeler for her, and she said, "Can you walk me home? It's such a nice evening, and I ate so much that I should probably walk it off."

"Buwaba is upstairs by himself."

"You'd be home within half an hour."

He felt cornered, so he quietly agreed. They headed toward New Road, where the store lights were still bright. He didn't know what to say to her, and it seemed she felt the same. As they reached the New Road Gate, she abruptly said, "Do you like Manisha Koirala?"

He winced but tried to say casually, "She's a good actress."

"Do you consider her an Indian or a Nepali? You know, she was born in Nepal. Her grandfather was our prime minister—"

"I know, I know," he said. They entered the parade ground of Tundikhel. "I don't think about whether she's a Nepali or an Indian," he said. "I really don't think about her too much."

The area had grown dark, so he couldn't see her face, but he could almost hear the question she had in mind about his magazine. He contemplated telling her that Manisha was the kind of beauty he wanted to marry, but even in his head it sounded ridiculous. As they approached her flat, he tried to think of something to say before they parted. "You don't have to bring your mother by my house," he said. "Buwaba doesn't know what he's talking about."

She nodded. A moment later she said, "It was just small talk."

Outside her flat, she thanked him again for dinner and bid him good night.

Back home, Buwaba was already asleep, or so Chintamani thought until he turned off the lights and slid into his bed.

"She's the perfect woman," Buwaba spoke into the darkness.

For the next few days, Buwaba asked him many times about Sushmita. Chintamani didn't tell his father that he had been avoiding her, that he tried never to make eye contact with her, and when he did, he pretended to be lost in thought. He had already decided that if she came to him and said anything about coming back or bringing her mother, he'd tell her to forget about it. He would not even offer her a reason. Why should he? Her mother's visit would signal that there was something more to their relationship than there actually was.

Then she began to avoid him too. During the rare times when he glanced at her across the office, she was either busy with her work or chatting with the man who shared her desk. In the afternoons, she and this man, Prabhakar, lingered behind as the others headed out in a group for tea; only then did the two of them leave together. Once Chintamani casually walked to the window and looked outside after they'd gone: he saw them enter a tea shop across the street, not the shop where the others usually went. Buwaba's perfect woman has found a perfect man, he told himself. Well, good riddance.

When he turned around, he saw Mr. Somnath standing by his desk, a folder in his hand, looking at him. Chintamani quickly walked back and sat in his chair. "I thought I heard an accident out there," he said.

Mr. Somnath handed him a sheet from the folder. "Check to make sure that these numbers are correct. The last time you ran them, I received complaints from the distributor."

Chintamani took the sheet from him and immediately started punching numbers into his calculator. He breathed regularly again only after Mr. Somnath shut the door to his office.

At home that evening, when Buwaba asked him about Sushmita, Chintamani said, "She hasn't mentioned coming here again or bringing her mother." When Buwaba inquired further, he told his father that Sushmita didn't speak much to him these days.

Buwaba looked puzzled. "You sure you didn't say anything rude to her?"

Chintamani laughed. "Why would I do that?" A moment later he said, "She's begun to spend time with another man in the office." He realized with a start that he sounded almost resentful.

Buwaba was obviously disturbed by this turn of events: he began to complain continually about Chintamani's being unmarried, and his mood turned darker—he spoke more and more about his own death. Chintamani soon regretted telling Buwaba about Sushmita's not speaking to him. After all, what if this led to another emergency trip to the hospital, and what if Chintamani was late for work again? He worried about this for a day or so, then grew defiant. He wasn't about to start something with Sushmita just for Buwaba's sake. What would his life be like if every move he made was determined by Buwaba's desires?

One evening near the end of that week, Chintamani was at his bedroom window when he saw the Red Bag Girl enter Sarla's shop. He went to the bathroom, checked his face and his hair, forced himself to keep moving, to just go ahead and do this, then told Buwaba he'd be back in a second. He rushed down the stairs. Outside, he took a deep breath and crossed the street. Sarla sat behind her counter, and when he stepped inside, she asked anxiously, "Something wrong with Buwaba?"

He shook his head and said that he needed some tea. He looked around and saw the girl in the corner reading a magazine, an alu dum in one hand, a glass of water in front of her. She wore glasses today; they were small and delicate and accentuated her slender nose and soft lips. The table next to her was empty, and after Sarla handed him a glass of tea, he walked over to the table and sat down, making sure that he faced her. His heartbeat quickened, his palms were sweaty, but he was determined to make a move. The Red Bag Girl seemed to be engrossed in her reading, and she ate her potatoes without glancing at them. At one point she lifted the magazine a little, and he noticed that it was a film magazine. Manisha was on the cover—her arms crossed over her bare shoulders, her hair blown by the wind. He smiled to himself, took a large gulp of tea, swallowed it, and spoke.

"She's an excellent actress, isn't she?"

The girl continued reading.

He spoke loudly, "Is that Manisha Koirala on your magazine?"

She looked up, then glanced at the cover. "I hadn't noticed her."

"You like movies?" he asked, wondering if he sounded like an idiot.

"I tend to read about them more than watch them," the girl said. "I'm too busy with work."

"Where do you work?"

"I have two jobs, one during the day and one in the evening."

"You could always go to a movie on the weekend."

"I have other things to do on weekends." She turned back to her reading, and he felt his face grow warm. He tried to think of other things to say but couldn't come up with anything, so he turned around and asked the waiter for another glass of tea. When he turned back, the girl was standing, getting ready to leave.

"Going already?" he asked hastily.

She nodded and picked up her red bag.

"Manisha's new film is playing at Kumari Hall. If you're free sometime, maybe you and I could go—" He couldn't seem to stop himself.

She looked at him, her face suddenly transformed, and spat out a string of English words so fast that he didn't understand them. Then she turned and left, and he sat there, numb. Without waiting for his second glass of tea to arrive, he stood and moved toward the door, keeping his head down. Sarla was talking with someone, and she called to him as he went by. "Chintamani babu, one second. I need to talk to you."

His face reddened again, and he continued walking. Sarla joined him as he crossed the street, and at the entrance to his house, she whispered, "So, what is happening with Sushmita?"

"Buwaba talked to you about her?" he asked hoarsely.

"Last week he was going on nonstop about her—Sushmita this, Sushmita that—but the past few days he hasn't said a word." She touched his arm. "I saw her go into your flat. She looked quite nice in that pink sari."

Chintamani watched her eyes to see whether she was being sarcastic—it didn't look as if she was. "There's nothing between us. We're just friends. Buwaba is making a big thing out of it."

"Well, not to be intrusive or anything, but you know, you're not getting any younger."

"You too?" he said. "What is wrong with everyone?" He sighed, and realized that he was at least relieved Sarla hadn't wanted to talk about the girl in the shop.

"Babu, let me tell you something. It's hard these days to find someone who'd be good for you. Sure, there are plenty of pretty young girls in the city, but who knows what they are really like? When you find someone nice, you shouldn't let go of the opportunity. Take the advice of a woman who's seen a lot in life."

"Okay, okay, Mother of Wisdom."

Playfully, Sarla pinched his cheek and said, "I want to go to your wedding soon, okay?"

One morning a few days later, as he sat at his desk, staring out the window, trying not to think about the fact that Mr. Somnath was probably watching him, he suddenly felt someone's presence. It was Sushmita, standing by his desk, breathing insistently. "How is Buwaba these days?" she asked him.

He was actually somewhat glad to hear her voice. "The same as always," he said, shaking his head. "Although thankfully there haven't been any more emergencies."

"Thank God for that," she said. Then, a moment later, "You want to go out for tea with me today?"

He glanced past her to her desk, where Prabhakar quickly averted his gaze. "Yes, why not? It's been a while since we've talked."

At two o'clock, Prabhakar left with the larger group, and Sushmita and Chintamani followed a few minutes later. They went to the shop across the street.

"You look awfully pensive these days. Something on your mind?" she asked after they ordered tea and laddoos.

"I've just been kind of depressed about this whole thing with Buwaba," he said. "He acts like such a child sometimes. It's difficult."

The waiter brought their tea and sweets. "Eat," she said, handing him a laddoo. "They're very tasty here."

"It doesn't look tasty," he said, glancing down at it. It looked like any other laddoo—a round ball of flour and sugar.

"Try it, you'd be surprised."

He took a bite and was in fact pleasantly surprised. It was very soft, with a creamy center that tasted of almonds.

"You like it?" she asked, and he nodded and took another bite. They talked about their colleagues, how one of them had won an immigration lottery to move to America. They discussed the latest headlines about bus and truck drivers striking to protest high fuel prices, about the sudden popularity of yoga and health clubs in the city.

By the time they left the shop, his mood had improved. He jokingly said that he hoped Mr. Somnath wouldn't revoke his probation and fire him for going out for tea. Then he flinched: she didn't know about the probation.

"You know," she said, "Mr. Somnath is not as bad as you make him out to be. That probation was your idea, not his."

She seemed to realize that they'd never talked about it, and her face grew red. "I guess I should just tell you—Mr. Somnath told me the day after it happened."

"He said he'd keep it a secret! He must have told everyone by now."

She put her hand on his arm. "Listen, it was only me. He's not like that. He did tell me recently that he came very close to firing you that day, though he admitted that he doubted he'd have actually done it. I think he was feeling that you weren't taking your job seriously, and he said that the probation was a good way to keep you on your toes."

"But he knows my father is sick." They were standing at the entrance to their office building, and he looked at his watch and saw that it was five minutes past three. Everyone else had probably gone back up to work already. Would being five minutes late count as a violation? But Mr. Somnath had also broken their pact, and Chintamani decided that if his boss said anything, he would confront him about this.

"Listen, he thought you were exaggerating about your father," Sushmita said. "I told him I'd met Buwaba and he was indeed very ill, and now he believes you."

Chintamani stared at her. He couldn't believe that she had been so free with his personal business. Yet she had done him a favor, probably even saved him from getting fired, and she certainly didn't owe him that or anything else, especially after he'd acted so distant with her lately. "Buwaba keeps talking about you," he finally said.

They were leaning against the building, now facing the sidewalk that was busy with people. He noticed that she was wearing a pair of red crystal earrings he hadn't seen on her before — they gleamed in the afternoon sun.

"After meeting him," she said, "I couldn't stop thinking about my own father."

"Do you want to see Buwaba again?" he asked, then wondered why he'd said that. Only a couple of weeks ago her visit had made him miserable. Now here she was, saying what she was saying, and she'd done him this favor — it seemed unfair to deny her another visit, if that's what she wanted.

"I'd love to," she said. "But he's going to ask to meet my mother again, and it'll be back to square one."

She was right, and he thought a moment. "Maybe the three of us could go to see a movie sometime," he said. "That way he wouldn't have the opportunity to harp on about your mother."

"That one with Manisha Koirala that's playing at Kumari Hall? Is that what you're thinking?"

He turned away from her, smiling. "It's not what you think. Just because a man reads magazines doesn't mean anything."

"You have some kind of silly crush on her, don't you? Tell me the truth."

"I think she's pretty, sure," he said, and strangely, he felt relieved having admitted this. "She is very pretty," he repeated. "But that's it. Even if I have a foolish crush on her, which I'm not saying I do, it doesn't mean anything. Don't tell me that when you see a good-looking man you don't feel something."

"What would I feel for a man I don't know? I can tell you this much," she said. "I don't stare at pictures of actors in magazines."

"All right, all right," he said. "You win."

"Thank you," she said. She took his hand and pulled him inside. "I like the idea of us three going to a movie. There's one out right now with Naseeruddin Shah that looked interesting to me. Would Buwaba like to see that, you think?"

"Provided it's not too serious. He needs some cheering up."

They made a plan: that Saturday afternoon, she'd meet him at Jai Nepal ten minutes before the movie started, and leave as soon as the movie was over. This way the conversation would be kept to a minimum.

Upstairs, Mr. Somnath was standing in his office, his arms crossed, watching them as they walked to their desks. Chintamani sucked in his breath. "He's looking at us," he whispered from the side of his mouth. She glanced at Mr. Somnath and waved, then lightly placed her hand on Chintamani's back. She kept her hand there until they reached his desk, and then stood chatting with him about how she was learning to make laddoos at home. She laughed about the way they'd turned out the last time she made them, and told him that since he was such a good cook, perhaps he'd be much better at it. He kept his eyes on his files, pretending to jot down notes and be busy working while she talked. Finally she stopped, and he raised his head for a quick glance at Mr. Somnath's office. He had disappeared from view. Chintamani leaned back against his chair and looked at Sushmita, who was smiling at him.

"Your Prabhakar is waiting for you," he said in a silly voice.

She sighed. "He's such a handsome man. I should take a picture of him with my new camera and send it to a magazine."

"All right, all right," he said as she turned and went back to her desk.

Toward the end of the day, he rushed to finish a letter that needed to be signed by Mr. Somnath first thing tomorrow. Once it was done, he clasped his hands behind his head and thought about how Buwaba's face would light up at the prospect of seeing Sushmita again. He imagined his father all dressed up in his brown pants and a light coat, looking forward to this rare outing.

Then he began to imagine what it'd be like to sit in a movie theater with Sushmita alone, just the two of them, watching Naseeruddin Shah—or better yet, Manisha—on the screen. He saw himself reaching out for Sushmita's hand in the darkness, and his pulse quickened. He tried to imagine Manisha up on the big screen, her dark hair, her soft, swimming eyes, and suddenly he felt self-conscious. He glanced at Sushmita: she was talking to Prabhakar, and the two were getting ready to leave. Chintamani quickly stood, gathered his things, and faced her desk so she'd know that he, too, was ready to go. He kept his gaze on her until she looked back, then he raised his eyebrows and gestured toward the door.

Father, Daughter

EARLY ONE MORNING, Shova walked into her father's room with a glass of tea and the newspaper. "Did you sleep well, Daddy?" she asked.

Shivaram didn't answer. He had barely spoken to her since the day she left her new husband and returned to their house—she'd been married for only a few weeks. It had taken Shivaram months to find her a husband because everyone in town knew about her earlier relationship with the cobbler's son. Just when Shivaram and Urmila had thought that their only child would die an old maid, this doctor with a thriving practice in town, someone who'd apparently seen Shova at a gathering and had taken a liking to her, had stepped forward, and they'd gotten married right away. Then one morning about a month ago she came back home, suitcases in hand, refusing to say anything about why she'd left. Shivaram went to his son-in-law to find out what had gone wrong. Rajiv lived with his parents in Bansbari, in a large house that had a beautiful garden and a newly paved driveway. His parents weren't in, and he and Shivaram talked in the living room.

"I think she was just unhappy with me," Rajiv said, his eyes on the floor. "I wish I knew more." He said that at first he thought his parents were getting to her—they were old-fashioned and expected their daughter-in-law to act like a proper and obedient housewife, to cook and clean and tend to all their needs. "I reminded Shova that I was about to buy a house and we'd soon move out of here and she wouldn't have to listen to them anymore." He shook his head. "But it turned out my parents weren't the problem—I was." Although Rajiv didn't say it, Shivaram sensed that Shova had not allowed her husband to consummate their marriage.

Now Shova put the tea and a copy of *Kantipur* on the bedside table and said, "It was too hot last night. I was tossing and turning all night." Shivaram wished Urmila had brought him his tea, but these days she always asked Shova to do it, obviously hoping that it would help the two begin to reconcile. Throughout her childhood and into her teens, Shova had brought him his tea and paper, and the summer she'd gone to America, he'd missed this morning ritual terribly and complained to Urmila that the tea didn't taste the same without his daughter. Now, of course, everything had changed.

He picked up the newspaper and pretended to read. Shova stood there watching him, then asked, "Anything interesting, Daddy?"

He thrust the paper toward her and picked up his tea. She sat down next to him on the bed and scanned the headlines. "Things never change in this country," she said. "Always one skirmish or the other."

He loudly slurped his tea. Shova set aside the newspaper and pulled her legs beneath her on the bed. After a brief silence, she said, "I dreamt about you last night. You were standing in front of me, and I kept calling your name, but you wouldn't respond. Then you raised your hand, and I woke up."

"Well, what do you want me to say about that?" The last time Shivaram had had any real conversation with her had been when he informed her of what her husband's face looked like when he'd visited him. It aggravated Shivaram that she didn't see the damage she'd done.

Shova looked at him, wounded. "Daddy, why don't you understand my perspective? I was not happy there."

"You've never really told me why you were so miserable. And anyway, what would happen if every newlywed who felt the slightest bit unhappy just up and left?"

"People have a right to their feelings."

Sighing, Shivaram stood and went into the kitchen, where Urmila was cutting vegetables at the counter. "Did you hear that? Your daughter says her feelings are more important than anyone else's."

"You finally talk after so many days and you are already fighting?"

"Why am I the only one here who thinks this is a problem?"

Urmila raised her knife. "What do you want me to do? Give her time, she'll come to her senses." She turned to her cauliflower and split it in two, then said softly, so that Shova wouldn't hear, "Perhaps we were a bit hasty with the wedding. Perhaps we should have tried to find out more about what she was feeling beforehand."

The wedding had been arranged in a rush — that much Shivaram admitted. He and Urmila had been so afraid that Rajiv might change his mind, especially after it became clear that he was well aware of Shova's past, that they'd pressed for an early wedding date and sped through the preparations. Still, it didn't justify what Shova did. "She is lucky we found someone for her," he said.

"I know, I know," Urmila said. "She could have objected before the wedding instead of now."

"What was there to object to, Urmila? Help me understand. Rajiv babu had even started building a house for her so she wouldn't have to live under his parents' thumb. How many newly married women here have that luxury?"

"I don't know what she's thinking," Urmila said helplessly. "You know she's always been stubborn. You used to admire that about her, boast to everyone about how independent-minded she was and how she was going to become someone great one day, a diplomat or a prime minister, remember? Now I'm supposed to understand her more than you do?"

Suddenly Shova was at the kitchen door. "Please, don't argue over this. I will leave this house, go live alone, and you can tell everybody you've disowned me."

"Shova, don't talk this way," Urmila said.

"What do you want me to do, then?" Shova said angrily. "You want me to go back to that loveless marriage and be unhappy all my life?"

Shivaram tried to speak calmly to her. "But love needs time to grow. You don't simply give up after a couple of weeks. Look at your mother and me."

Shova moaned, stalked off to her room, and shut the door.

Shivaram watched Urmila put the vegetables in the frying pan and turn on the gas. "I bet she's still thinking about that cobbler's son," he said.

Urmila stirred the vegetables and didn't respond.

"It's been nearly a month since she came back. I'm sure Rajiv babu is thinking about getting the marriage annulled. His neighbor Raghuji told me the other day that he's already considering trying to find a new wife."

Urmila sprinkled salt over the pan. Shivaram sighed and went to his room to change his clothes.

"Come back soon," Urmila said when he returned and told her he was going for a walk. "The food will be ready in half an hour, and I have to be at work early today for a meeting."

It was only eight o'clock, and he had a couple of hours before he himself had to head for work. He wandered aimlessly around the neighborhood, mulling things over. Each day he held out hope that Shova would change her mind. He wondered whether he should visit his son-in-law again, plead with him to go to Shova and try to persuade her to return. But when Shivaram went to Rajiv the last time, his mother had come home as they were talking, and she was livid. "Look," she said, "we'd heard about your daughter's past before the wedding, and to be honest we were pretty much against this marriage. But our son said he was a modern man, and young people have romantic flings all the time these days. We caved in to our son's wishes then, but now we're standing firm. There's no question of going back — this marriage is over." Still, Rajiv came by Shivaram's house later that evening, and he and Shova talked in her room for about half an hour. But when he emerged, he looked disappointed. "She won't really talk to me. She just keeps saying she can't go anywhere with me." Urmila asked him to stay for dinner, but of course he refused.

Now Shivaram decided that he didn't have the fortitude to return to Rajiv and his parents. At least not today — maybe some other day he'd muster the courage. As he walked along the street, he wondered what had gone wrong with his daughter. She had always been a bit strong-willed, and as Urmila said, Shivaram had been proud of her for that and had told everyone that headstrong people usually went on to achieve something significant in life. As if confirming her father's dreams for her, Shova had done extraordinarily well in school. Immediately after graduating from high school at the top of her class, she won an essay contest sponsored by the Nepal-U.S. Foundation and got to travel to New York for a summer seminar. There she became passionate about global politics, and when she got back home, she and Shivaram talked excitedly about the possibility of her returning to America after college and going to graduate school for political science or international studies. But the scandal with the cobbler's son had deeply injured Shivaram's faith in her.

He remembered that day about two years ago when he received a call in his office from the police station in Hanuman Dhoka, saying that Shova was in their custody. Thinking that she'd been mistakenly apprehended during some political demonstration, as she sometimes took part in them, he rushed to the station. He found her sitting inside a jail cell, her head down, fiddling with her necklace.

"We arrested her for indecent exposure," said the officer

who'd accompanied him to the cell. "In the park of Gokarna, in the bushes. With that boy." He pointed to a young man in the cell across from hers. At first Shivaram didn't believe the officer, but when he questioned Shova, she wouldn't meet his eyes. Her lower lip was swollen and split, and a small clot of blood had formed there. He couldn't bear to ask what had caused it.

"How do you know him?" Shivaram whispered to her.

"He's a student at Ratna Rajya too," she said.

Shivaram had to bribe the police to get Shova released, and as soon as they got home, he told her he'd never felt so humiliated in his life. When she confessed to him and Urmila that the boy's father was a lowly cobbler, even Urmila became indignant. Shivaram went to the boy's house in Samakhusi, where he confronted the father about what had happened, saying his son had ruined his daughter's reputation. The man apologized profusely, said he too wasn't exactly happy about what had happened, that he too had had to bribe the police to free his son. He hauled the boy, whose name was Mukti, out of his room by his ear and forced him to apologize to Shivaram. "I don't want his apology," Shivaram said. "I want him to promise me that he'll never look at my daughter again." After his father slapped him, Mukti promised, then wrote a note to Shova—dictated by his father—saying that their relationship was over. When Shivaram presented the note to his daughter, she read it and tossed it to the floor. "It doesn't mean anything," she said. "I can only imagine what you did to get him to write this."

For a moment Shivaram questioned whether he had overreacted. Had the boy been of another caste, perhaps a Brahmin or a Chetri, he might not have acted so aggressively. With some dismay, Shivaram came to realize that he actually wished the boy had been of a higher caste; then he could have simply gone to Mukti's parents and insisted that the two get married. This new self-awareness troubled him, as he'd always considered himself fairly open-minded, someone who paid little attention to notions of the purity of caste and other traditions that demeaned people. Despite his own parents' objections, he'd encouraged Urmila to find a job right after they got married. And later, after Shova was born, when his parents didn't stop criticizing Urmila for being unable to bear any more children and thus depriving them of a grandson, he'd moved his wife and daughter into a separate flat, away from them. He had several friends and colleagues who came from lower castes: just the year before, he'd attended the wedding of the son of a lower-caste colleague when many of his coworkers had come up with excuses not to go. Yet there was no denying that the discovery of his own daughter's liaison with Mukti had brought out something deeply embedded in him, and he found himself unable to wish away the revulsion he felt in his stomach.

Gradually he convinced himself that some traditions survived centuries because they had important functions. When people kept to their own role, their own station, society functioned more smoothly. You could see this, Shivaram told himself over and over, in many intercaste marriages—they got no support from their families or their culture, and the couples gradually turned bitter toward each other. Shivaram knew of several such marriages that had soon resulted in divorce. And while a divorced man had little trouble remarrying, the woman ended up being shunned by friends and relatives for the rest of her life.

That was not the future any father would wish upon his daughter, and for nearly a month, Shivaram, worried that Shova would reconnect with Mukti secretly, didn't allow her out of the house unless Urmila was by her side. He was on constant watch for Mukti, and he monitored Shova's phone calls. When both he and Urmila were at work, he enlisted a relative to stay at home to watch her. Perhaps because of the shameful manner in which she'd been caught with Mukti, Shova remained subdued during all of this, not speaking to her parents but not doing anything to rebel either. After a few weeks, she approached them and said, "I want to get back to my studies," and fought them when they responded that she'd have to attend a different college. They categorically refused to pay her tuition at Ratna Rajya, and reluctantly she agreed to transfer. After starting at her new college, her mood seemed to improve, and she didn't object when they began talking to Rajiv babu's family about a possible marriage. She did, however, turn a little quiet and withdrawn.

Those days Shivaram could feel her eyes following him, as if she were waiting for just the right moment to say something important. Once when Urmila wasn't home, she came into the living room, where Shivaram was looking through old photo albums. She sat down next to him and leaned her head against his shoulder. "Look at this one—it was taken the day you left for New York," he said, and glanced at her. Her eyes were suddenly teary. He hugged her and asked, "What's wrong? What's bothering you?" She kept shaking her head, and he stroked her hair and said, "Everything will be fine, just fine. Believe me, Shova, this marriage will be a new beginning for you. Do you understand? You deserve to be happy." She nodded, then wiped her tears and smiled at him. Perhaps she was just anxious about her impending wedding—such nervousness was to be expected. That night he told Urmila about her crying, and she agreed that such prewedding jitters were normal for any woman. They both expressed relief that their daughter finally seemed to be coming around.

But now here she was, willfully headed for divorce. Why didn't she understand that all marriages needed time to work? Four weeks was all she had given Rajiv. Shivaram was convinced that if only Shova stayed with her husband for a longer period, say six months, she'd get used to him, and he'd eventually make her so happy, especially in that new house, that she'd look back and laugh at the fact that she once thought of leaving him. Six months—that's all that was needed. And if after six months she still wanted to leave him, which Shivaram doubted she would, he himself would tell her that she'd made the right decision. Now Shivaram wondered whether he should try to talk to Shova again and mention the idea of a six-month trial period. He sighed. She wouldn't listen to him. She'd merely shake her head and say that one month was enough, that her mind was made up.

But he had to do something, and after walking around a bit more, Shivaram pointed himself toward his brother's house.

Damodar lived in Thapathali, not far from Shivaram's office, and was watching television and eating dal-bhat and chicken in the living room when Shivaram knocked on the door. His wife, Anita, let him in.

"Dai, what brings you here?" Damodar said, turning off the television and getting up. "Have you eaten?"

The smell of chicken made Shivaram hungry, but Urmila would be expecting him to return home to eat, so he said he'd already eaten and sat down. A year ago, he and Damodar had squabbled over a piece of land they'd inherited from their father. Since then, Anita and Urmila had stopped speaking to each other, because Anita thought that Urmila had incited Shivaram to argue with his brother; but Shivaram had gradually patched up his differences with Damodar and, to a lesser extent, with Anita.

"Why such a gloomy face?" Damodar asked. "Nothing's changed with Shova?"

Shivaram looked at the ceiling. "I don't understand what's going through her head."

Anita said, "What can we say to people about her? You have no idea the kind of things we hear. People are starting to say nasty things about us too."

"Can you be quiet?" Damodar said. "Dai has come here worried, and you're concerned about what others think of us."

"Remember," she said, "we were the ones who acted as the go-betweens for that marriage. Just the other day Rajiv babu's mother called and told me bluntly that I had hooked her son up with a crazy, spoiled woman."

"I didn't want this to happen, Anita, you should understand that," Shivaram said. "I'm sorry you've had to deal with all this, but you know as well as I do that Shova is far from crazy or spoiled. She's basically a good girl. I'm just as baffled as everyone else at what's happening."

"You should do something," Anita said. "If she were my daughter, I'd drag her by her hair back to Rajiv babu and forbid her to leave him again."

Her words made Shivaram cringe.

"Will you stop this drivel about dragging people by their hair?" Damodar said. "This is a serious matter and needs a serious solution."

"That's why I came to you, brother," Shivaram said. "Maybe you can talk with Rajiv babu, persuade him to visit Shova."

"Of course, I will try."

Shivaram soon felt better, and he ended up eating dal-bhat with them after all. If Urmila found out, she'd be annoyed, but he didn't feel quite ready to leave yet. The three chatted about politics and television programs, and after they finished eating, Shivaram told Damodar he was glad to have a brother he could depend on at a time like this, and stiffly apologized again to Anita for what she'd had to put up with. Since it was already time to go to work, he headed straight to his office.

Late that afternoon, Shivaram was talking to his colleague Yograj when he spotted his son-in-law at his office door. Surprised, Shivaram rushed over to him. "Rajiv babu, I was just thinking about you."

Rajiv ran his hand through his hair and said, "I need to talk to you in private."

"Let's go up to the roof where it'll be quiet."

Shivaram told Yograj that he'd be back in a few minutes, and he and Rajiv climbed the stairs to the roof. They leaned against the wall that overlooked the busy street below. At first neither man spoke, then Shivaram said, "It's good you came. I was thinking about paying you another visit, and Damodar was even going to talk to you."

"It's been nearly a month," Rajiv said.

"That's why I wanted to talk to you. I think you should try coming to the house one more time, try to persuade her again."

"I want to come, but my parents would be furious." He paused. "They already have someone else in mind for me to marry."

Shivaram shook his head and said, "You're still married to Shova. Don't act rashly." He tried to sound confident. "She'll come back to you, you'll see."

"But," Rajiv said, his expression pained, "why is she acting this way?"

Shivaram wished he had an answer. He placed his hand on top of Rajiv's. "Listen, son-in-law, you shouldn't give up so easily. A marriage shouldn't be taken so lightly."

"It's not me who is taking it lightly," Rajiv said. "It's your daughter."

"I know, I know, but please, Rajiv babu, talk to Shova. She's your wife. Problems come up in all marriages. In your case this happened early, and maybe it means that the rest of your lives together will be happy."

Rajiv's eyes followed a speeding taxi below, then he looked down at his feet. Finally he lifted his head and spoke. "All right, I'll give it one last try. I'll come by this evening. If she acts like she did last time, though, I'm going to do what my parents want."

Shivaram patted his back and attempted a smile. The two left the roof and walked down the stairs. Outside his office door, Shivaram clasped Rajiv's hands and told him how glad he was that he came, then went back inside to his desk. But he had a hard time focusing on his work. Yograj stopped by and asked in a whisper how it went with his son-in-law.

"I just don't know what my daughter is doing," Shivaram said dejectedly.

"You might try to be more strict with her." Yograj was a staunch Brahmin who performed an hour-long prayer ceremony at home every morning, and he refused to join his co-workers for snacks because he feared becoming what he called "polluted" by eating "impure" food.

"But how? She's a grown woman."

Yograj shook his head. "This is probably because of the time she spent in America. No one has any sense of tradition or rules there."

Rajiv had said he'd come around six that evening, and Shivaram wanted to make sure that Shova was in a good frame of mind for his visit. When he got home, she was shut in her room, and Urmila, back from her office, was watching television in the living room. She didn't speak to him when he entered, presumably annoyed that he hadn't returned home to eat before going to work this morning. He stood behind her and massaged her shoulders. "Why is my dear Urmila frowning?" he asked. When she didn't respond, he said, "I have some news. He's coming to talk to her."

Urmila turned to face him. "Rajiv babu?"

He nodded, leaned down, and whispered that Rajiv had come by his office. "Do you want to tell her, or should I?"

"Should we even let her know? What good would that do? She hasn't left her room since this morning. Hasn't eaten a thing. With both of you not eating, why do I slave away in the kitchen? I was late for my meeting because I waited for you."

Shivaram adopted an apologetic tone. "I just wasn't feeling good this morning, and I would have been late for work if I came back here. Listen, I really want to make sure she's prepared for his visit. She's more receptive to you than me, so would you talk to her?"

Urmila sighed and slowly stood up just as Shova opened her door. She spoke as if she'd been rehearsing her words all day: "I have decided I am going to leave this house. I was just on the phone with my friend Bimala. I'm going to move in with her."

"How can that be?" Urmila said. "Shova, Rajiv babu is coming here to talk to you soon."

"You can send him away. We've talked through everything already, and there's no way I'm going back to him."

With a controlled voice, Shivaram said, "Daughter, there's still time to fix this before everything gets more out of hand."

He was about to mention his idea of a six-month trial when Urmila said, "What's the harm in talking to him, Shova? Listen to what Rajiv babu has to say, then decide what you want to do. Your father is right—you should give it one more chance."

"You two are deluded," Shova said. "Nothing is going to change my mind."

Shivaram fought the urge to slap his daughter; he'd never laid a hand on Shova, and he couldn't see himself doing it even now. Instead, he stammered, "Go prepare yourself for Rajiv babu. He'll come, you two will talk, then you'll leave with him." He took a deep breath. "If you disappointment me again, Shova," he said, the words seeming to float from his mouth, "you can't call me your father anymore."

Shova didn't respond, didn't move.

He turned and walked out of the house. It was already a quarter to six, so he didn't have much time before Rajiv would arrive. He wandered around the neighborhood, replaying the conversation he'd just had, hoping that actually seeing Rajiv in person would change something in Shova. When his anger dissipated, he returned to the house and stood by the gate.

Soon Rajiv pulled up in a taxi, and Shivaram ushered him into the house. Urmila was standing outside Shova's closed bedroom door. Her eyes indicated that she hadn't had much success in talking to their daughter. Urmila and Rajiv exchanged greetings, and Urmila offered to make tea, but Rajiv declined, saying that he'd rather "just get this over with." Urmila tried to open Shova's door, but Shova had locked it. "Rajiv babu is here, Shova," Urmila said. "Please open the door."

They waited, then Shivaram called, "Open the door, Shova. Don't act like a child."

There was no sound from inside.

"Well, that's it, I guess," Rajiv said with a rueful smile.

"Wait," Shivaram said, and he pushed his shoulder against the door, but it wouldn't budge. He took a few steps back and was about to ram the door when Rajiv raised his hand and said, "Enough! What is this, a circus? I've had enough. I understand now."

"Don't say that, son-in-law," Shivaram said, pressing his palms together in supplication.

Rajiv rushed toward the front door. "She can start the divorce process. That way she'll be able to do what she pleases."

Shivaram and Urmila sat stunned in the living room after Rajiv left. Finally Urmila said, "What else can we do? We've tried hard. But if she's not willing —"

"Stop," Shivaram said, holding his head.

Urmila went to the kitchen and began cooking dinner. Shivaram stayed on the sofa, leafing through a magazine but not seeing anything.

After nearly half an hour, the door to Shova's room creaked open. She stood there holding a suitcase in her hand. "I'm leaving," she said.

"Shova," Urmila said, "don't make such a rash decision."

"Let her go," Shivaram said.

"She's my daughter. I can't just let her go like this."

"I don't want to see her face anymore." His whole body felt hot.

Shova walked slowly to the front door, as if she half expected her father to get up and try to stop her, but Shivaram stifled his desperation and continued flipping the pages of his magazine. Urmila kept pleading with her until Shova slammed the door shut behind her.

Later Urmila called Shova's friend's house, where she said she'd be staying. Bimala assured Urmila that Shova had indeed arrived, and Urmila briefly talked to her daughter, then told Shivaram that Shova had been crying on the phone. Shivaram said nothing. When Urmila said that Shova would undoubtedly get homesick and come back in a few days, Shivaram flicked on the television and turned up the volume.

For days Shivaram didn't say much, at home or at work. When his colleagues asked him about Shova's situation, he said, "I'd rather not talk about it."

Damodar came to the house one morning. "What happened?

Rajiv tells me it's all over, that there's no possibility of reconciliation now."

Shivaram said, "He's right."

"I still have hope," Urmila said. She confessed, as she had to Shivaram, that she'd gone to visit Shova twice since she moved out. Their daughter had already gotten a job at a newspaper, and she was planning to take night classes to complete her master's degree. "She's getting back on her own feet. Maybe that's what she needs right now, and maybe she'll eventually come around."

Damodar and Shivaram shook their heads. "You know they're actively looking for another bride for Rajiv?" Damodar said.

"Brother-in-law, isn't there anything you can do to stop them?" Urmila said. "They are still a married couple, and it's wrong for Rajiv babu to move on so quickly."

Shivaram laughed bitterly. "When will you learn? A young doctor with a growing practice, a respected family — other parents will line up to introduce their daughters to him. Why should he wait around when Shova doesn't even want to look at him?"

Urmila had no answer, and the three of them stood there silently. Damodar promised that he'd talk to Rajiv, although his tone conveyed that he too thought the matter was hopeless.

Urmila visited Shova regularly on her way to work and back, and Shivaram turned a deaf ear to his wife's updates about her. One evening after dinner, Urmila said that she'd broken the heel of her shoe on her way to Shova's flat that afternoon, and she needed to go to a cobbler.

Shivaram went on reading his book. Then he looked up at her. "What did you say?" he asked her sharply. "What about cobblers?"

She was sitting on the sofa next to him, darning a sweater for him, and she kept her head down, but he noticed that her ears had turned red. "Oh, nothing," she said. "Let's hope this sweater won't tear again."

"You need to find a cobbler?"

She didn't respond.

"Is there something you're hiding from me?"

"I'm not."

Shivaram took her arm. "Something is up. Come on, tell me!"

Urmila gazed at him, then said, "If I tell you, you'll get mad. I shouldn't have said anything—it just slipped out."

"Is it about that cobbler's son, that Mukti, again?"

It took her a few seconds to get her words out: "I saw him at Shova's flat the other day. Don't get angry, please."

"What was he doing there? Did you tell him to leave?"

"What could I say?" she said. She tossed him his sweater. "If this tears again, we'll buy you a new one."

Shivaram flung the sweater aside. "Things are only getting worse with her. Soon people on the street will be laughing at us." It struck him that he'd never worried about what others thought of him before the scandal with Mukti. He expected Urmila to challenge him, but all she said, in a commiserating tone, was "Who would have known that things would turn out like this?" She stood and picked up the sweater from the floor. "But we, and especially you, have to handle this calmly. She's our daughter no matter what she does."

Early the next morning, Shivaram told Urmila he was going out for a walk. Still half asleep, she nodded and went to take a bath. He headed straight for Tangal, where Shova's flat was located. Just before her wedding, Shova had stopped by Bimala's place to borrow a blouse while Shivaram had waited outside, so he knew where she lived. The house was tucked away in an alley, and he climbed the stairs to the second floor. He felt his heart beating rapidly, partly at the thought of a confrontation with Shova, partly in anticipation of simply seeing her again. It had been several weeks since she'd moved out. When he knocked on the door, Bimala opened it and took a quick step backward. "Shova's still asleep."

"Can you wake her? I need to talk to her."

She led him to a rattan chair in the corner of the living room and went to fetch Shova, who soon appeared in her nightgown. Shivaram recalled nights during her childhood when, disturbed by a nightmare, she appeared at her parents' door, asking if she could sleep with them. A lump rose in his throat.

"Daddy?"

Careful not to seem too aggressive, he said, "I thought I'd drop by for a cup of tea."

Bimala said she'd make it, and walked off.

Shova stood there, her arms crossed. "You've probably come to fight with me, haven't you?"

Shivaram shook his head. He felt weary, his head thick. "I don't want to fight with you. I don't know what to think about anything anymore."

"You just aren't listening to me or trying to understand me, Daddy," Shova said. "That's what hurts me the most."

"I don't know how much more you want from me," Shivaram said. "I married you to probably the most eligible man in town. And now I hear you're spending time with that Mukti again."

"Ah," Shova said. "Now I know why you came. Not to talk to me but to scold me again, tell me what a disappointment I am."

She was right, he supposed. Strangely, here in her flat, her space, it felt as if his authority was beginning to diminish. "I'm your father," he said, "and I do care about your happiness. I've come here to talk about the choices you're making and how they'll wind up making you unhappy." He spoke slowly, thinking about each word before he spoke it.

"How do you know that? Do you live inside my mind? My body?"

He shook his head. "I'm just your father. That's all I know.

Just tell me, Shova," he said gently. "What's wrong with Rajiv? Why don't you like him?"

"I don't dislike him. I just don't feel anything for him."

"Then why didn't you object before you got married?"

"As if you'd have listened." After a pause, she said, "I looked at your face, and you were so thrilled about me getting married, especially to a doctor. So I told myself that I'd learn to love Rajiv, but every day, no matter how hard I tried, I felt nothing for him. Not a single thing."

Shivaram began to feel weak. "What do you want me to do, Shova? You advise me on how to proceed. You tell me what to do."

Shova smiled ruefully. "As if you'd agree to what I'd say."

Shivaram swallowed. "Tell me and I'll do it." He sensed where this conversation was headed, and it terrified him, but there seemed to be no backing out now.

"Really?"

He nodded.

Shova sat down next him and took his hand. She searched his eyes, and with difficulty he held her gaze. "All right," she said. "Mukti and I want to get married."

Seconds ago, he'd imagined her exact words. Still, when she said them, they sounded unreal.

"We've already discussed it," she said. "All this time he's remained unmarried because of me." When Shivaram didn't respond, Shova said, "I'm telling you what I want, Daddy."

"Have you been in contact with him all this time?"

She shook her head. "He came to see me just a few weeks ago."

"And you've already made the decision?"

She nodded. "Mukti works as a teller at the Arab Bank now," Shova said. "He plans on getting a master's degree soon too."

Shivaram pretended to think, but all he could do was listen to the pounding in his chest. Then he shook his head. "I'm sorry, but I just can't be a part of it, Shova. I can't have people say that I had an active hand in ruining my daughter's marriage so that she could wed a cobbler's son."

"He has a name, Daddy."

"I know, but that's not the point." He stood. "You two go ahead and do what you want to do. Just leave me out of it."

Bimala appeared with tea but immediately turned around and left the room.

"So much for your promise to do whatever I ask you to do," Shova said.

"Forgive me, daughter," Shivaram said, then opened the door and walked out.

Glumly, he headed home. A part of him wanted to go back to Shova, talk to her more, but he knew that if he returned to her flat now, he'd end up submitting to her and regretting it later, so he gritted his teeth and kept walking. Yes, she was stubborn, but maybe she forgot that he was too. He simply wasn't going to put his stamp of approval on her flagrant strike against what was proper: she was already planning to get married, and to a cobbler's son, when her first marriage hadn't ended yet. He could already see people staring at him, at Urmila, his colleagues snickering as he walked by. Damodar and Anita would be furious, and they'd probably never speak to them again. If he didn't participate in the wedding, he decided, people would say less, say that he'd at least attempted to protect his dignity.

At home, Urmila had already eaten and was getting dressed for work. She adjusted her sari in front of the mirror and asked, "Aren't you going to be late? Your food is ready." Then she turned to look at his face and seemed to guess where he'd been. "What happened?"

He gazed out the window of their bedroom. "Did you know she was going to marry him?"

She came to him, and he could smell the sweet perfume she always wore to work.

He turned to her. "You knew, didn't you?"

"I can't fight with her," Urmila said. She wrapped her arm

around his waist and put her head on his shoulder. "What do you want me to do? I feel like I'm caught between you two, and to be honest, I'm suffocating."

He let her hold him for a while, then gently disengaged himself and trudged down the stairs.

In the days that followed, Urmila went to Shova's flat every day, and sometimes when Shivaram got home from work, she was still gone. Urmila would always arrive before long, though, breathless and looking exhausted, and say that she had to stop at the market or that she ran into someone she hadn't seen in a while. She never mentioned Shova or the wedding, but it was easy for Shivaram to guess where she'd really been.

The news of Shova's imminent wedding spread, of course, and Shivaram soon had to weather barbs and innuendoes at work as well as in his neighborhood. One evening, as he and Urmila were watching television after dinner, someone knocked on the door. It was Anita, and she spoke softly to Urmila in the doorway. "Although you and I have had our differences, I still thought of you as my own sister-in-law and a friend, but now I see how wrong I was."

"Get out of here," Urmila said. "You have some nerve coming to my house and talking to me this way!"

Anita continued speaking softly, as if it were beneath her to raise her voice. "You know what? It'll take a year for the court to approve the divorce, and Rajiv babu says he'll file charges against Shova if she gets married before that."

"Enough!" Shivaram said. "Please leave, Anita."

Urmila shoved Anita out the door and locked it. She and Shivaram looked at each other but didn't say anything until they heard Anita's footsteps down the stairs. Then she said, "The gall. Let's see if he even does anything." But she paced the room—clearly she was worried, and Shivaram too became anxious that Rajiv might follow up on this threat. Urmila had told Shivaram that Shova had already filed for divorce in the district court, but he knew that remarrying before the approval, which often took months, was a crime under the law.

Anita's words turned out to be empty, because the very next day a messenger delivered an invitation to Shivaram — to Rajiv's wedding, the word "chulhey" handwritten on the card to indicate that the whole family was welcome. It was meant as a taunt, of course, but Urmila laughed when she saw it. Shivaram also felt relieved: Rajiv's getting remarried without the divorce papers meant that he was equally culpable and that no one would be taking anyone to court. "Anita will say anything," Urmila said to Shivaram, and he merely nodded.

In order not to lose the game of one-upmanship with Rajiv's family, Urmila responded with an invitation to Shova's wedding. Shivaram watched her as she licked the envelope and set it on the pile with other invitations that would soon be sent out. He'd already peeked at the invitation, and Urmila had tried to tell him about the wedding plans, always speaking in a hesitant tone, as if she were furnishing information about a distant relative: the ceremony would take place in the Gueswori temple; there would be a dinner party later that evening; there would be no wedding band because both Mukti and Shova felt that would be a frivolous expense. Shivaram learned that Mukti's father had agreed to bear all the costs of the wedding, and that Urmila had only helped Shova buy her saris. That the groom's father was paying for his daughter's wedding burned Shivaram a bit, but he reminded himself that he had no reason to fund something he had been against from the start. He also gathered from Urmila that Mukti's parents had initially objected to Shova, saying she had already been someone's wife, but Mukti had remained obstinate, and his parents were forced to submit to his wishes. "He's as strong-willed as she is," Urmila declared.

The day before the wedding, Shivaram left home early in the morning and went to Samakhusi, where the cobbler lived. The neighborhood was much more crowded than when he'd visited last, and for a while he had trouble locating the house, which now was two stories instead of one, the bottom floor entirely given over to a shoe shop. A thought entered his head that at least Shova wouldn't be poor. Then he told himself that he was being ridiculous—money or no money, Shova would be treated like an outcast for the rest of her life.

He slipped into a tea shop across the street and looked out at the house. Colorful ribbons had been strung across the place in celebration of the wedding. A few women carrying baskets entered and exited the house through a side door, and at around eight-thirty, Mukti emerged from the front door. He had a small goatee now, and wore a leather jacket and carried a helmet. He walked over to a motorcycle, got on, put on his helmet, and zoomed off. That man would be Shova's husband tomorrow, and everyone would have ammunition for a lifetime of taunts and putdowns.

A little later, Mukti's father appeared in the yard, smoking a cigarette. He shouted to a boy on the balcony, who began throwing down rolls of what looked like strings of small lights. One of the women nearby said something and laughed, and Mukti's father went to her, grabbed her by the waist, and began dancing with her in the yard. The other women soon set down their baskets and, clapping their hands, joined them.

At work Shivaram developed an intense headache and was thinking about leaving early when his colleague Yograj appeared at his desk. Stroking his mustache, Yograj said, "The wedding is tomorrow, isn't it, Shivaramji? What's the feast going to be like?"

Shivaram was used to Yograj's jabs, and thus far he'd just smiled and changed the subject, but today something boiled up inside him. "Don't you have work to do? Why do you need to give me a headache with this gibberish?"

Out of the corner of his eye he saw another colleague signal to Yograj to drop it. But Yograj continued, "Daughters are always big headaches, aren't they? It's hard to know how they'll turn out."

Before Shivaram could respond, another coworker came over and led Yograj away. Shivaram stared in their direction, then left his desk, then the office, without informing his supervisor.

All the way home, he thought about what he should have done to Yograj—grab him by the collar and slap his insolent face. *My daughter is not a bad woman,* he should have hissed. He walked fast, afraid of his own anger. He felt an urgency, as if he needed to do something, go somewhere, anywhere but home. He considered going to Damodar's house, even asking if he could spend the night there, but immediately he realized how smug that would make Anita feel, and he didn't want to give her the satisfaction.

When he got home, Urmila wasn't there, which didn't surprise him. He went straight to bed, and despite his headache he quickly fell asleep. He woke to the evening darkness, a bit calmer now. He assumed that Urmila had left him some food in the refrigerator, and all he'd have to do was heat it up, but he didn't have the energy. He stayed in bed, in the dark, thinking about what was about to happen.

The shrill ring of the phone jolted him. It was Urmila. She said that there was so much work to do for the wedding that she'd have to stay over at Shova's flat. "Have you eaten?" she asked.

He said that he was not hungry.

"I've left some chicken and rice for you in the refrigerator." After an awkward silence, she asked, "Do you want to talk to your daughter?"

He didn't say anything, but he didn't hang up.

The phone was passed to Shova, who said, "Daddy?"

"Yes?"

"How are you?"

"To be honest, I have a headache."

"You should take an aspirin, okay?" she said. "You wouldn't believe how much work there is to do here." She laughed.

Shivaram swallowed hard.

"Daddy," Shova said softly, "how long are you going to stay so distant from me?"

He cleared his throat and mumbled, "What do you want from me, Shova?" He heard Urmila in the background, asking her something.

Shova responded, "If you don't come to my wedding—" Her voice broke. "Daddy, don't do this to me."

"I haven't done anything."

"I need your presence. Otherwise it won't mean anything."

Fearing that he might break down and cry, he said, "I'll talk to you later," and hung up.

All that night he stayed awake. Now and then he went to the window and gazed at the darkness outside. He attempted to read, then gave up. He finally went out for a short walk in the neighborhood, his shawl around his shoulders, shivering a bit from the chill. After some time, he went back home and slipped into bed, but he remained wide awake. He remembered his own parents, how unrelenting they'd been in their disapproval of Urmila for not giving birth to a son. They'd even suggested to Shivaram, after it became clear that Urmila couldn't bear any more children, that he consider getting a divorce and finding a new wife. That's when he told them, "There's nothing wrong with Urmila or my daughter," and moved his young family away from his parents, into a new home.

By the time light began appearing in the sky, he felt disoriented, tired. He closed his eyes and suddenly remembered Shova as a child, coming to their room after she'd had a nightmare. When she crawled into their bed, Shivaram would always have trouble getting back to sleep. And if he did manage to doze off, Shova thrashed her arms and legs so much in her sleep that she'd jolt him awake. The next morning, groggy and irritable, he always complained to Urmila, who'd go and whisper something to Shova, who in turn would go to him, wrap her arms around his neck, and plant a wet kiss on his cheek.

The sun began to show itself more, and its heat on his face through the window calmed him and threatened to lull him to sleep. So he made himself sit up, feeling light, almost airy. He went to the bathroom, washed his face, and changed his clothes. Then he realized that he hadn't shaved, and the circles beneath his eyes made him appear haggard. But what did it matter? Shova wasn't going to turn him away.

A Servant in the City

SOON AFTER STARTING WORK as a servant to Laxmi Memsab, Jeevan discovered that she was having an affair with a married businessman. A couple of times a week, he came to visit her in the evening, then went back to his wife in another part of the city. Jeevan, who was seventeen, learned about his wife by eavesdropping on arguments that his employer and Raju Sab got into. They were not loud, boisterous arguments, but quiet, melancholy ones that featured Laxmi Memsab pleading with him to divorce his wife. Jeevan gathered that Raju Sab's wife knew about Laxmi Memsab, and had confronted her one day in his office, where Laxmi Memsab used to work. "Mona refuses to grant me a divorce, Laxmi," Raju Sab said once. He was a big man with a mustache, and he always wore tailored suits.

"But how long can we go on like this, Raju?" Laxmi Memsab said. "Everyone is calling me names. My uncle has disowned me. My friends don't speak to me."

And so they argued, Raju Sab asking for more time, Laxmi Memsab complaining that she'd given up everything for him and now she had nothing. "A whore, that's what they call me," she said.

"I can't prevent people from calling you names, Laxmi,"

Raju Sab said. "And anyway, the divorce is just going to take time. You've known this all along."

"But nearly a year has passed since we first started."

"Please, Laxmi, I'm working on it."

Through their arguments, and through snippets of conversation Jeevan himself had with her, a story emerged. Laxmi Memsab used to work as a secretary in Raju Sab's travel agency, and despite the fact that he had recently gotten married, they'd fallen in love. When Raju Sab's wife discovered the affair, she stormed into his office one day and, planting herself in the doorway, glared at Laxmi Memsab, not saying a word and not even flinching when Raju Sab came out of his office and tried to lead her away. Finally it was Laxmi Memsab who stood up, left her desk, and went out by the side door. She headed straight home and curled up in bed for the rest of the day. Soon Mona pressured him to fire her, but Laxmi Memsab quit before he could. She tried finding another job, but at the other travel agencies where she applied, she was turned away. She suspected that all these people had heard about her affair, or that in the small circle of travel agents in town, Mona had made some phone calls; anyway, she eventually gave up looking. Since Raju Sab's firm was so well known in the city, news of the affair spread quickly. Laxmi Memsab's landlord knocked on her door one evening and asked her to move out, saying that because he had a family, he could rent his rooms only to "respectable people." Raju Sab found her this flat and agreed to pay the rent until she got on her feet again.

Now she'd been waiting for months for him to divorce his wife. He kept reassuring Laxmi Memsab that Mona would soon see that their marriage wasn't working and give up, but as the days passed and nothing changed, Laxmi Memsab grew more and more depressed. The few friends she had avoided her, and her uncle, who'd been her guardian after her parents had died in a bus accident, refused to have anything to do with her. The last time she'd gone to visit him, he wouldn't even open his door.

On the evenings Raju Sab didn't visit her, Laxmi Memsab was dejected. She wondered aloud to herself why he hadn't come. She paced the floor of the flat and sometimes picked up the phone to call him. She'd hang up immediately, presumably when Mona answered the phone.

Jeevan watched her and wished he could do something about her loneliness. He'd come to like her. She was generally a considerate woman, and was patient with him when he didn't know how to do something. Whenever he thought about the day he'd met her, he reminded himself how lucky he was.

At that time he had been in the city for two weeks and hadn't been able to find work. He was considering going back to his village and his ill mother. Her only child, he hadn't wanted to go to the city, but ever since his father died a year earlier, leaving them with a large debt, life had been difficult. His mother's medical expenses were piling up, and his father's creditors were threatening to confiscate their house if they couldn't start making regular payments on the loan. He'd had no choice but to leave home and look for a job. For some time he'd hauled merchandise on wooden carts, but the work was strenuous, and his lower back throbbed in pain at night as he lay on his straw mat in the room he shared with other laborers. Two of his roommates, veterans at this work, laughed at him, called him a mama's boy, and said that he'd have to get used to living with a screwed-up back. He was indeed a mama's boy, he'd admitted to himself. He thought about her all day as he pulled carts and at night in bed as he listened to his roommates snore. He prayed that the neighbor woman he'd entrusted to look after his mother was doing a good job.

The day he met Laxmi Memsab, he'd been wandering around the Basantapur vegetable market, thinking he'd catch the afternoon bus back to his village in Dhunche and be done with this city. Then he overheard a young woman talking to a vegetable vendor about how she was looking for household help. Hesitantly, Jeevan approached her.

At first she'd said that she was not about to hire just any

stranger, but he was persistent, saying that he had fallen on hard times.

Her face changed. "Have you been able to eat?"

"I have, but my money is running out."

"Poor boy," she said. She had a soft face and kind eyes, and he remained hopeful.

"I'll do anything you ask me to do, Memsab."

"Anything?" she said, smiling. "I suppose what I need is someone like you, someone who'd swim the seven seas for me."

Back at her flat, she showed him the small storage room adjacent to the kitchen, where she kept some boxes and suitcases. "You'll sleep there. As you can see, I'm the only one living in this place, so the work is easy." She told him she'd pay him four hundred rupees a month, which wasn't much, but it was better money than he'd gotten for pulling carts, and his food and clothing would be taken care of. "There's a man who comes here often," she said at one point. "He pays for all my household expenses, including your wages. We are going to get married, understand?" She looked at him as if she were daring him to challenge her.

That night Jeevan wrote a letter to his mother, telling her that he was fine and had found a good job as a servant. He didn't tell her that Laxmi Memsab lived by herself.

Soon after, Jeevan learned that Laxmi Memsab's neighbors didn't think highly of her. One evening, on his eighth day working for her, he was leaning against the stair rail outside her flat when a man, someone he had seen around the building before, stopped and said, "Eh, does your memsab give it to you every night?" At first Jeevan was confused, then he understood what the man was talking about, and he scowled and hurried back inside.

"Who was that, Jeevan?" Laxmi Memsab asked. She was sitting in the living room, reading, but now she set down her book, sighed, and looked at the clock on the wall. She was expecting Raju Sab.

"Just a man from down the street."

"What was he saying?"

When Jeevan didn't speak, she looked at him. "Was he saying something bad?"

"He was just talking crazy."

"Come here," she said. He went and sat on the floor next to her feet. "You'll have to get used to a lot of nonsense from people around here if you work for me, all right?"

He nodded.

She smiled down at him. "You didn't get married in the village?"

He told her that he was too poor to get married.

"Surely there are girls from families that don't have so much money."

"Which father would give his daughter's hand to a boy with no money, Memsab?"

"Poor Jeevan," she said. "You'll find someone. But I'm so glad you approached me that day in the market. I was losing my mind in this house by myself."

"You must have some friends."

"I used to," she said. "But they all treat me like a pariah now. People are like that." She stared at the wall, and Jeevan wished he could think of something to say that would console her.

"Maybe you could start working again," he finally offered.

"Everyone in the city knows about my relationship with Raju, and even if someone were to hire me, I wouldn't be able to stand my coworkers talking behind my back or making rude comments."

"But if you stay in the house all day, you'll only feel more lonely and sad."

"Now you're here, Jeevan," she said. "And you won't treat me like the others, will you? Besides, it's just a matter of time. Once Raju divorces her, we can get married. Then I'll be accepted by this stupid world." But she doubted her own words, Jeevan could tell, for she then grew quiet.

He went to the kitchen to wash the dishes, and he could hear her pick up the phone and dial, then put the phone back down. She did this several times, then she walked through the kitchen and out onto the balcony, which afforded a view of the street. In a few moments she went back to the living room. After Jeevan was done with the dishes, he boiled a glass of milk and brought it to her. The door to the living room was shut, and when he pushed it open, he saw her lying on the sofa. Her sari had fallen open at her chest and the top few buttons of her black blouse were undone, revealing the bra underneath. The fan whirled nearby. She held a glass of something, and a magazine lay on her lap, its pages flapping in the breeze from the fan. He froze in the doorway.

When she became aware of his presence, she looked up. "You should always knock," she said, setting the glass down. She buttoned her blouse and adjusted her sari. "I don't think Raju is coming today," she said.

He put the glass of milk down on the coffee table and saw that she was drinking alcohol of some kind. She watched his face, then said, "You don't like to see women drink?"

"Who am I to tell you not to drink, Memsab?"

"If I don't drink a peg or two, I'll go mad," she said. "What's wrong with Raju? Why doesn't he come?"

His impulse was to tell her not to depend so much on Raju Sab, but he kept his mouth shut. She asked him to join her. He went to sit on the floor, but then she gestured for him to sit next to her on the sofa. "Why should I treat you as if you were beneath me when the world treats me like that?" He sat on the edge of the sofa, his hands between his knees. She asked whether he was missing his mother, and Jeevan said, "Sometimes." Actually, last night he'd dreamt that he learned she had died in the village, and the thought had terrified him. If she died, he'd have no family left in this world. For some time, he had felt weepy.

"In a couple of weeks you should go back and visit her," Laxmi Memsab said. "She must really miss you." She drank from her glass, and after a moment said, "Tell me, Jeevan, do you think I'm a bad woman?"

"You've been like a savior to me."

"Savior!" she said. "I wish I felt like a savior. Right now I feel worthless."

"If you keep reminding yourself of that," Jeevan said, "you're bound to keep feeling that way."

She eyed him. "True, true. Do you think it was wrong for me to let myself fall in love with Raju knowing that he was married?"

"People have their reasons, hajur," he said. "How can I judge you?"

"You're quite a diplomat, Jeevan," she said. "Where did you learn all of this? From your mother?"

He kept quiet, and they sat in silence for a while. He was about to get up and go back to the kitchen when she said, "Jeevan, do you think I'm beautiful?"

He'd never known anyone who spoke as she did, and he couldn't look at her face. How did she expect a servant to answer such a question?

"Please tell me. Don't be shy."

Without meeting her eyes, he nodded.

"Look at me and tell me that. I want to hear it from your mouth."

His heart was hammering, and he managed to lift his face, look into her eyes, and say, "Yes, Memsab."

"No, no, say it."

He wanted to flee the room. He felt a stirring in his crotch, and he became afraid that she'd notice. When his voice finally emerged, it was shaky, almost giddy. "Memsab, you're beautiful."

She stared at him, then said, "It's good to hear you say that. I never hear that from Raju anymore." She was sliding deeper into the sofa, her eyes watery and small.

"Memsab—"

"Jeevan, did I show you my wedding sari?"

He shook his head. His mouth was dry.

She rose from the sofa and went into her bedroom. As he waited, his eyes fell on the glass of milk that he'd boiled for her. It had probably turned lukewarm by now. He considered going to the kitchen to drink some water, but he was suddenly afraid to move, so he reached for the milk and took a few gulps. He waited; it seemed an eternity.

At last Laxmi Memsab emerged, wearing a red sari. A diamond necklace glittered on her chest. She'd combed her hair and put on some lipstick, and she looked different, younger, happier. He muttered, "Memsab, you look beautiful."

"You don't have to say that if you don't mean it, Jeevan."

"No, no, I mean it," he said, getting up and approaching her. "You look absolutely beautiful." His own words began to excite him.

She stood in front of him, smiling. Her eyes glistened as if she might start to cry. "Raju says that he doesn't want another formal wedding, just a court wedding. Says the big one he had with his wife was enough. But I've told him that I want it all, a band and a party and everything. I want the whole world to see."

The front door creaked open and Raju Sab entered. For a moment he stood there, taking in the scene. "What's going on?" he asked.

"I thought you weren't coming tonight," she whispered.

"What's the occasion?"

"I was showing Jeevan my wedding sari."

Raju Sab shook his head. "We've talked about this before. I don't want another wedding like that, Laxmi. Look where it got me."

Laxmi Memsab turned to Jeevan. "Didn't I tell you?"

"But you look good," Raju Sab said. "Doesn't she, boy?" He went to Laxmi Memsab and put his hand on her shoulder. "Here you are, looking so beautiful. I think I should do something about it. Jeevan, isn't it time for you to go to sleep? Don't folks in the village go to bed at sunset?"

His face warm and his mouth still dry, Jeevan left, feeling as if he had been rudely awakened from a pleasant dream. Raju Sab and Laxmi Memsab went into her bedroom, and Jeevan soon heard their laughter and whispers. He went to his room, shut the door, and stared at the poster of Lord Krishna that he'd tacked to the wall. He found the letter he'd begun writing to his mother, and as he read over what he'd written about his life in this house, how he planned to bring her gifts from the city, he realized that he missed her terribly. Then he reminded himself of their struggles after his father's death and how fortunate he'd been to land this job. He knew that he had to be strong and stop pining for home.

Jeevan heard a familiar thumping noise from Laxmi Memsab's bedroom, and he pushed his forehead against his pillow and pulled the blanket over his head. But he was too agitated to sleep, and he tried to calm himself by reciting a hymn he'd learned as a child.

The next morning, Laxmi Memsab looked happier than Jeevan had seen her in days. "Today Raju is going to Singapore on a business trip for a week," she said, sipping her tea, "and after he returns, he's going to hire a lawyer to finalize the divorce. He says he's not going to take no for an answer from Mona this time."

Her confidence bothered him. She was too trusting of Raju Sab, who, Jeevan increasingly suspected, wasn't as serious about her as he told her he was. All morning she chatted with Jeevan in the kitchen, her hands moving restlessly from one utensil to another. She even helped him cook, something she had never done. "If you stay with me, Jeevan," she said at one point, "I'll send you to school. You want to go to school, don't you?"

His father's death had forced Jeevan to quit studying for the School Leaving Certificate exam, and he had wished that he could finish it. So he nodded, but when he spoke, he was unable to mask his annoyance at her gullibility when it came to

Raju Sab. "Easier said than done, though. How would I work and still go to school?"

She eyed him. "What's the matter? Are you thinking about your mother?"

He muttered an excuse about needing to buy some ginger, and left the house. Outside, he ran into the shopkeeper who owned the shop across the street, a talkative fellow who had taken a liking to Jeevan, and now he asked in a low voice, "So, how's your Laxmi Memsab? Is Raju Sab going to leave his wife for her?"

Jeevan said sullenly, "How would I know? I only work for her."

Walking back inside, he decided to ask Laxmi Memsab if he could visit his mother in a few days. He'd broach the subject with her later today, because she seemed to be in a good mood.

That afternoon, however, something happened that changed everything. Laxmi Memsab and Jeevan had gone to a crowded supermarket in Bhatbhateni. Jeevan was walking behind her, holding a shopping basket, when a large woman approached them and snapped at her, "Whore! Are you happy sleeping with my sister's husband?" Her voice was loud enough so that people stopped and looked at them. Laxmi Memsab stared at the floor. The woman seemed to occupy the whole aisle. "Slut!" the woman barked. Her face was heavy with makeup, and her round eyes bulged in rage. A teenage girl beside her touched her hand and said, "Mummy, let's go. What's the point in talking to people like her?"

The woman flung the girl's arm away and said to Laxmi Memsab, "Do you know that right now Raju and Mona are flying to Singapore for their honeymoon? The honeymoon that you deprived them of because of your slutty ways?"

Laxmi Memsab kept her head lowered. Jeevan could only gape at the woman.

"Don't think it's that easy to ruin someone's marriage, a marriage sanctified with God as its witness. Raju babu will soon get tired of you. I'd love to see your face then."

Jeevan was about to respond angrily but the woman and the girl turned abruptly and left. He got a whiff of perfume as they went past. Her face crimson, Laxmi Memsab studied the label on a can while other customers sneaked glances in her direction. Finally, after what seemed like minutes, she said, "Let's go." She told Jeevan to put the basket on the floor, and they left the supermarket.

In the taxi on the way home, she kept her eyes on the road, her head against the seat. Jeevan sat awkwardly with the driver in the front seat. He wanted to turn his head, tell her not to worry, that she shouldn't listen to what that woman had said, but it seemed improper to break the silence. The evening traffic was heavy, and on such trips Laxmi Memsab would have commented on something outside—the pedestrians, the new stores, the aggressive drivers—but today she said nothing.

At home, she locked herself in her bedroom. Jeevan made tea for her and knocked on her door, but she didn't answer. He stood there, trying to listen for any sound inside, but heard nothing, so he went back to the kitchen. He imagined Raju Sab and his wife on an airplane, flying to Singapore.

Jeevan decided to make dinner—Laxmi Memsab's favorite, chicken and eggplant—then remembered that they hadn't bought anything at the supermarket. He looked around the kitchen; there was very little food left. He needed to ask her what to do about dinner, so he went to her door. But she had moved to the living room and was sitting on the sofa, massaging her temples.

"Do you have a headache, Memsab?"

She nodded and looked at him. Her eyes were clouded. "I think I need a glass of whiskey," she said.

"I'll pour you one."

He went to the cabinet in the corner of the room and found a bottle of Jack Daniel's. He poured her a glass, and when he brought it to her, he said, "Memsab, you shouldn't pay attention to what that woman said. She only wanted to rile you."

"Oh, that Ramita?"

"Her name is Ramita? That means spectacle, a show, doesn't it?" Jeevan said, laughing. "Did her parents really name her that?"

She smiled. "You really have to wonder what they were thinking, don't you? Maybe they sensed that she'd create a circus like the one in the supermarket today."

"And what big eyes she had."

"Didn't she?" Laxmi Memsab said. "Like the fanged goddess Kali." She made her eyes big and stuck out her tongue. Jeevan pretended to be scared, and they both laughed, but Laxmi Memsab's laughter soon turned gloomy.

"Forget about this, Memsab."

"I've ruined my life with Raju."

Jeevan didn't know what to say.

"He's gone off with Mona. He's going to stay with her—I can feel it. It would make sense."

"That Ramita woman was just being hurtful."

"Jeevan, I've been feeling it for a while. Raju is losing interest in me. I was just a diversion for him."

"You shouldn't be thinking these thoughts. You should talk to him about it when he comes back."

"Now I'm beginning to think I really am worthless. I wreaked havoc on a man's marriage, created a bad name for myself, and look at what has happened to me. I have no one."

"Memsab, I am here for you."

She shook her head. "One day you too will go, Jeevan."

He took her hand. "Memsab, I'll never leave you. I'll go if you kick me out, but I'll never leave your side." He thought of his mother, but right now he badly wanted Laxmi Memsab to feel better about herself.

"You're just trying to console me."

"I swear, Memsab," he said. "You took me in when I was desperate. And I will stay with you."

She ran her finger over his chin. "You are a very sweet boy, Jeevan. The woman you marry will be a lucky one."

Impulsively, he kissed her hand. He felt his eyes grow teary as he did.

In the middle of the night, he was woken by her screaming. He rushed to her room, where she was sitting upright in her bed, looking terrified. "Someone was just in my room, Jeevan. He said something, then disappeared."

To satisfy her, Jeevan checked underneath the bed, then went out to the balcony and surveyed the yard. When he came back inside, she was still in the same position, anxiously waiting for him.

"You had a nightmare, Memsab," he said.

"It didn't feel like a nightmare. He was calling me names and his face was all twisted. Feel my heart, feel how fast it's beating." She took his hand and put it against her chest. He could feel the thud-thud-thud of her heart, like a tiny bird against his palm.

"It was only a nightmare. You'll be fine, Memsab. Now try to sleep again."

"But I know I won't be able to. Please Jeevan, can you sleep in my room tonight? I beg you. You could sleep right here on the floor."

Though he knew better, he couldn't think of a way to say no to her. "All right, let me get my things."

He transferred his straw mat and blanket to the floor in her room, right below her bed. "Now nothing will happen," he told her, "so try to go to sleep." For a long time, he heard her tossing and turning, the bed creaking as she moved. Once or twice it sounded as if she were whispering to herself.

He dozed, then woke a short while later to see her sitting up in bed again. He asked her what was wrong, and she said she needed to use the toilet but was too scared. Half asleep, he accompanied her to the bathroom and waited outside until she was done. Back in bed, her tossing and turning continued.

+ + +

Raju Sab had said he would be back after a week, and each day that he was gone Laxmi Memsab seemed more and more tormented by her own thoughts. Every night Jeevan slept in her room, and during the day she started drinking early in the afternoon. She stopped taking her daily baths, he noticed, and her hair often went uncombed. She ate erratically, sometimes devouring everything Jeevan set in front of her, and other times not eating for the entire day. When there was a knock on the door — the postman or the laundry woman or someone trying to sell something — she'd run to her bedroom, frantically signaling to Jeevan to tell whoever it was that she was not home. She'd stay in her room for a long time, and when Jeevan went to her afterward, he'd find her in bed, lying face-down. "Memsab, you need to get a hold of yourself," he finally told her one day. "You can't live your life like this."

"What do you know about life?" she replied. "You come from the village and in two days you understand everything?"

Her words stung him, and he mumbled that although he was from the village, he was not stupid.

The night before Raju Sab was to return, Jeevan woke to Laxmi Memsab sliding under his blanket. She didn't say anything, just rested her head on his chest. He stroked her hair. He wished she wasn't so miserable, wished there were something he could do to truly help her. "I'll never leave you, Memsab," he whispered in her ear. Her eyes were closed, so he didn't know whether she heard him.

When Raju Sab came the next evening, he was clearly stunned to see the state Laxmi Memsab was in. Her hair was a mess, and the dhoti she wore had food stains all over it. "What have you done to yourself?" he asked.

At first she didn't answer, but he was persistent.

Finally, in a clipped voice, she said, "How was your honeymoon?"

"What honeymoon? I was on a business trip, I told you."

When she glared at him, he took her hand and said, "What

could I do, Laxmi? At the last minute she threw a fit. I had to take her. But honeymoon? I barely touch her these days."

"Your sister-in-law said you two were on the honeymoon that I prevented you from taking."

"Ramita will say anything. For me it was business from morning to night. Mona was in the hotel by herself all day. Some honeymoon!"

She stared at him. "You're not lying?"

"Why would I lie to you? Why are you in such a state? Jeevan, didn't you take care of your memsab?"

You're supposed to take care of her, not me, Jeevan wanted to say, but he just muttered, "Shall I make tea?" Laxmi Memsab nodded, and he went to the kitchen. When he returned, she and Raju Sab were sitting on the sofa, holding hands. Laxmi Memsab had apparently just told him about the supermarket incident, for he was saying, "Don't pay any attention to Ramita. She's a real witch."

Soon they went to her bedroom and shut the door. Earlier that afternoon, in anticipation of Raju Sab's arrival, Jeevan had taken his bedding back to his room. Now, unable to bear the thought of listening to them, he went out.

The moon was full, and he looked up at it as he walked along narrow streets where the shops were closing for the night. He headed toward New Road, where the lights were still bright and people were still shopping. But his mind stayed on what was happening in the flat. When would she come to her senses? No wonder Raju Sab had been able to keep her in limbo for so long. If she hadn't understood by now that he wasn't leaving his wife, she might never understand it. Perhaps Jeevan was better off getting out of this mess. Yet the thought of leaving Laxmi Memsab made him anxious. He tried to sort out his feelings for her: yes, his heart beat louder when he was close to her, but there was something more — he'd become strangely possessive of her, as if he were the only one who truly knew her. And he felt that he needed to guard her from people like Raju Sab and Ramita. If he were to leave Laxmi Memsab and find a job in another household, he could see himself continuing to worry about her, becoming racked by guilt that he'd left her at the mercy of these people.

When he returned about an hour later, Raju Sab was already gone, and Laxmi Memsab was sitting on the sofa reading a book. She had combed her hair, washed her face, and changed into a new dhoti. "Where did you go?" she asked him.

"For a walk," he said curtly, and went to the kitchen to cook dinner.

She followed him. "Are you angry at me about something?"

"Why would I be angry at you?" he snapped.

"No, you're angry. What's wrong, Jeevan?"

He turned to her. "Don't you see, Laxmi Memsab? Raju Sab is lying."

"How do you know?"

"Can't you sense it? Don't you see it in his eyes?"

"You think you know everything, Jeevan? I've known Raju longer than you have."

"But you yourself said —"

"Listen, things are difficult for Raju, but I know he wants to be with me."

"Is he going to leave his wife to marry you?"

"Who are you to question me like that?" she said loudly. "You think you've become such an important person? Don't forget, you're still a servant in this house."

She stormed away from him, and he heard her slam the bedroom door. He turned off the gas, scooped her food onto a plate, and carried it to her room. He put the plate down outside her door and announced, "Your food is ready." He walked back to the kitchen and sat on the floor. She was right: he was only a servant in this house, and he was deluding himself if he thought that he could actually protect her from anyone. Was he trying to be *her* savior? He had to return to his village, at least for a visit, to remind himself where he came from. Seeing his mother again would help him reclaim his true self, and he'd come back to Laxmi Memsab with a renewed sense of who he was and who he was not. *Tomorrow,* he said to himself, *I'm going to go whether she approves of it or not.*

That night he woke up and saw, by his door, her figure, illuminated from behind by moonlight streaming into the kitchen.

"Jeevan," she said. "I can't sleep."

"Are you hungry?" he asked. "Do you want me to heat up some leftovers for you?"

She shook her head. Then she came and sat on his mat. "I shouldn't have blown up at you, Jeevan. Are you still angry at me?"

"Not really. You're right, Memsab. I forgot that I am just a servant in this house."

"You're not just a servant. You're my friend."

He clasped her hand. "Memsab, do you seriously think Raju Sab will leave his wife for you? Do you believe it in your heart?"

She sighed and lay down beside him. His mat was narrow, and their bodies pressed against each other. "Can we not talk about it?" she said. She rested her head on his chest, and her breath smelled of alcohol—obviously she'd been drinking in her room. She closed her eyes. "Let's sleep, Jeevan," she said.

He wanted to tell her, right now, that tomorrow morning he planned to catch the first bus to Dhunche, but as he felt her warm breath on his chest, his resolve weakened. *Maybe not tomorrow,* he told himself, *maybe the day after.* Perhaps better to write to his mother first, informing her of his visit.

He stayed awake thinking about what might happen in the days to come. He didn't know what would transpire between her and Raju Sab—Raju Sab would never leave his wife to marry her, of that Jeevan was certain. But he also knew that every moment he himself spent with her, every night they slept together, his village seemed to move farther and farther away from him. That this could happen in such a short time surprised him. He could hear his mother saying, This is what you went to the city for?

This thought unsettled him and, gently disengaging himself from Laxmi Memsab, he sat up. Outside, the moon was big. He looked at Laxmi Memsab's face, white in the moonlight, a crease across her forehead. Somehow he knew that this was how things would continue for a long time to come: Raju Sab would keep her hanging, and she would turn to him, Jeevan, for comfort. Even if he were to visit his village, he would keep worrying about her, and return to her as quickly as he could.

The Royal Ghosts

THAT JUNE MORNING, a Saturday, the whole country woke to the news of the killings inside the
palace. People walked the streets bewildered. Ganga said to
the regulars at Saney's tea shop, "What do you expect?
They're royalty. It's their destiny to do things like this once in a
while. Remember Kot Parba?" Ganga had failed history back
in school, but somehow the lesson of Kot Parba returned to
him vividly now: the brutal massacre of 1846 that propelled the
Ranas to power and shackled the country with a dictatorship
for more than a century. When he'd studied it, he'd found the
images intoxicating: the men clanking swords in the cobble-
stone courtyards of Hanuman Dhoka, the old palace; the whispered rumors, brother against brother, mother against son; the
heads chopped off and presented as gifts to the avenger; the
spies and messengers traveling on horseback in the middle of
the night; the king and queen eating dinner while their own
children plotted their demise.

He began regaling the others with the story. "Queen Lax-
midevi's favorite military commander, Gagan Singh, was found
murdered, and she had a fit. She blamed the Pandeys and ordered everyone to assemble at the palace armory. Everyone

drew their swords and knives, and fighting broke out. Now, Jung Bahadur Rana was the only one not taken by surprise. Some say he had it all planned out. By the time the fighting was over, dozens and dozens of corpses—"

"Be quiet, Ganga!" shouted one elderly regular, who had known Ganga's father. "Who cares about Kot Parba now?"

"Why are you shouting, Nati ba?" Ganga said. "I'm just seeing parallels, that's all." But it was obvious that no one in the tea shop was interested in feudal Nepal when they'd just learned on CNN that Crown Prince Dipendra had shot himself after wiping out his entire family last night inside the palace. Ganga didn't dismiss royalty out of political conviction. And it wasn't just royalty he scoffed at—his mistrust of those in power spread to many levels. He hated the policemen who demanded bribes for minor traffic violations. He despised the bureaucrats who slyly extracted "tea money" to process licenses, permits, and other documents, which required so many government stamps that you could hardly read the words. He dreaded the days when rich English-speaking ladies hired his taxi for picnics in Gokarna or Dakshinkali, when he had to listen to them complain about the smell in his cab or how his jerky driving gave them headaches. A year ago, he'd taken a group of NGO workers to Nagarkot for an office picnic. Toward the end of the day, his passengers had insisted that he wash their dirty dishes as part of the fare, and after arguing with them, he warned that he'd leave without them if they didn't stop their nonsense. When they didn't, he abruptly got into his taxi and drove away. He relinquished his fare, but the sense of satisfaction he experienced had been worth it. On the other hand, he felt an absolute solicitude toward the old and the sick. He'd taken a number of people to the hospital free of charge, something his younger brother, Dharma, didn't understand. "This is your job," he chided. "Why would you do that?"

Now Ganga drank his tea and wondered what Dharma thought of the news. Dharma would have appreciated his Kot Parba story, seen the similarities between the two massacres, wondered how Ganga could remember this, especially since it was Dharma—not Ganga—who had been a good student, especially in history, and who ended up going to college and getting a degree. Dharma was probably weeping at the news—he was such a softy. Tears welled up in his eyes easily. During festivals he pleaded with Ganga not to slaughter goats, asking why he couldn't let others bloody their hands. In their school days, Dharma had been the brunt of much teasing because of his long eyelashes, higher voice, and effeminate walk. Ganga, older by a year, had fought for his brother, taking on even the most fearsome of bullies.

Everyone in the tea shop was discussing the palace carnage. Since the government media hadn't announced anything, people were watching CNN on the small TV on the counter. Some customers were claiming that the prime minister was behind it. Others were certain that the mastermind was the king's brother, Gyanendra, who—it was being discovered in bits and pieces—had been out of town. "How can we be sure that anything at all happened inside the palace?" the tea shop's owner said. "How do we know that this all isn't just a rumor? It could be the prime minister's conspiracy to upset and distract the country, then grab power." The others reproached him, saying that CNN never lied.

Ganga bought his secondhand taxi a couple of years ago, after his father died and left him four lakh rupees, a sum he didn't know the man possessed. Ganga loved driving the taxi—he loved speeding through the city, overtaking trucks and lorries at blind corners, squeezing through narrow alleys, blasting his stereo as he drove past pretty girls. Owning his own taxi provided him a freedom that other taxi drivers didn't have. He didn't have to answer to anyone or adhere to any schedule.

Dharma's life was quite different. He worked as a bookkeeper for a local merchant who owned several copy shops in the city. Customers came in to use copiers, fax machines, and telephones that had long-distance connections. It was a booming business, and the merchant opened new stores every year. Ganga was happy for his brother; at the age of twenty-three, he already had a respectable job. Many of his classmates still hung around street corners, looking for drugs.

Back at home, Ganga washed his face and changed, then got into his taxi and drove toward town. Across the city, people had gathered in groups, their faces betraying their shock. Most of the shops that had opened earlier had now shut down, and in Lagankhel, by the side of the road, Ganga saw a number of people getting their heads shaved, as if the deceased king had actually been their father. This amazed him, but then he realized that this was the kind of thing his brother would do—shave his head in mourning for a king who didn't even know that he existed. Ganga imagined a bald Dharma, and he smiled. If he had shaved his head, or was contemplating it, Ganga would say to him, "Who was that king to you, huh? You probably wouldn't shave your head if I were to croak tomorrow." And of course Dharma would ask him not to say such things about his own death, and of course he would say that Ganga was more important to him than anyone else.

In Jawalakhel, a group of women milled about in front of a house. As Ganga slowly drove past them, his window rolled down, he could hear them weeping. He swerved to the side, stopped, and asked them, "Someone died in this house?"

The women looked at him. "Haven't you heard what happened in the palace?" one asked. He rolled up his window and stepped on the accelerator.

Ganga turned on the radio. It was playing the syrupy music—a slow, tortuous violin—that was always played when some national tragedy had happened, so he turned it off. He slipped in a cassette of Ram Krishna Dhakal's music and sang along. The song reminded him of Anu, a teacher at the English boarding school in his neighborhood. He'd driven her around in his taxi a few times and played this song, one of his favorites, for her. He'd liked Anu immensely and had felt good about how their relationship was progressing. But after about a month, she began to avoid him. Whenever he called her, she conjured up excuses not to see him, and then one day he saw her with another teacher from her school, sitting inside the restaurant opposite her flat, laughing. He confronted Anu near her school the next day, and she told him that there was nothing between the teacher and her, but also that there was nothing between her and Ganga. "You have to understand—you drive a taxi," she told him, "and I am an educated woman." His astonished face seemed to prompt her to soften the blow. "If I've misled you, I'm sorry." "My fault," he said, trying to hide the hurt. "I misunderstood you." These days he saw Anu with the teacher all the time, and there was talk in the neighborhood that they were going to get married. One afternoon, after a particularly trying morning in the taxi, he pulled up beside them and asked whether they needed a ride. She glared at him, and he scoffed and drove off. He'd soon felt embarrassed for what he'd done, and the next day he waited at the restaurant across from her flat, hoping to catch a glimpse of her. But the only person who came to her window, a cigarette between his fingers, was the other teacher.

Ganga parked the taxi right outside the shop where his brother worked. Dharma lived in a small flat at the back of the shop. Ganga didn't understand why his brother would want to sleep in such cramped quarters in Putalisadak when he could have continued staying with Ganga in his roomier flat near Godavari. "It takes too long to commute to the city," Dharma complained before he moved out a few months ago. He didn't have to go to work until nine-thirty; Ganga headed out at around seven, so he couldn't give Dharma a ride. When Ganga offered to start later, his brother added, "But my boss wants me to sleep in Putalisadak so I can keep an eye on the place." He explained that shops in the Putalisadak and Baghbazar areas had recently suffered a series of break-ins.

"I should guard the place," Ganga said. "Look." He lifted his arms like a bodybuilder and flexed his biceps. He exercised obsessively, and his muscles were knotty and impressive.

Dharma said, "You're an idiot, dai. It's psychological, something you wouldn't understand. How would a robber know that I don't have a knife or a gun?"

He was right, of course.

On Saturdays, Ganga usually stopped by the shop around noon to chat with his brother. Sometimes the two went out for lunch, and today, guessing that Dharma was depressed over the palace news, Ganga was thinking that he'd treat his brother. It might be hard to find a place that was open, but there was a new Punjabi restaurant in Kalimati that Ganga had been want-ing to try — maybe they could see if it was open. Another taxi driver had told him that the food was terrific, quite spicy, and Dharma loved spicy food.

The door to the shop creaked open when Ganga placed his palm on it. Inside, it was dark, but he felt his way past the fax and copy machines. The door to Dharma's flat was ajar, and Ganga gently pushed it open. In the light seeping through the small window that overlooked a courtyard, he saw his brother, stark naked, and another man, also naked, sleeping together on the narrow bed. On the edge of the bed, Ganga spotted a used condom, its mouth in a knot. Both men were sound asleep — the other man was actually snoring near Dharma's forehead.

Ganga closed the door behind him, rushed out of the shop, and stepped onto the pavement. He felt nauseated, and put his hand on the roof of his taxi for balance. He didn't want to lin-ger, in case he had woken Dharma, so he quickly got into the taxi and drove off, nearly smashing into a three-wheeler close by.

About a month ago, Dharma mentioned that another man, a relative of his boss, had started sleeping at the shop too. Ganga suggested that since now his boss had found another man to guard the shop, Dharma could move back in with him. But Dharma had said, "My boss wants both of us there to keep an eye on things." Ganga wondered if Dharma was just mak-ing excuses, if his brother was simply tired of living with him. After all, a week before that Dharma had criticized Ganga for getting into a shoving match with the neighborhood butcher.

"Every problem doesn't need to be tackled like a bull, dai. Everywhere I go people complain about you."

Ganga asked his brother who'd been complaining.

"What does it matter?" Dharma asked. "How can you be so hot-tempered all the time?"

It's better than being a softy like you, he wanted to say, but he knew it would hurt his brother's feelings, so he just smiled and punched Dharma on the shoulder.

Dharma grabbed his shoulder and hopped around the room shouting, "Aiya!" Ganga moved toward him to apologize, and Dharma kicked his leg. "Donkey!" he said. "That hurt. You don't realize how strong you are."

Ganga felt like an idiot. This had happened plenty of times before. He'd hit Dharma as a sign of affection, and Dharma would howl in pain.

Now Ganga drove aimlessly around the city, refusing to stop for customers who tried to hail him. He couldn't focus on anything, and he was relieved that the streets didn't have much traffic; otherwise he probably would have gotten into an accident. At times he drove slowly, at other times at breakneck speed, gunning the engine, scaring people who'd gathered on the sidewalks and in the streets to discuss the day's news.

Over the past few weeks Dharma had frequently mentioned his roommate, Jeet, and how funny he was. "He has me laughing all the time, dai," Dharma said. "I've never met anyone like him." Ganga felt a strange pang, and said, "How's there enough room for both of you in that tiny flat?"

Dharma shrugged dismissively. "We don't have that much stuff—it just works out somehow. Jeet is such a fun man. You'll see when you meet him."

Ganga pressed harder on the accelerator. Near Dashrath Stadium, a policeman waved his baton at him, motioning for him to stop, but Ganga swerved toward him, nearly hitting him, then floored it. His taxi brushed against a pole before hurtling toward Thapathali.

+ + +

As he climbed the steps to his flat, his landlord, Gaurishanker, called to him, asking him what the situation was in town, whether he'd learned anything more about what had happened at the palace. "Nothing," Ganga said. The landlord, his lungi wrapped around his waist, came out his door and ambled after him. "There are rumors that the funeral is tonight," Gaurishanker said, following Ganga into his flat. "Can you imagine? Killing off your entire family? I still don't believe it. There's something fishy here. Eh, Ganga, you have anything to drink? This is too mind-boggling—I need something to calm my mind." He spotted the bottle of Ruslan vodka on Ganga's windowsill. "Let's have a drink, okay?" Dumbly, Ganga agreed.

Before long, both were tipsy. Gaurishanker had been going on nonstop about what might have happened in the palace. He'd tiptoed down to his room to grab his transistor radio and was playing with the dials now, attempting to get the BBC. Radio Nepal was still playing religious tunes of mourning. The old transistor wasn't working that well, and Gaurishanker was cursing it. Finally Ganga stopped him and asked, "Dai, what do you think of chhakkas?"

Gaurishanker, still fiddling with the dial, asked, "Why? Was the crown prince a chhakka?"

"No, no, I'm just asking. Looks like the population of chhakkas is increasing in Kathmandu."

"Are you one?" Gaurishanker grinned.

"If you don't want to answer, that's fine."

"Disgusting, that's what I think. They should be rounded up and locked away, that's what I think. I've heard there's even a chhakka club in the city—can you believe that? You know who's a chhakka?"

Ganga's heart pounded.

"That Parmendra who runs the Internet café by the school. His two employees there are his lovers. Both of them. And I've heard he also likes very young boys, gives them money to come to his shop at night."

"Parmendra?" Ganga had driven the man into the city a few

times in his taxi. He was always very cordial, asking Ganga about his business, inquiring about how Dharma was doing. Suddenly, with a shudder, Ganga wondered if Parmendra and Dharma were involved; why else would Parmendra have asked after his brother that time?

The rest of that afternoon, Gaurishanker drifted in and out of Ganga's flat, bringing him news updates. The state television and radio had finally admitted that the king and queen and several other members of the royal family had died in an "unanticipated" event at the palace last night. Crown Prince Dipendra, now officially declared the king, was in a coma, so Prince Gyanendra had been named regent. The dead would be cremated at the Pashupatinath temple that evening. Their bodies would be carried in a procession starting at the Chhauni military hospital. "I'm going to go," Gaurishanker announced. "Do you want to come?"

Ganga shook his head.

"Are you just going to sit here all day and mope? Come, let's go. And call Dharma. Where is he today, by the way? Did you see him in town?"

Ganga mumbled that the booze had given him a headache and that he needed sleep. After Gaurishanker left, he bolted the door, closed the curtains, and lay down on his bed. He should have known. Dharma had shown all the tendencies. In eighth grade, Ganga had stumbled upon a boy, pants down around his knees, rubbing himself against Dharma's buttocks. Tears streamed down Dharma's face, but he hadn't cried for help. Ganga yanked back the other boy's head so hard that for weeks he had to wear a neck brace. To the crowd that had gathered that afternoon to watch the "action," Ganga had warned, "Any of you do anything to my brother or tease him anymore, you'll have to deal with me," and he'd shown them the large knife he'd stolen from a neighbor. That afternoon as the brothers walked home, Ganga scolded Dharma. "Why didn't you scream for help?"

"I was just scared," Dharma said, teary-eyed.

"You still should have fought back," Ganga said gently. As they neared home, he put his arm around his brother, rubbed his head with his knuckles, and said, "Don't worry. As long as I am here, no one can do anything to you. And I won't tell Father."

Dharma wiped his tears and looked at him gratefully. Later, when Ganga was alone, his own eyes grew moist at the thought of his brother so helpless at the hands of that bully. He vowed that he'd always protect Dharma. And he did, even from their own father.

Baba had been overly strict with his two sons, especially after the death of their mother when they were still young. When they disobeyed him, he beat them with his cane. He was especially harsh on Ganga, whose aggressiveness frequently got him into trouble. He accepted these beatings with a clenched jaw, unlike Dharma, who whimpered and bawled, begging Baba to stop. Ganga's heart broke when he saw his brother's misery, and soon he began to step in front of Dharma when his father brandished his cane. As the boys grew older, Baba softened, mainly because he found a formidable opponent in Ganga, who once wrestled the cane away from him and smacked him on his own behind. On his deathbed Baba wheezed and coughed and apologized to Ganga for being too tough on them. Ganga held the man's hand, but said nothing.

Now he turned on the television, which showed the state farewell at the hospital. People were placing flowers on the royal corpses, which were wrapped in white cloth. The faces of the dead looked ashen and twisted, caught in their final moments of horror. Ganga turned off the television when he heard a loud knock at the door. "Dai, dai." It was Dharma.

Ganga kept very still and held his breath, but the banging on the door continued, and Dharma shouted, "Dai, open the door. I heard your television just now."

Ganga finally went to the door.

"Dai, everything okay?" Dharma asked.

Ganga ignored him and walked back to his bed.

"You heard about what happened in the palace, didn't you?" Dharma asked.

"I don't want to talk to you right now."

"What happened? Did I do something wrong?"

Ganga lay down on the bed, unable to look at his brother. Dharma sat next to him. "Dai, what did I do?"

"I saw something today that has turned my mind upside down."

Dharma looked confused.

"You go now. And don't come to visit me anymore."

"What did I do? At least tell me what I did."

"I didn't know you were like this."

"What—?" An understanding seemed to dawn on his brother. "Did someone tell you something about me?"

"No one needs to tell me anything. I saw it with my own two eyes." Ganga pointed to his face.

"You came to the shop?"

Ganga didn't respond, and Dharma kept quiet, staring at him. Then he wiped his face with both palms and stood up. "All right. If that's the way it is, then what can I do?" He moved toward the door, but he didn't leave. He just stood there for a moment, then returned to the bed. "I've always been like this, dai. Hasn't it been obvious? Why are you pretending as if the sky has fallen on you now?"

Ganga maintained his stone face.

"What makes you think you're better than me? You're driving a taxi because you can't hold a real job. Look at you—you get into fights all the time, women shy away from you. When people talk to me, they don't have a single good thing to say about you. At least people don't say bad things about me."

"That's because they don't know you're a chhakka," Ganga said. He sat up. "Tell me, how long has this been going on?" He couldn't help himself—he grabbed his brother's collar. Dharma squirmed to get out of his grasp, but Ganga held tight. As Dharma struggled to break free, his shirt ripped. One sleeve now hung by a few threads. They punched and kicked and fell to the floor, Ganga on top. He pinned Dharma's arms with his knees and pressed his forearm against his throat, increasing the pressure as he spoke. "What the fuck am I supposed to say to people, huh? Chhakka's brother, they'll call me." Then, suddenly realizing what he was doing, Ganga let go, and Dharma began to massage his throat to normalize his breathing.

There was a loud knock at the door, and Ganga stood and went to see who it was. His landlady, Gaurishanker's wife, was standing there, and Ganga kept the door partly closed so she couldn't peek inside. "What is all this banging and shouting?" she asked. She had never bothered to pretend she liked Ganga, although she always spoke sweetly to Dharma. "You're not beating up your own brother, are you?"

He shut the door in her face and locked it, then went to check on his brother. Dharma was still lying on the floor, breathing heavily, but the color had returned to his face. "Dai," he croaked.

"You better leave, Dharma," Ganga said.

Shakily, Dharma stood up. He looked down at his shirt without its sleeve, then at his brother again. He turned around and walked out of the flat.

The rest of the evening Ganga stayed inside his flat, drinking. At around seven o'clock, Gaurishanker knocked on his door, demanding that Ganga open it, that he needed to talk. Ganga simply ignored him. By eleven he was pretty drunk, and he opened his door and stumbled down the stairs. He wandered around the neighborhood. It had rained a bit, so the streets were wet, and a couple of times he slipped and fell into puddles. Under the big tree near the shops, a group of young men had gathered, Dharma's old school friends, Ganga soon saw. They stopped talking when they saw him approach.

Tottering, Ganga asked, "What are you donkeys doing out so late?"

"Talking about what happened in the palace."

"What's the scoop?"

"It's pretty confusing, but everyone is saying Gyanendra is behind it."

A brother killing his own brother. Ganga made a pistol out of his right hand and, aiming it at them, shot them one by one, making a *phoosh* sound with each shot. They all laughed at him, and one mumbled something about him that he didn't quite catch.

"How is Dharma doing?" another asked. A couple of them exchanged glances.

Had they known all along? Whatever the case, he wasn't going to take the bait. How many people was he going to have to fight with over his brother? "Dharma is fine," he said, and moved on. Soon he passed Parmendra's Internet café. The light was still on inside, so he went to the window and peeked in. Parmendra was sitting in front of a computer, his eyes fixed on the screen. Every once in a while he'd type something, and the screen would change. At one point, he glanced toward the window and gave a start. He raised his hand questioningly, then came to the door.

"Any further news?" Ganga asked.

"Dipendra did it," Parmendra said. "Our news might not say it, but it's all over the Internet." He paused. "You're drunk, aren't you?"

Ganga sat on the steps of the shop and asked Parmendra if he had a cigarette. He rarely smoked, but knew that Parmendra did. Parmendra fetched his pack from inside, sat next to Ganga, and lit both their cigarettes. The smoke burned the inside of Ganga's mouth.

"Who would have imagined," Parmendra said, "that Dipendra would do such a thing? But who knows? Maybe it was a giant conspiracy."

"Maybe, maybe," Ganga said. "Or maybe the crown prince did it. These people in power are crazy. How can we know what goes on behind closed doors? We cannot even know with our own relatives." His words were slurred.

"Yes, yes," Parmendra said. "What really happened, you

and I might never know. But it's sad. King Birendra was such a good king, wasn't he? He let us have our democracy when we wanted it a decade ago."

"For me, it doesn't really make a difference. One king or another—one politician or another. They're all the same."

"Then why do you look so sad? And why are you so drunk tonight?" Parmendra put his arm around Ganga. "Didn't know you were so sentimental. Everyone thinks you're such a tough guy."

Parmendra's touch made Ganga uneasy, and he shifted a bit. He stubbed out his cigarette on the stairs and stood up, swaying. He said, "I want to ask you something. It's a bit personal."

"What is it?"

"Don't get angry with me. I only heard it from someone else and am just curious." It took him a while to formulate the words. "I've heard that you're a chhakka. Is that true?"

Parmendra stared at him for a second, then burst out laughing. "Who told you that? Is that what people say about me?"

"So you're not?"

"I'm going to Janakpur to get married next month. When I bring my wife back here, you'll see."

"So why are people calling you chhakka?"

"Go ask them," Parmendra said. "This is Nepal. It doesn't take anything for people to start talking here. Look at what happened today. How many theories have we heard already? Did you hear the one about that astrologer? He supposedly warned King Mahendra that his grandson Dipendra's birth date was so unlucky that *it* would destroy the royal family. You can't live your life always listening to what other people say. Besides, even if I were a chhakka, what's the big deal? What business is it of anyone's?" Parmendra carried on about people meddling in other people's lives, but Ganga had already tuned him out. He felt tired and now merely wanted the comfort of his own bed.

Over the next few days, an ugly picture emerged of what Crown Prince Dipendra had done: drugged and drunk, he'd fought with his mother over a girl he wanted to marry, and after tending the palace bar that evening, he went to his room, then returned in full military gear and killed everyone. But people refused to believe it. They burned tires on the streets and chanted slurs against Gyanendra, who, after Dipendra died of self-inflicted wounds two days later, was named the next king. The police tried to control the rioters and eventually used tear gas. Curfews were announced, and soon the streets were empty at night.

For Ganga, all of this held only mild interest. Gaurishanker later confronted him, saying that although he understood his wife was not the most polite woman in the world, she was still the landlady, and Ganga had to show some respect. "You can do your fighting outside," he told Ganga, "but no banging or smashing people in my house." Ganga slammed the door on him, thinking that he would move out of the flat soon anyway, maybe leave the city, just get in his taxi and drive off to a place where he wouldn't have to see Dharma anymore. The more he thought about it, the more the idea made sense to him. Who else did he have in the city? When Anu used to ride in his taxi with him, he'd imagined having a family here, a nice little house of his own where he could raise his children. But now what was the point in staying?

He packed his clothes and other belongings in two suitcases. He had about twenty thousand rupees in the bank, and he'd return to the city some other time to withdraw the money. Right now it was important to leave, get far away from it all. He left a note for Gaurishanker, telling him that he'd be back to pay him the next month's rent, and that he was free to use or discard whatever was left in the flat — which wasn't much, just some pots and pans, a chair, his bedding, and an empty steel trunk.

Even as Ganga loaded his suitcases in his taxi in the late afternoon, he didn't know where he would go. He had no friends anywhere else; most of his friends were taxi drivers who worked here in Kathmandu. He suddenly recalled an old friend who now lived in Hetauda and drove buses from there to Biratnagar, something like that. Ganga had heard that the friend was doing well, and perhaps he could stay with him for a few days. Or he could stay in a hotel—he didn't care. He had enough money for now, and what would be the worst thing that could happen to him if the money ran out? He could always sell the taxi. Whatever it took, he would not look back.

Well after he'd driven beyond the city, past the town of Thankot, as he was climbing the steep, meandering hillside that would take him out of the valley, he began to grow teary. He pulled over to the side of the road and rested his head on the steering wheel. He couldn't do this. He simply couldn't leave Dharma. He had protected his younger brother all his life. Who would fight those people who made Dharma's life hell? Ganga looked out the window. It was beginning to get dark outside, and trucks moved slowly up and down the hilly highway. The city was stretched out below him and was beginning to flicker with dots of light. He sat in his taxi until it became dark, then turned around.

As Ganga sped along the streets of Kathmandu, he decided he'd go directly to Dharma's shop, knock on the door, and ask for his brother's forgiveness. But what if Jeet was there? Could he face him? He didn't think he could, so he drove back toward Godavari. Tomorrow morning he'd phone Dharma, ask him how he was doing. They could meet somewhere, perhaps in that Punjabi restaurant. Ganga would tell him that he was sorry for what he'd done, and that Dharma was right: Ganga sometimes didn't realize how strong he was. He wouldn't bring up Jeet again, or what he saw.

Maybe over dinner they'd talk about what had happened inside the palace, what would happen to the country now, whether the Maobadis would take advantage of this uncertainty, raid the capital and take over. "Dipendra killed his own parents and his pregnant sister and his brother, dai," Dharma would say. "How can people be like that?" And Ganga would console him: "Don't dwell on it, Dharma. There are things that happen with the raja-maharaja we'll never understand. Leave it be." And he would tell him all about Kot Parba, the men on horses, the bloodstained courtyards, guns booming in the middle of the night.

On second thought, he would not. What would be the point of bringing up those royal ghosts? Instead he'd tell Dharma, "Eat, eat. You're all skin and bones," and Dharma would dig into the food—mutton curry or lamb masala or whatever they'd ordered—and say that eating well was probably the best thing to do in times like these.

ACKNOWLEDGMENTS

I would like to thank the following people for their support and guidance: my editor, Heidi Pitlor, whose faith in my work has remained a constant source of nourishment for me; the folks at Janklow and Nesbit, especially my wonderful agent, Eric Simonoff; Indiana University's English Department and my students and colleagues in the MFA writing program; Buwa and Ammi in Nepal; and my first reader, my wife, Babita, whose generous spirit breathes life into every word I write.